Stephen Edger has been writing crime thrillers since 2010. An avid reader, Stephen writes what he likes to read: fast-paced, suspense thrillers with more than a nod to the darker side of the human psyche. In all, he has published twenty novels – four trilogies, and the rest standalone psychological thrillers.

The one common location to each of the novels is the city of Southampton, where Stephen has lived since attending the university there. This local knowledge gives each of the stories a unique and edgy realism that few can match.

Stephen was born in the north-east of England, but grew up in London, meaning he is both a northerner and a southerner. By day he works in the financial industry using his insider knowledge to help shape the plots of his books.

He is passionate about reading and writing, and cites Simon Kernick and Tony Parsons as major influences on his writing style.

www.stephenedger.com

/AuthorStephenEdger

@StephenEdger

ALSO BY STEPHEN EDGER

<u>The DI Kate Matthews Series</u>
Dead to Me
Dying Day
Cold Heart

<u>The PI Johnson Carmichael Series</u>
Trespass
Fragments
Downfall

<u>Standalones</u>
Snatched
Blackout
Then He Was Gone
Little Girl Gone
Till Death Do Us Part
Déjà Vu

# STEPHEN EDGER

snapshot

This novel is entirely a work of fiction.
The names, characters and incidents portrayed in it are the work of the author's imagination. Any resemblance to actual persons, living or dead, events or localities is entirely coincidental.

All rights reserved. No part of this publication may be reproduced, stored in a retrieval system, or transmitted, in any form or by any means, electronic, mechanical, photocopying, recording or otherwise, without the prior permission of the author

Copyright © 2020 Stephen Edger

ISBN: 9781672254632

Dedicated to my wife and children.

ONE

The copper-like tang in Hannah Davenport's mouth was familiar, but not welcome. The alarm screeching overhead was neither wanted, nor helping with the thought-splitting ache in her head. Running her fingers over the rough fibres of the carpet, her mind struggled to identify if this was just part of a dream, or whether she'd just woken up on the floor. Pushing her hands into the thick pile, she winced at the stabbing pain in her chest; directly in front of her the charcoal-coloured cupboard and drawer unit by the front door; her feet resting on the bottom step of the staircase.

Had she fallen? Is that what had happened?

She couldn't remember falling, but in that moment a thick smog filled her mind as she tried to recall any last fragment of memory.

What time was it now anyway?

Rolling onto her back, she was breathless at the realisation of pain flooding her system. Her entire body ached, and she could feel her left cheek swelling beneath her eye. It was like no pain she could recall, and staring back up the staircase, she could only deduce that she must have fallen, but there was still no recollection of tumbling.

The smoke alarm continued to shriek above her, and as she turned her head towards the cacophony, a black cloud billowing from the kitchen told her the cause of the alarm. It took all her effort to get her body into a sitting position, and as she pushed herself onto her hands and knees, she had to accept it would be too much effort to get to her feet. Placing one aching hand in front of the other, she did her best to shuffle along the carpet towards the kitchen door.

She must have been cooking before the fall, but again her memory failed to offer any enlightenment. The smoke was thicker as she trundled in, keeping her face as low as she could manage, and only taking breaths when necessary. She could barely see the oven through the thick black smoke, and the dark night sky beyond the glass pane of the patio door told her it was late evening or night.

Had she been cooking John's dinner?

That had to be it, but why had she allowed it to burn? John wouldn't be happy if she'd burned dinner; money was tight enough as it was without food wastage. Struggling to breathe, she coughed as she made it to the patio door, and fiddling with the key in the lock, she just about managed to drag herself into a standing position using the cold metal door handle, and the side of the work surface. The door opened, and she welcomed the fresh blast of icy wind, like a vacuum sucking out the smoke. She remained where she was for as long as she could, the wind cutting at her sore cheeks, eyes closed and just trying to inhale as much as her aching ribcage would allow.

The alarm was still shrieking, and God only knew how long it had been sounding for. The only answer was to remove the burning item from the oven. Wrapping her hands in towels from the radiator, she pulled the oven door open, a fresh plume of black filling her face and stinging her eyes. Gripping both sides of the large roasting tin, she dragged it out, not stopping to consider whether the charred bird could still be saved. Hobbling unsteadily towards the open door, she flung both the carcass and tin into the darkness, hearing the tray clatter against the patio stones further away. The neighbour's cats would be in for a treat later.

The relentless ringing of the alarm continued, as she returned to and slammed the oven door shut, before raising and wafting the towels in the immediate vicinity below the small plastic box on the ceiling. After what felt like minutes, but was probably only ear-splitting seconds, the alarm faded, leaving Hannah to survey the mess in the kitchen.

A stabbing pain in her head made her teeter, and reaching for the edge of the countertop, she just kept herself level. The stench of smoke hung in the air, despite the cool, wet air blowing in from the back garden. Closing her eyes, she concentrated on steadying her breathing, trying to push thoughts of the present from her mind and focus on the last thing she could recall.

John had messaged to say he'd be home by seven, and she'd decided to cook his favourite meal: roast chicken with all the trimmings. There'd be leftovers for days, but it hadn't mattered. There were still butterflies in her stomach from the excitement of what she'd planned to tell him. With the roasting tin in the oven she'd prepared the vegetables: swede, peas, carrots, cauliflower, and mashed potatoes. She'd been planning to go upstairs and change when the doorbell had sounded, but that was the last memory, before fresh pain erupted behind her temples.

Catching a glimpse of her reflection in the swinging patio door, she shuddered; her hair, always so tidy in a ponytail, was all over the place, as if she'd been dragged backwards through a bush; the dark crimson smears around her mouth couldn't be lipstick; and as she looked at her left forearm, the sleeve torn, she gasped at the bloody scars of scratches.

A haunting terror slowly enveloped her body: what the hell happened?

She needed John. She had to tell him; he'd look after her; would take away the pain.

Limping out of the kitchen towards the phone panel in

the hallway, she was surprised to find the cradle empty. Had she left it somewhere? She couldn't remember receiving a call, but maybe in the shock of falling down the stairs was causing some kind of temporary amnesia. She was no doctor, but it sounded logical enough to satisfy her curiosity.

Stumbling back towards the kitchen, she veered into the living room at the front of the house, assuming she may have left the phone in there. The television set was on, but muted, and one of the table lamps had been knocked to the floor. Fragments of glass surrounded the base where the bulb had smashed on impact. Several cushions were also lying haphazardly on the carpet. Picking them up, she grimaced as she put them back in place on the two sofas and single armchair, and returning the lamp to its usual place on the coffee table between the sofas.

She couldn't think of any reason the phone would be in the dining room between the kitchen and lounge, but forced herself onwards. John would want to know that she'd been injured. The door was ajar, as she'd left it, but as she pushed it open with her foot, she gasped. The table cloth was hanging from the table, the flute glasses knocked over and smashed, with half the crockery and cutlery now lying in a crumpled mess on the floor, as if someone had deliberately ransacked the place.

Her pulse quickened, the realisation of what had happened suddenly dawning. Someone had been at the door: had he forced his way in and robbed them? There was no other explanation for all this damage.

She needed to call the police, and to get hold of John as soon as possible. The phone couldn't be far; she must have left it somewhere and forgotten. It wouldn't be upstairs, as they had a separate handset up there. Returning to the living room, she decided to give it a second search.

Thundering footsteps on the staircase froze her still with

fear. She knew instantly it wasn't John's feet charging. She didn't dare turn around, willing whoever it was to go without attacking her, but also scanning the space immediately in front of her for any kind of weapon to protect herself.

Relief washed over her as she heard the front door quickly open and close. Had the thief still been in the property when she'd woken? She'd been stumbling around, and all the time some stranger had been upstairs. Bile bubbled at the back of her throat, and for a moment she thought she would retch, but managed to choke it down, closing her eyes and focusing on steadying her breathing.

Only one thought pushed its way to the front of her mind. She needed help, and the police would be able to sort out this mess, but she needed to locate the phone. It was times like this that she wished she still owned a mobile phone, but she'd hardly used her last one, and they'd agreed it wasn't practical.

Forcing herself towards the front door, terrified that the intruder could still be there waiting for her, she pushed her weight into it to make sure it was closed, before grabbing for keys from the unit drawer to lock it.

Her fingers tickled the leather photo holder on John's key ring. What was that doing there? Unless he was already home.

Looking back towards the kitchen, she returned to close and lock the patio door, no longer feeling safe in her own home. The ache in her knees was worsening, and as she now considered what she'd learned couldn't escape the possibility that she'd been pushed down the stairs; that would explain why she didn't remember falling.

Her breaths coming in short, shallow bursts, she stumbled from the room, climbing the stairs on hands and knees, the dread growing in the pit of her stomach as her eyes fell on red splotches on the carpet leading to the main bedroom.

'John?' she called out, unable to keep the anxiety from her voice.

Pausing at the top of the stairs, she listened for any sound to indicate whether he was in fact home. The door to the main bedroom was open, and beyond it she could see the glow of the bedside lamp.

'John?' she called again, as loud as she dared.

Still no sound from within the room.

Taking a deep breath, she crept along the landing, pushing the door open with her outstretched fingers.

Her hand shot up to her mouth as her eyes fell on the lifeless corpse splayed in the centre of the mattress, his abdomen a torn mess of blood and tissue. A large kitchen knife, coated in sticky red had left a huge stain on the duvet cover near his right knee.

Hannah collapsed to the floor, her mouth wide as she silently screamed, the tears bursting from her eyes, as she continued to stare at her dead husband.

TWO

Her eyelids were heavy, but there was no way Hannah would sleep tonight; not in that house. Even if the police examiners weren't combing over every inch of the floor and furniture, it wouldn't feel right to stay. Not without John.

The mug of tea remained on the table in front of Hannah. Probably cold now, but she had no desire to drink it.

'It's loaded with sugar,' her neighbour Sandra had said. 'Supposed to be good for shock.'

Hannah wasn't in shock. She felt numb, and she'd run out of tears to cry. Two hours had passed since she'd made the gruesome discovery in the bedroom, but it felt as current as her neighbour buzzing awkwardly around offering drinks and biscuits to the two detectives who were sitting across from Hannah, offering sympathetic nods and apologies for having to ask their difficult questions.

They had relocated to Sandra's house next door in order to preserve the scene. That had been how they'd phrased it. She'd wanted to remind them that it was a loving home – her home – not just a crime scene. It wasn't their fault; maybe they'd become desensitised to the pain of such a loss.

'Tell us again: what's the last thing you remember?' the detective with olive-coloured skin said.

Hannah considered him for a moment. Thirty at most, his chin bore the designer stubble so popular with men of his age. He was dressed in a light grey suit – a supermarket make, rather than tailored – with a white shirt and navy blue tie. It wasn't a look that suited him, and Hannah could only guess the tie was an effort to impress the more straight-faced woman sat with him.

'I told you,' Hannah said, taking a deep breath. 'There was someone at the door; the bell had rung.'

'And then?'

'I don't remember anything until the smoke alarm woke me at the bottom of the stairs.'

'What time did the doorbell ring?'

'Just before six, I think…I'm not sure.'

'What time did you wake at the bottom of the stairs? Please try to be exact.'

'I – I – I don't know. A few minutes before I called you.'

The detective eagerly typed a note into the iPad he'd brought with him and had been updating throughout the course of taking her statement.

The woman next to him – Detective Inspector Chandler – was much older. Her unkempt hair was a mess of long curls, with streaks of grey counter-balancing the natural dark colour. The skirt and jacket she was wearing looked ready to burst at the seams, and the way in which she'd been devouring the biscuits Sandra had supplied, it was hardly a surprise.

'Mrs Davenport, do you remember what happened to your arms?' the woman asked, her accent more Yorkshire than local to Salford, if Hannah had to guess. 'There are cuts consistent with a knife of some kind. Did Mr Davenport do this to you?'

Hannah's eyes widened at the question. 'How dare you? John would never… no, John didn't do this.'

The woman raised her hands in a pacifying gesture. 'Forgive me, we see a lot of cases like this where the victim of abuse can't take anymore, and snaps suddenly.'

Hannah stared at them both incredulously. 'I'm not a victim of abuse. My husband never hit me. We had a happy, loving marriage. Ask anyone.' She fired a look at Sandra. 'Tell them.'

Sandra's cheeks flushed as the two detectives turned to see her response. 'Uh, as far as I... uh, no I've never seen Hannah with bruises before. John's not like that; he's a nice guy who wouldn't hurt a fly. Honestly.'

The olive-skinned detective turned back to Hannah. 'You said you heard heavy footfalls on the stairs right before you discovered the body.'

The thundering sound echoed through Hannah's brain again; a noise she was certain she'd never forget. 'Yes.'

'You didn't see who was in the house?'

'No.'

'Why didn't you turn to see who it was?'

She glanced at Sandra for reassurance. 'I – I – I was terrified... the state of the place told me something bad had happened, and... I was scared he'd attack me again.'

Chandler's head snapped around. '*Again?*'

'Well, yeah, if John didn't do this to me, *he* must have been responsible.'

'You went from the kitchen to the lounge, and then to the dining room looking for your phone?'

'Yes.'

The woman frowned. 'When you heard someone thundering down the stairs your immediate thought was that there was an intruder in your house?'

'Yes,' Hannah replied, less certain this time.

'The thing is, Mrs Davenport, what I can't understand is why you didn't think the footsteps belonged to your husband. You said yourself he should have been home at seven, and when you woke it was at least an hour and a half later. So why was your first thought of an intruder and not the man you shared the house with?'

The wind left Hannah, and no amount of inhaling seemed to refill her lungs. What were they suggesting, that she'd made up the sound of the intruder? Did they think that she could have…? She couldn't finish the thought as she tasted bile in her throat.

DI Chandler pressed her palms flat against the table. 'What I'm trying to ascertain is whether there is something you're not telling us, Mrs Davenport. I know this has been a huge shock for you and I can't imagine how you must be feeling. It's my responsibility to investigate what has occurred tonight and to identify the person who took John from you. I'm on your side.'

It didn't feel like it. What did they think she was hiding?

'If I could remember anything else, I would tell you,' Hannah said when her breathing had steadied. 'I want you to find whoever killed my husband and then I want to see them punished. I swear if there was anything else I would tell you.'

The two detectives exchanged glances, before Chandler nodded, sliding a business card across the table to Hannah. 'You can reach me on this number at any time. You've taken a nasty bump to the head and that can temporarily disrupt short-term memory. There's a good chance you will start to remember other details from this evening, and all I ask is you give me a call the moment you remember something else. However minute, please call.'

Hannah picked up the card, holding it close.

'You can stay here tonight,' Sandra offered, suddenly perking up. 'I'll make up the spare room so you can get your head down.

Hannah forced a thin smile of gratitude, and then turned back to face the two detectives. 'When will… what I mean is, how long will it take until… when I can get my things from the house?'

Chandler stood, and nudged her colleague to do the same. 'It will probably take several days for our team to finish their investigations. As soon as they're done I'll let you know. In the meantime, you're not permitted within the cordon or tent that we've set up. Do you understand? I'll have one of the team bring you a change of clothes.'

Hannah nodded, the scene from the bedroom stabbing at her mind like a photograph. It didn't feel real. Murder wasn't something that happened to families like theirs. It was something that happened in books and on the television. Or in inner city gangs culture. This part of Salford was affluent and targeted at law-abiding families.

'I think it would be a good idea to go to the hospital and let the doctors have a look at your injuries. I can arrange for someone to escort you if you'd like?'

Hannah looked down at the scratches on her arms, before nodding.

Sandra showed the detectives to the door, and as she returned, leaned against the doorframe of the kitchen just staring at Hannah, her face plastered with pained empathy.

'I'm going to have to phone John's dad and brother and let them know what happened,' Hannah suddenly said as her pragmatic nature took control. 'His brother will have to be told. Oh God, his niece and nephews are going to be so devastated.'

She remembered the reason she'd been planning the surprise romantic dinner, and heart shattered into a thousand tiny pieces, and her hand fell to her abdomen. She couldn't stop the fresh tears pooling in her eyes, and as if sensing a fresh downpour, Sandra rushed to her side, draping a sympathetic arm around Hannah's shoulders.

'Oh, sweetie, it's okay, you let it out,' Sandra said soothingly. 'I'm here for whatever you need.'

'I'm pregnant,' Hannah sputtered between aching sobs.

Sandra's arm tightened at the shock of the news. 'Oh my darling, I'm so sorry. I wish there was something else I could say. Oh you poor thing.'

There was nothing anybody could do. Not now. She'd

been robbed of a normal life; one she'd planned to spend with John, growing old together and building a home full of loving memories. Nothing in her life would ever be the same again. She couldn't imagine a life without John, not hearing his sarcastic jokes, never breathing in his rugged masculine scent, never feeling his touch, or tasting his sweet kisses.

All so some lowlife could steal a few precious items. Hannah had known the world wasn't fair, but she'd never appreciated just how cruel it could be.

ONE YEAR LATER

THREE

The sharp edge of the blade glinted as it caught the autumn sun's rays through the window. Coiling her fingers tightly around the handle, Hannah raised it to the wall and began to hack at the clump of stale wallpaper once again.

'It's a fixer-upper,' the estate agent had proclaimed when they'd entered some ten weeks earlier.

As understatements went, that had been a corker!

Hannah had been prepared to overlook the stained and outdated wall coverings, seeing through the grime; imagining what it could be with a little love and attention. For the large amount of floor space, the loft apartment had been a bargain, even if it did need modernising. Now as she pulled and scraped at the stubborn paper which refused to come away from the wall, she wondered whether she should have hired someone to gut and redecorate the place.

She'd wanted to prove everyone wrong.

'Why don't you move back home with us for a bit?' her dad had offered warmly. After four weeks of home cooked food and her mother's never-ending fussing, she'd had to find something she could call her own; for the sake of *everyone's* sanity.

She knew how lucky she was to have both parents still alive, and fit enough to worry about her, but at twenty-nine, she was simply too old to be parented. That's why she'd jumped at the chance to buy this apartment in an area of Eastleigh that was undergoing its own modernisation project. There were streets of new-build townhouses and flats a stone's throw away, but she'd opted for a block with character, even though it was tucked away inside a cul-de-sac.

Catching her reflection in the pane of glass to the right of the wall, she considered herself for a moment. Wearing blue dungarees and a paint-spattered t-shirt, her hair was tied in a bun, and the top of her head protected by a hat made of newspaper. To any passer-by she was just a new homeowner coming to terms with her new purchase.

Anonymity was a welcome friend. Nobody in the building, road, or area would know who she was or what had happened nearly twelve months before.

The hairs on the back of her neck stood as she recalled the piercing sound of the smoke alarm that night. Taking a deep breath she drove the scraper at the clump of wallpaper, and this time it gave way, landing on the dusty floorboards with a plop.

Taking a step back she wiped her forehead with the back of her arm. Finally, one wall of the wide living room was free of the yellowing paper. Not for the first time, she wondered whether it would have been better just to have painted over the existing wallpaper, burying it. It would have been easier, but she wasn't someone who buckled at a challenge, which is why she'd uprooted her life and left the Salford suburbs for this growing town in Hampshire. With its own airport and access to both the M27 and M3 motorways, it was an ideal spot to rebuild what remained of her life.

John would be proud of her. She'd faced the toughest circumstances a person can suffer, and she'd fought back from the edge.

Out on the road below she spotted Nigel, the neighbour who lived on the floor below. They'd only passed on the stairs a couple of times and she knew very little about him.

Dark hair with deep-set eyes, he had to be in his late forties, but still dressed like his mother was buying his clothes. Today he was in maroon corduroys and a white and navy checked shirt.

'Never trust a man who keeps such odd hours,' Bea – the neighbour who resided on the ground floor – had concluded. 'Doesn't go to work until after eleven, and isn't home much before ten most nights.'

'Maybe he works a late shift?' Hannah had countered.

'I saw inside his flat once: floor-to-ceiling books on every wall: copies of bibles and books on theology and whatnot. I'm telling you: people like that, they're the ones the police investigate when strange things happen.'

Four gentle footsteps padded into the room, and before Hannah could turn she felt Barney's furry head nuzzling against the side of her knee. Rescuing a bearded collie, like the one they used to use in the paint commercials, for company had seemed like a logical step, and as soon as she'd spotted Barney's muffle of grey and white fur and his two dark eyes, she'd known she had to take him home. John had always said she was overly-sensitive when it came to animals. She'd put it down to his endless list of allergies, and had once mooted the idea of them buying a puppy or kitten for company at home, but he'd simply told her he was all the company she needed.

Growing up, Hannah had been neither a cat, nor dog person. With her father away so much with work, a pet wasn't practical, though she remembered taking care of a goldfish for a period until she'd discovered it floating on its side one morning.

Having fitted new door locks and an intruder alarm, in the new place, she'd headed to a dog shelter and almost instantly fallen in love with Barney's soppy face. When she'd heard his backstory, she'd known she would do anything to give him a loving home. After weeks of background checks, and home inspections, they'd finally agreed for her to adopt him, and they'd been virtually inseparable ever since.

Barney was just as likely to lick a burglar to death as he was to bite them, but he'd provided something else she hadn't realised had been missing from her life since the incident: companionship. He didn't judge her when she suddenly burst into tears while watching television; nor did he criticise when all she could stomach eating was pasta from a can. He never answered back when she chatted nonsensically to him.

Yet every night when she cried herself to sleep, and every morning when she woke and temporarily forgot that John had been snatched from her, Barney was there with his lopsided smile and gaze of pure love. She'd chosen to rescue him, but he was the one who'd rescued her.

The shelter had recommended giving him his own space for sleeping, suggesting she put his bed in the kitchen or spare room, but that first night he'd whined so much that she'd relented and moved his cushioned bed to her room. That's where he'd slept every night since. At no point during those nights did he venture from his bed, until she was awake and welcomed him up onto her mattress for a morning snuggle.

Hannah's hand instinctively moved across her abdomen, and the bitter pain of that sonographer's office came flooding back. After all that had happened the night John died, and the weeks of inquest that had followed as the police had at first treated Hannah as a suspect in John's murder, before arresting the real culprit, to learn that she'd lost their baby had shattered her heart into a million pieces.

She'd allowed herself to become withdrawn from the cruel world around her. Struggling to even get out of bed for more than an hour a day; barely eating or functioning. The days that had followed were a blur now, but her mum had refused to watch Hannah sink any lower. With counselling, nutrition and unrelenting love, somehow she'd made it back from the brink.

Barney caught her staring at him and barked once to tell her to stop messing about and take him for a walk.

Watching Barney scampering after the stick, and cocking his leg next to any weed that took his fancy, Hannah felt at peace. The grass underfoot was wet, and she had to be careful not to slip on a couple of occasions, but it didn't stop Barney tearing through the taller grass like he'd been unleashed and didn't know where to go next.

The parkland stretched as far as the eye could see, and felt so removed from the built-up Manchester skyline she'd been so used to seeing. John would have hated it. He was a city boy through and through. IT companies like his thrived in inner-city locations, so whenever she'd suggested they move somewhere more peaceful, he'd always met it with resistance.

Barney suddenly tore off towards a clump of woodland at the far side of the parkland where two much larger German Shepherd dogs were playing, their owner nowhere in sight.

'Barney, come,' Hannah shouted breathlessly, as he slunk into the distance. It was impossible to know whether he was choosing to ignore her commands, or genuinely couldn't hear them.

Hannah broke into a sprint, cutting through the ankle-length grass, regretting letting him roam off-lead. Her heart skipped a beat as one of the other dogs turned and snapped at Barney, and he pulled back abruptly, no longer so confident in his actions. The owner of the two dogs, wearing bright red overalls and heavy boots, did what he could to pull his dogs away as Hannah managed to catch up to Barney, relieved he hadn't raced off again. She quickly reattached the lead, and chastised him for disobeying her command.

'I'm... so... sorry,' she panted, barely able to get the words out, as she wheezed for breath.

'That's okay,' the man said, before adding, 'Are you okay?'

His voice was deeper than she'd expected. Looking up, her vision fell upon his tall frame, closely cropped dark hair and deep brown eyes, she found herself gulping down the air in a desperate attempt to compose herself. For the briefest of moments it was like John was standing before her, but he was gone in a blink.

'He... doesn't usually... run off,' she stuttered, feeling heat in her cheeks.

He smiled warmly at her, revealing a dimple in his left cheek. 'They're a law unto themselves sometimes, aren't they? Perhaps you should do some recall training with him.' His smile widened to show he meant no offence.

'I only adopted him a few weeks ago,' she said, uncertain why she felt the need to justify her actions.

'Well that makes him a lucky boy,' the man said, transferring the two dog leads to his left hand, before extending his right. 'I'm Steve, by the way.'

She shook the hand without thinking twice. 'Hannah.'

'It's nice to meet you, Hannah. You're local? I can't quite place your accent?'

'I am now. I was from Southampton originally, but lived in Manchester until very recently.'

'Ah, well welcome back.' He paused. 'You know there's a really good dog class that meets at the church hall down the road. Do you know where I mean? At the end of the main road. You should try taking him there. It's a great class, lots of friendly dogs and a good way for them to socialise, particularly if they're not used to doing it.' He paused again, this time reaching into his pocket, pulling out a small flyer and passing it to her 'I run the class actually. It's on every Thursday and Sunday night at seven. You should come along.'

She looked at the leaflet advertising "Williams' Woofers", recognising the address, as the hall up the road.

'It's a silly name, isn't it?' he said, pulling an awkward face. 'A mate of mine reckoned I should give the business a name, and suggested that. I'm Steve Williams, you see.'

She folded the leaflet and placed it in her pocket. 'I'll think about it.'

'Great. Anyway, I'd better get these two back,' he added, starting to turn. 'Maybe see you tonight at the class?'

'Maybe,' she said, keeping Barney close, as she watched him head away across the field, wielding the two large dogs as if they were only puppies.

Hannah looked down at Barney, ready to chastise him for running off, but then it wasn't really his fault; she'd been naïve to think his attention wouldn't be drawn to other animals.

Looking back up, she saw Steve disappearing into the distance, and immediately felt guilty about their exchange. John had been dead less than a year, and even talking to the handsome stranger felt like a betrayal of some kind. Withdrawing the leaflet from her pocket, she dropped it into the nearest litter bin, and was about to continue her journey when she felt her phone vibrating in her coat pocket. DI Jeanette Chandler's profile filled the screen, and Hannah knew almost immediately it wouldn't be good news.

FOUR

The wind was stronger as Hannah rounded the corner back onto the main road. 'Hi Jeanette, now's not a great time, I'm just on my way home.'

Despite Hannah's initial reservations about DI Jeanette Chandler's attitude on that night in Sandra's kitchen, the detective had proven herself to be the sort of person you'd rather be fighting with than against.

'Won't take two minutes,' Chandler replied, not one who liked to be put off. 'It's about Seamus Fahey: his appeal has been rejected.'

The very mention of *his* name still sent a shiver down Hannah's spine. Even though she hadn't been able to face him following the arrest, she'd seen his picture in the newspapers, and when Chandler had asked whether Hannah could identify him as the intruder. Now as she closed her eyes, Hannah could still hear the sound of his heavy footfalls on the staircase.

'Hannah? Did you hear what I said?' Chandler said, louder down the line.

Hannah shuddered against the cold. 'Um, yeah, that's good isn't it?'

'Yes, it's excellent news. I just thought it would be better you hear it from me.'

She'd grown used to Chandler's broad Yorkshire accent, which didn't sound out of place in Lancashire, but stood out a mile compared to what Hannah was growing accustomed to in Hampshire.

'Thank you for letting me know,' Hannah said, not sure whether she should be relieved that his appeal had been rejected, or angry that he'd been given the right to appeal his conviction in the first place.

The defence barrister had openly claimed that his client should never have been allowed to stand trial on account of diminished capacity. One of the tabloids had printed a two-page spread on Fahey's backstory. Hannah hadn't wanted to read it, but John's brother Patrick had brought it round and had ranted angrily for half an hour that the paper was deliberately trying to justify what Fahey had done. Hannah had managed to calm Patrick down, and had then read the piece herself, and couldn't deny feeling pity for what had befallen the man who stole everything from her.

Hannah had refused to attend the trial, unable to stomach being in the same room as Fahey, but Patrick had attended every day, the family's sole representative there. Their mum had passed away not long after Hannah had met John, and the trauma of losing John was too much for his dad to handle. A heart attack had followed shortly after Hannah had made *that* call, and he'd still been recuperating when the trial had begun.

Joining the army at sixteen, Fahey had completed tours in the Falklands as well as Northern Ireland, before he'd been caught in a blast during the first Gulf War. His unit was ambushed and tortured, before being rescued, but by then the damage was already done. Honourably discharged, he'd returned to the UK with no qualifications, and a country in recession. No family to support him, he'd fallen on hard times. With no job, limited benefits, and suffering undiagnosed PTSD, he'd ended up on the streets.

A forensic examination of the property had found Fahey's palm print on the knife's handle, a strand of his hair on the bed next to John's body, and his bloody boot print on the staircase. A vagrant, Fahey was already known to the local police for drug possession and theft offences, and when they picked him up in one of his regular haunts, they found several dried patches of John's blood on his overcoat. Evidentially the case had been as sound as it could have been, but Fahey's inability to properly answer any of the questions at interview had raised questions about his capacity to stand trial. He'd been drunk and high when he was arrested and had spent almost a day sobering up in custody. Even when he was sober, he still couldn't provide an explanation of how the blood had wound up on his coat.

At trial the barrister had tried to challenge the evidence, claiming many of the homeless frequently swapped clothing, and that given Fahey's state when he was arrested, there was no way he'd have been able to carry out the attack. After all, John was a strong man, and Fahey – despite his military background – wasn't in good health. The jury had seen through the barrister's parlour tricks and had returned a majority verdict.

'Hannah? Are you still there?' Chandler's Yorkshire baritone cut through the memories.

'Yes, was there anything else? I'm in a bit of a rush.'

There was a pause on the line. Chandler wasn't one who minced her words. 'Are you still in touch with your counsellor?'

'Jeanette, I'm fine; honestly I am. The loft is starting to take shape, I'm getting plenty of exercise with Barney the dog, and I'm about to start a new job on Monday. You don't need to worry about me. I'm not your problem anymore.'

Hannah hadn't meant to sound so curt, and hoped Chandler wouldn't take it personally.

'New job? You going to be starting up your photography business again?'

It was a fair question, and one Hannah had spent weeks contemplating herself. She'd always been creative, enjoying art and design at school, and when the opportunity to study photography as part of her college course arose, she'd leapt at the opportunity. Nothing felt as powerful to her as snatching a moment in time.

John had never seen what she had in her photographs. He'd tease, 'You'll never make any real money out of it,' but it had never been about making an income for her. It was about capturing a million possibilities in a single frame. He'd been right, of course he had, and the business had folded. It seemed that people just weren't willing to pay for the beauty of a snapshot.

She was sure he wouldn't have approved in her accepting a part-time job at a local supermarket, and would have insisted she live off his life assurance and the proceeds of the house sale, but she needed a distraction in her life; something to force her from the safety of the loft. It was fine to be a homemaker when he'd been there to provide, but she was on her own now.

'Something like that,' Hannah replied, opting not to admit the truth, assuming her path was unlikely to cross Chandler's again.

'Okay, okay, I'll let you get on,' Chandler huffed, 'but don't think you get to cut me out of your life that easy, girl. My job doesn't stop just because Fahey's behind bars. You were a victim of his malicious act, and I will do everything within my power to help set your course straight.'

'I'm grateful to have your support. I don't know how I would have made it through the last year without you.'

'Remember what I said about your counselling. The fact that your memory hasn't returned should be as concerning for you as it is for me. The doctors have said that medically there is no reason for the amnesia to continue. I can understand you not wanting to relive that nightmare, but no good comes from burying the truth.'

The line disconnected, and with her cheeks flushing,

Hannah headed back into the wind, with Chandler's words still ringing in her ears.

FIVE

Barney snuggled close as Hannah scraped the last of the lasagne from the plastic container with her fork.

'Sorry, no leftovers for you little man,' she said ruffling the fur on the top of his head.

Resting his head on her leg, he stared up at her with his shiny dark eyes, and in that moment she knew no other male would ever love her as much as he did.

Pushing up off the sofa, she carried her plate through to the kitchen, dropping the container in the bin and lowering the fork and plate into the bowl in the sink. The dishes could wait for morning. She'd yet to draw the blind in the kitchen, and so the cul-de-sac filled the window. With the kitchen light off, she had full view of the properties on both sides of the street, delicately lit by occasional street lights lining the pavement, it felt as though the shadows were alive, moving in and out of the light as the wind blew.

A knock at the door startled her, and moving across to the viewing hole, she squinted at the figure on the other side.

'It's Bea,' her neighbour called out, holding up a bottle of wine for Hannah to see. 'You busy?'

Hannah felt too tired to entertain, but opened the door, and tried her best to smile at her neighbour. Wearing an overly large and colourful scarf, Bea was only a couple of years older than Hannah, but carried herself with a bohemian air; in control of her life, yet not caring where she ended up. In many ways a polar opposite of Hannah who craved structure and direction.

'I'm not disturbing you, am I?' Bea asked, edging closer to the doorway. 'I was supposed to be hanging out with some friends tonight but they've cancelled last minute because one of their children has the pox or something. I have wine and a bag of snacks,' she added, a grocery bag appearing from behind her back.

Hannah's counsellor Dr Yenny had encouraged her to be more sociable, especially in a new area, so, stepping back, Hannah ushered her neighbour in. 'You'll have to excuse the state of the place,' Hannah apologised, 'it's mid-renovation, and I wasn't anticipating company.'

Bea headed through, looking around her at the half-papered-half-scraped plaster. 'It's not all that bad,' she smiled. 'You ought to see my place!' Patting Barney on the head as she passed him stretched out on the sofa, she added, 'Have you got a couple of glasses?'

Muting the television, Hannah collected two tumblers from the cupboard beneath the set, and handed them over. 'I haven't bought any wine glasses yet. Sorry.'

Bea pulled a surprised face. 'No wine glasses? Right, definitely need to get you trained up. It's a rule of living in this block, you see. We're all wine drinkers in this place. You can't go wrong with white or rosé, but best to avoid red; brings me out in hives.' Filling both glasses, Bea handed one to Hannah, before squashing herself in next to Barney. 'He's cute, what breed is he?'

'Bearded Collie,' Hannah said, sitting in the single uncovered chair at the small round table near the window. 'Thanks for the wine,' she said, sipping, and grimacing at the bitter taste.

'It's just the cheap plonk from the local shop,' Bea said, taking a large gulp from her glass. 'It's good for two things: lowering inhibitions, and de-icing cars.' She cackled at her own joke, stopping when she spotted the bulky digital camera on the sideboard. 'That yours?'

Hannah's eyes fell on the Canon EOS Digital SLR Camera and wide zoom lens, a fresh layer of dust having settled since she'd cleaned it yesterday. She had a bag full of lenses and a tripod under the bed, which she hadn't touched since moving in. It did seem a waste keeping hold of such expensive kit. It had taken time and money to purchase the valuable set, and if she truly would never use it again, she was better off selling it. Capturing nature had been a hobby as much as a career choice, but then she'd met John and her priorities had changed.

'I used to be a professional photographer,' Hannah admitted, surprised at how easy it felt to speak with Bea.

Bea reached for a framed photograph from the coffee table next to her. 'This one of yours then?'

Hannah nodded, remembering the moment they'd been on safari and she'd snapped the shot of the mother giraffe tending to her offspring. 'It was a different life.'

Bea returned the frame to the table and took another drink from her glass. 'You've got a good eye. I always wanted to do something creative with my life, an actress, or a performer of some kind, maybe it will happen one day. For now, I'll continue answering phones at the call centre. What do you do? How come you've ended up here alone?'

Hannah looked away, not yet ready to share her immediate past. 'I was born in Southampton as it happens, but I went to Manchester for university, and settled there, but now I'm looking for a fresh start.'

Bea raised her glass in toast. 'Oh I know that feeling. God knows how many times I've tried to reinvent myself. Different flat, different town, but I continue to fall into old habits. Sometimes I wish I could just totally reinvent myself; new name, new ambitions, no history; just wipe the slate clean.'

That had been Hannah's intention, but it seemed it

wasn't so easy to escape the past.

'I reckon that Melanie Fowler had the right idea.'

Hannah frowned, not recognising the name. 'Am I supposed to know who that is?'

Bea gave her a puzzled look. 'Oh, you don't know, do you…? I probably shouldn't say any more; I don't want to freak you out.'

It was like Bea was trying to bait her, and Hannah succumbed. 'Who is Melanie Fowler?'

Bea pushed herself off the sofa, refilling her glass from the bottle on the table, before leaning closer to Hannah. 'She used to live in this apartment. Maybe four to five years ago. She was pretty: blonde with sparkling emerald eyes; looked like the sort who could have been a model but had chosen education over glamour.' Bea retook her seat, Barney rolling onto his back, encouraging her to rub his belly. 'I didn't know her that well, but she was always friendly whenever I'd pass her on the stairs, and then one day, she just disappeared.'

Hannah couldn't ignore the sense that like all good ghost stories, this one had been shared many times between friends, each adding their own unique embellishment to the facts.

'The police were swarming all over the place once her disappearance was reported. Treated it as suspicious, because of the way she'd just fallen off the planet. She'd been quite active on social media – Facebook, twitter, and the like – but hasn't logged into any of that since the last day she was seen. Didn't close the accounts, just left them to live on perpetually. Hasn't touched her bank accounts since either, from what I've heard.'

The wind blew against the frame of the window, and Hannah shuddered involuntarily, despite the warmth of the room. 'That's impossible. You can't just disappear in this day and age. With the number of traffic and security cameras, and GPS signals on all smart devices, they'd be able to track her, surely?'

'Apparently not. The last person to see her said she'd looked upset – teary – when she'd gone into the loft that night, and that she had never reappeared. I'm surprised you didn't hear about it; it was in the newspapers, and all over the television down here.'

'What do you think happened?'

'At first I reckoned she'd been offed by that weirdo downstairs, but the police interviewed him, and ruled him out as a suspect, so I now like to think that she'd just had enough and decided to start again.'

'Wait, why would you assume Nigel had something to do with it?'

'Well, I've told you what he's like: a religious nut! Plus, they were seeing each other for a few months before she disappeared, so he was the logical suspect. Apparently, she ended it with him, and he didn't take it well, but as I said, the police let him go.'

Hannah pictured Nigel's dark eyes watching over their every move, but quickly dismissed the thought; if the police had suspected him of harming this Melanie Fowler, he wouldn't be roaming the streets. In her limited experience with law enforcement, they didn't stop searching until they found the culprit.

'Are you on Facebook?' Bea suddenly asked, sitting forward. 'I should add you as a friend in case Nigel takes a fancy to you too.' She burst out laughing, though Hannah didn't see the funny side.

'I'm not, no. I'm not that tech savvy, my husband used to deal with things like…' her words trailed off, as she realised what she'd said.

'You're married then?'

It was too late to correct the mistake. 'I was.'

'Ah that explains it,' Bea said, with an understanding

nod. 'Did the dirty on you, did he?'

'No. he didn't cheat on me,' Hannah corrected. 'He… he died. Last year.'

Bea's expression instantly changed to one of regret. 'Oh, I'm so sorry, I didn't realise.'

Hannah stood suddenly, not wanting to linger. 'It's not something I like to talk about. Too raw.'

Bea pointed at a frame on the sideboard near the camera. 'Is that him?'

The sting of tears threatened to spill as Hannah turned and saw where Bea was pointing. It had been taken by John's brother Patrick the day John had proposed. They both looked so happy, so strong and so in love. Neither of them could have predicted what would come or how their lives would be permanently altered by Fahey's attack.

'Yes, that was my John.'

'Handsome,' Bea commented. 'You both look very happy.'

Hannah dabbed the corner of her eyes. 'He was my whole world.' She paused, craving solitude. 'Listen, Bea, I appreciate you coming over to keep me company, but I should probably get to bed; busy day tomorrow, you know?'

Bea's face said she regretted broaching such a sensitive subject, but she didn't argue, ruffling Barney's fur, and standing. 'If you ever want to talk or just put the world to rights, you know where I am. Okay? Oh and keep the wine, you look like you need it more than I do.'

Hannah showed her to the door, fastening the three locks and attaching the security chain in place. Transferring the glasses and bottle to the kitchen draining board, she returned to the living room and was about to switch off the television, when she froze. The volume was still muted, but it was clear what the newscaster was describing, as Seamus Fahey's face filled the screen.

Despite months of therapy, sessions of hypnosis, and

memory-aiding stimuli, her view of that night was still marred in confusion. She could remember the doorbell ringing and her reaching for the door. She had flashes of her head crashing against the floor and the feeling of her body being thrown about, but no vision of Fahey's face until the point where the police showed her his profile picture and explained that they were charging him with John's murder.

The face on the television screen finally disappeared, and a wave of relief washed over her. He couldn't get her. Not now. He'd made a mistake in leaving her alive, and now he would spend the rest of his life in prison because of it.

Hannah completed a circuit of the loft, double-checking the windows and front door were locked, before heading to bed, leaving the hallway lights on.

SIX

Staring out of the upstairs bedroom window, Hannah was surprised at how dark it was already. There was no sign of John's car on the driveway, but he would be home soon, and then she could share her news. Pulling the curtains closed, she stepped backwards and admired her reflection in the tall mirror in the cupboard door, gently holding her abdomen, knowing that her baby wasn't even the size of a bean yet. She could feel it inside of her though, growing and she tingled at the excitement of telling John what the doctor had confirmed earlier.

Although they hadn't been trying for a baby, it had been six months since she'd stopped taking the prescribed contraceptive, and John would be thrilled to find out he was going to be a dad. They'd talked many times about starting a family, and now their chance had arrived.

She knew it was too early to start thinking about baby names, but she couldn't help but smile at the thought of cradling her baby one day soon. Hearing a noise downstairs, she turned and headed towards it, a feeling of dread crawling over her as she made her way slowly down the stairs.

For some reason, the front door was wide open, but there was no sign of John approaching. A cool breeze was blowing outside, so she closed the door, but neither her keys, nor John's were in sight. Moving towards the kitchen in search of her handbag, she'd barely made it eight yards when she heard the front door opening behind her. Turning, the door swung wide, but there was nobody on the doorstep. Moving back, she closed it again more forcibly, wondering how she'd failed to close it properly the first time. As she turned back towards the kitchen, her eyes widened as a dark figure appeared in the shadows of the room by the patio door.

As she continued to watch him, his arm slowly rose and he put a finger to his lips.

Dread turned to panic, and suddenly she was racing up the stairs, even though she knew it would limit her options. He was in pursuit, just behind her, and as she reached the top step, he lunged at her ankle, pulling it from under her, and then she was falling fast and to the floor. The musty smell of carpet filled her lungs.

One thought raced through her mind: she needed to get away. If she remained where she was, she would be at his mercy.

He was on top of her now, forcing her face further into the pile of the carpet, before pulling her head back by her ponytail, and then slamming it back down again. A pain tore through her nose, but her agonised screams were muffled by the pile

The adrenaline coursing, she struggled and battled, using her elbows to manoeuvre her body, so she'd have a chance of getting him off her. Suddenly his weight shifted enough for her to push herself up, and dart away. Diving into the main bedroom, she slammed and locked the door behind her, desperate to keep him out, yet knowing she was only delaying the inevitable. Killing the lights, she rushed around the edge of the bed, and ducked down, hoping John would return and put an end to this nightmare, or that the intruder would give up.

A sudden thud was followed by the sound of wood splintering as the door flew open. The intruder was in the room. Hannah held her breath, willing him not to come closer, his breathing laboured as he stomped into the room.

Blindly searching for anything she might use as a weapon, there was nothing within grasp. Where was her phone? It had to be in her handbag, and if she could just get to it she could call the police and they could save her.

His heavy footsteps moved closer, and it wouldn't be long until he'd be able to see her cowering behind the bed. Her only chance of survival was if she could take him by surprise.

Taking a deep breath, she shuffled quietly into a hunched position, trying to compose herself, before launching up and forwards, crashing into the large figure and catching him off-guard. He stumbled backwards, reaching out for her, but she narrowly managed to avoid his grasp.

The light of the landing beckoned, and she made no attempt to close the broken door as she dived through it, and raced back down the stairs. At the bottom, the front door was now closed, and as she tried to unfasten the latch, she found it locked and, despite her best efforts, it wouldn't open.

Realising her only exit was out through the patio door in the kitchen, she rushed along the hallway and into the kitchen, but he was soon upon her again, tackling her to the ground. His large warm hand coiled around the back of her neck and then something sharp and cold was pressed against her throat, and the fight instantly left her body.

Hannah shot up in bed, screaming, her heart racing and her whole body dripping with sweat. A large object bounded onto the duvet, and it was only his warm tongue that told her Barney had come to her rescue. Ruffling his fur, she remained still, trying to steady her breathing, before reaching for the light switch, relieved to see the unpainted walls of the loft staring back at her.

It was only a dream, she reminded herself, but that didn't mean she was safe.

Rolling out of bed, she turned on the main light, and moved out to the hallway, heading straight for the kitchen, and pulling a large carving knife from the block. Although nightmares had been a common occurrence since that night, this one had felt so real that she wasn't prepared to take any chances, especially after what Bea had said about Melanie Fowler.

Tiptoeing to the front door, she checked again that the three locks and security chain were fastened, and that the external intruder alarm hadn't been sounded. Then moving to the living room, she undertook her regular checking of all the window locks, and only when she was absolutely satisfied that nobody had nor could get in did she return to the bedroom.

Barney was back in his bed, though he did open his eyes as she entered. The room felt stuffy, but there was no way she would open a window for air. Instead, she peeled the nightdress from her body, tossing it into the laundry basket and pulling the shower cubicle door closed behind her. She allowed the cool water to wash over her. The night sky beyond the frosted window was pitch black, giving her no indication of how early or late it was.

Stepping out of the shower, her fingers were still trembling as she reached for the towels on the back of the bathroom door, tying one around her head, and the other around her body. Barney gave her a curious look as she slumped down on the bed, unsure whether he should join her or remain where he was.

Checking the clock, she growled in frustration. Three thirty was too early to get up, but she wasn't sure she could handle falling back to sleep and suffering another nightmare. With nobody she could phone and talk to, she finally gave up, and headed out to the living room, beckoning Barney to come and join her. He wouldn't care whether he slept in his bed or on the sofa. Sitting, she turned on the television and flicked through the stations until she found a late night movie channel, and settled in.

SEVEN

Combing her hair for the third time since waking, Hannah scanned the immediate layout in front of the laptop, which was precariously rested on a stool, about two metres from the sofa. Did it look like she'd gone to too much effort to convey normality? Would Dr Yenny see through the façade Hannah was projecting?

In the bathroom, she opened her makeup bag, searching for the red lipstick, which would perfectly compliment the crimson dress she'd chosen to wear. She didn't tend to wear a lot of makeup. John had always said she didn't need it. In fairness, her skin was smooth, and although she moisturised it every night, she didn't have to do much else to maintain it. However, on this occasion, she needed to make a good impression, and the autumn weather had done little to add much colour to her skin. Staring at her complexion in the misty mirror, it was hard to ignore how pale her skin tone looked.

Continuing to scramble her fingers through the bag, she couldn't find the red lipstick. Carrying the bag out of the bathroom and into the living room, here the light was stronger, she tipped the contents onto the sofa. There was mascara, blusher, eyeliner, a pink and maroon lipstick, but not the red one.

She hadn't used it up, she was certain, but where else could it be. She was so meticulous about putting it back, out of fear that Barney might inadvertently mistake any of it for food. Turning to look at him dozing in his basket, she said, 'You haven't seen my lipstick have you?'

He raised his head as she was addressing him, but made no movement towards her.

Carefully returning each item to the bag, she inspected the two lipsticks to make sure she hadn't missed it. Neither the maroon nor the pink would complement her outfit, and the last thing she wanted to do was go to the hassle of picking something else out.

Huffing, she returned the bag to its usual spot in the basket on the windowsill, searching for anywhere the lipstick might have fallen at some point, and trying to recall the last time she'd used it. Sighing, she checked her skin tone in the mirror again. It would just have to do.

Barney had been patiently sitting in his basket in the corner of the living room watching her fussing here and there, gathering magazines and moving them out of sight, before realising that the space behind her looked too neat. Dr Yenny knew she'd only just moved into the loft, so it would be natural to expect some kind of disarray, wouldn't it? Too much chaos and Dr Yenny would be concerned that Hannah wasn't coping.

Perching on the edge of the sofa, she examined the viewing window displaying what the laptop's built-in camera would capture. Hannah had decided to hold the video call in here, even though she had yet to finish removing the previous owner's hideous taste in wallpaper. It was the largest room in the loft, and was where Hannah would expect any normal, rational person to host a video call. Hosting in the bedroom was too informal, and hosting in the kitchen would lead Dr Yenny to wonder what Hannah was trying to hide.

Hannah had already rehearsed what she would say when Dr Yenny inevitably asked about the wallpaper.

'It's hideous,' Hannah said smiling at herself in the

viewing window, as if she was speaking directly to Dr Yenny. 'I knew the apartment would need some work, but I hadn't realised just how shocking it was. This is the last room I need to finish and I'm just taking my time with it.'

She exhaled, replaying the words in her mind, looking for any triggers that Dr Yenny might pick up on. Had she delivered it at the right pace? Had it sounded rehearsed, or had she managed to deliver at a natural pitch and pace?

Something glinted in the corner of the viewing window, and Hannah suddenly realised the large carving knife, which she'd taken from the kitchen in the middle of the night, could be seen on the coffee table next to the sofa. How had she missed it?

Picking up the knife, she carried it back through to the kitchen and returned it to the block. With the morning autumn sunshine now streaming through the loft's large windows, the space didn't look nearly as scary as it had last night. Even so, she made a mental note to take the knife through to the bedroom that night. She was defenceless once before, and would never make that mistake again.

'Hi Hannah, so wonderful to see you looking so happy,' Dr Alison Yenny exclaimed, when her call came through two minutes later.

The two women had first met six weeks after John's murder. With disrupted sleep, and grieving heavily, Hannah had been diagnosed with mild PTSD, and referred to Dr Yenny, an expert in her field. Hannah hadn't been keen on sharing her situation with a stranger, but Dr Yenny had immediately put her at ease, striking up an informal conversation, with no mention of the incident at that first meeting.

Born in Hong Kong, Dr Yenny had been raised in the UK from age three, and there was no longer a trace of her mother tongue, though Hannah had overheard what she assumed was Cantonese once when Dr Yenny had taken a personal call during one of their sessions. In her late thirties, Dr Yenny had the face of someone much younger, and she had a wicked sense of humour. Their appointments together had been twice a month until Hannah had told her she was returning to Hampshire to start again.

Dr Yenny had urged caution, reminding Hannah that the best way to deal with the trauma of what she had experienced was to tackle it head-on. Moving to Southampton hadn't been an attempt to run away from her problems, more that she just could no longer handle the constant reminders of the life she'd lost.

'You look well, too,' Hannah said, stretching the smile a bit wider, one eye on Dr Yenny's face, and the other on the viewing window which was now much smaller and in the top left corner of the screen.

'Thank you. So is this the apartment you were telling me about when we last spoke?'

'That's right. Ignore the wallpaper – not my choice – but I'm in the process of removing it. Hideous isn't it?'

A flicker of a frown appeared on Dr Yenny's face. 'I quite like it actually. Does that make me old-fashioned? Probably. Have you hired someone to redecorate?'

'I'm doing it myself,' Hannah replied proudly. 'It's a bit more work than I'd anticipated, but I'm getting there.'

'I hope you're not taking on too much?'

There it was, the unmistakeable hint of concern in Dr Yenny's voice that Hannah had been anticipating.

'It's just a bit of wallpaper to be taken down, and then a couple of coats of paint. I'm actually finding it quite cathartic.'

'Good for you!' The concern was gone. 'Personally, the idea of decorating is enough to have me pulling my hair out, but if it's helping then that's great. How is the job hunting going?'

Hannah had been nervous about telling Dr Yenny her

plans to find work once she was settled, again because Dr Yenny was always so preoccupied with Hannah tackling too many challenges in one go.

'I had an interview for a supermarket job last week...' Hannah began, before the words trailed off.

'That's good to hear. How do you think it went?'

'Pretty well, I think,' Hannah lied. 'The manager said there'd been a lot of interest in the role, but they offered it to me, and I start on Monday.'

'That's fabulous! Congratulations. I bet they asked you lots of those "Describe a time when you did x, y, or z," didn't they?'

It was like Dr Yenny could read Hannah's mind. Maybe that was why they got on so well. 'Loads of them. Is it the same when you apply for jobs in medicine?'

'Not exactly, but my partner works in finance, and she asks me to help her prepare for interviews.'

It was rare for Dr Yenny to mention her partner. She'd always told Hannah that no subject was off-limits between them, but the sessions always tended to focus on Hannah's situation.

'Have you spoken with any of the counsellors I mentioned to you before you left Manchester?' Dr Yenny continued.

The printed list of names, addresses and phone numbers was stuck to the fridge with a magnet. Hannah looked at the list every time she got something out, but she had yet to contact any of them.

'I'm fine as I am. I really do think that I'm on the mend. Don't get me wrong, I still miss John every waking second of every day, but I'm learning to live with the feeling of loss.' Hannah had been reading the pile of books Dr Yenny had recommended, each listing different stages of the grieving process and suggesting methods for overcoming each stage, like following a set of instructions from a

Satnav.

'I've been through shock and denial, you were with me for the pain and guilt, and when I was so angry with Fahey. You recognised when I was at my lowest. This move has reinvigorated something inside of me. I really am fine.'

The flicker of doubt returned to Dr Yenny's face, but passed just as quickly again. 'I'm really pleased to hear that, Hannah. It's fantastic that you've made such great progress in such little time. I would caution you not to throw away the list just yet. The grieving process is different for everyone, and just because we – those who have observed others going through the same issues you are – have identified milestones, it doesn't mean that your journey will be textbook. It's still possible to go backwards when things get too much. Hopefully, you will continue to grow and improve, but just look out for the warning signs of things getting on top of you. Will you do that for me?'

Hannah stretched her smile wider again. 'Absolutely. I know there will be bad days as well as good.'

'I know I told you it would be awkward for us to continue our sessions via video calls, but if things get so bad that you feel you aren't coping, I want you to book time in with me. My door is never closed to you.'

The memory of last night's dream flashed through her mind, and she opened her mouth to speak before reconsidering, and taking a breath. 'I really do appreciate all your help, Dr Yenny. I promise that if I think things start getting on top of me, I will reach out to you or one of the counsellors on the list you provided.'

The concern vanished from Dr Yenny's face, and she smiled for the first time. 'Okay, well I'm pleased things have progressed for you. Keep me posted on how your first day goes.'

Hannah promised she would, and as the call ended, she sat back and let out a huge sigh of relief.

EIGHT

The heavy banging on the door continued as Hannah approached it. The whole reason she'd opted for an apartment was so that she'd have the safety of a main door and intercom system. Whoever was on the other side had obviously bypassed that security, leaving Hannah with two thoughts: either the person lived in the block – images of Nigel flashed through her mind – or the individual had tailgated someone inside. Either way, Hannah knew she wasn't about to open the door without confirming the individual's identity.

Barney continued to make his concern apparent, barking every time the door was struck.

Squinting through the peephole, she was surprised to see Bea on the other side, hopping from one foot to the other, her face deathly pale, and her wet fringe clinging to her forehead. Unfastening all the locks, Hannah opened the door, leaning against it and fixing Bea with an inquisitive stare.

'Oh, thank God you're home,' Bea panted. 'We need to talk.'

Bea didn't wait to be invited in, pushing past Hannah and hurrying into the living room, pacing frantically.

Closing the door, Hannah joined her neighbour in the room. 'Bea, what's going on? You're worrying me.'

'You're right to be worried. We both should be. Are you alone?'

The furrow in Hannah's brow deepened. 'Yes, of course. What is it? Has something happened?' Resting her hands on Bea's arms, she brought the pacing to an abrupt stop. 'Sit down and tell me what is troubling you.'

Bea reluctantly slumped onto the sofa, Hannah next to her, their knees practically touching. 'It's about what we discussed last night.'

Hannah tried to remember what they'd talked about when Bea had called around with the wine. Did she mean what Hannah had told her about John?

'I've been doing some research,' Bea said, biting the nails on her left hand.

Hannah's shoulders tensed. It had to be about John. Clearly Bea had gone home and dug up Hannah's past, and now knew what had happened almost a year ago. She braced herself for a flurry of questions.

Bea reached into her pocket, removing her phone and tapping the screen. 'Here you go, this is her Facebook profile.'

Hannah accepted the phone and stared down at the pretty young woman in the snapshot. She couldn't have been much younger than Hannah, with smooth skin, a low fringe, and hair tied back as John like it. After reading the post at the top of the page, she could only shrug. 'What am I supposed to be looking for?'

'Look at the dates,' Bea said, still chewing her nails.

Hannah glanced back at the phone. 'Okay, Guy Fawkes night, is that significant?'

'Not the day, but look at the year. 2015. She hasn't posted anything in nearly five years.'

Hannah still couldn't see the significance, having never had the urge to share the nitty-gritty details of her life for the world to see. 'If she was trying to shut herself off from the world, it isn't surprising that she'd cut herself off from social media, is it?'

Bea shook her head, and stabbed a finger towards the screen. 'If she wanted to stop social media, she'd close her account. Don't you see? She hasn't posted since 2015 because she's not able to. She's dead. He killed her.'

'He?'

Bea leaned closer, her voice barely more than a whisper. 'Nigel.'

Hannah thrust the phone back to her. 'This again? You said yourself that the police interviewed and released him. If he was guilty of anything they'd have charged him.'

'Not without evidence they wouldn't. The company I work for – the call centre – it's a legal firm. People phone up with legal queries, and those requiring general guidance we provide over the phone, and for more complex matters we make the caller an appointment to speak to a solicitor. Anyway, we see things like this *all* the time. Criminals are getting better at covering their tracks.'

Hannah could see how desperate Bea was to believe her own suspicions, and tried to let her down gently. 'Maybe she left the account open in case she wanted to return to it one day. Or maybe she didn't realise she could close it. You're jumping to all manner of conclusions with no foundation to support them.'

'She was here, and now she isn't,' Bea grizzled. 'Nobody knows where she is or why she suddenly disappeared. I found out from the previous landlord that Melanie had just paid her next two month's rent before she vanished. If she knew she was going to go, why do that? It makes no sense.'

'There could be any number of reasons.'

'Such as?'

Hannah opened her mouth to answer but was at a loss for words. 'Even so, it doesn't mean Nigel had anything to do with it.'

Bea suddenly froze, before pressing a finger to her lips.

'He could be listening in to us now,' she whispered. 'We don't want to alert him to the fact we know what he did.'

Hannah looked nervously around the living room, but anything of value was either covered with a dust sheet or still packed away in one of the pile of boxes in the spare room. She was allowing Bea's paranoia get the better of her.

'He sent me a friend request last night,' Bea said, her eyes watering. 'Why would he do that? We've barely exchanged more than two words, and then out of the blue – on the same night you and I discuss Melanie's disappearance – he suddenly reaches out to me on Facebook. Bit coincidental, don't you think?'

'Is it? I wouldn't know.'

Bea suddenly snapped her fingers together. 'We should set you up with a profile on Facebook, and see if he sends you a friend request too.'

The last thing Hannah wanted was to draw unnecessary attention to herself, let alone paint a potential target on her back. 'I'm not sure –'

'It's perfect!' Bea interrupted. 'I can do it now for you. All you need is an email address and a password, and you're away. It'll take a couple of minutes at most.'

'No, Bea. I'm not interested in any of that. I told you my husband was the technology expert in our household. Plus I don't want anyone to try and steal my information or identity.'

Bea snickered. 'It's perfectly safe, I promise you. You don't have to give them your address or bank account information, and you don't even have to post anything if you don't want to.'

Hannah's frown returned. 'How will setting up a Facebook account determine whether Nigel had anything to do with Melanie's disappearance? How would he even know I'm on there?'

'Exactly! *He* found me. We don't have any friends in

common from what I've seen looking at his profile, except for Melanie. All we have to do is add me to your friends list, and then if he sends you a friend request, we'll know he's been looking for us.'

'Hardly a smoking gun.'

'No, but it would be enough for us to know to take precautions.'

'This is assuming he had anything to do with her disappearing. For all we know, her family know exactly where she is.'

'You reckon? Well why don't we go and ask them and find out?'

Hannah gave her a puzzled look. 'How would we do that?'

Bea pulled a folded sheet of paper from her pocket. 'I found their address in the phone book. They live down the road in Fareham. Half an hour drive at most.'

Hannah couldn't keep the surprise out of her voice. 'How do you know the address is theirs?'

'Because I met them once, a couple of months before she vanished they came to visit her and I spoke briefly to them. Melanie mentioned that they lived in Fareham, and this address is the only one for the surname Fowler in the area.'

'Doesn't mean it's them.'

'I phoned the number and spoke for ten minutes with Mrs Fowler, Melanie's mum. I didn't tell her who I was, but mentioned Melanie by name, and that's when she hung up the phone.'

'You phoned her mum? What did you say?'

'It doesn't matter, she won't know who I was, but more importantly I got the impression that she still doesn't know where her daughter is.' Her voice dropped to a whisper again. 'What if he did kill Melanie because she rejected his advances? What if he does it again? One of us could be his next victim.'

NINE

Against her better judgement, Hannah was now stuck in crawling traffic, as the motorway exit slowly loomed into view. Having quickly showered, she'd told Bea she needed to walk Barney and get breakfast. Bea hadn't taken the hint and had followed her on the walk, talking non-stop about her theories regarding Nigel. It hadn't been easy listening, but Hannah couldn't doubt it wasn't the craziest idea she'd heard. Remembering how easily Seamus Fahey had penetrated her own home, she'd reluctantly agreed to drive Bea to Fareham.

'Imagine if we managed to solve a case the police weren't able to,' Bea continued, barely stopping for breath. 'We'd get our names in the newspaper, maybe set up our own detective agency. Here, what do you think?'

Hannah shrugged politely, but the thought of seeing her name in print filled her with dread. 'You do realise we need to tread very carefully,' she warned. 'Bear in mind, if you are right – by some weird stretch of the imagination – these people won't have heard from or seen their daughter in nearly five years. That can't be easy. We can't go stumbling blindly into their lives, and start making accusations about some guy they may never have heard about.'

'What do you take me for?' Bea challenged back, though with little conviction. They both knew Hannah was right, and that Bea's enthusiasm alone would no doubt get the better of her.

'Besides,' Hannah continued, 'if this is still an open case with the police, we could be in danger of interfering in their investigation. The last thing either of us needs is to be arrested.'

Bea didn't respond, staring down at the map on Hannah's phone. You need the third exit at the roundabout, then it's a straight road down to the next roundabout, which you need to go straight over.'

Hannah flicked on the car's indicator, and moved onto the slip road, able to increase their speed up to the roundabout.

The large bungalow was set back from the road, a small, recently cut lawn stretching out below a large bay window at the front, with a short patio stone driveway to the left of it. A brand new Jaguar saloon car was parked, shining beneath the sunlight which threatened to break through the even cloud coverage. A three foot brick wall protected the lawn from the pavement running the length of the road.

'That must be it,' Bea said, as Hannah pulled the car over on the road outside the property.

'Right then. How do you want to do this? There's every chance they won't even speak to us. You do realise that don't you? I mean: I didn't even know Melanie.'

Bea wasn't listening, out of the car a moment later, excitedly hurrying along the driveway and pressing the doorbell, stepping to one side when Hannah caught up.

The front door opened a moment later, and they were greeted by a woman with short, dark hair, her face a confusion of blusher and wrinkles, and her lipstick as red as any Hannah had ever seen. She looked from Hannah to Bea and then back again. 'I don't buy from the door, thank you very much.'

Bea pressed her foot down on the step to prevent the door being closed. 'Um, Mrs Fowler? My name's Bea, and this is Hannah. We were friends of Melanie's.

The older woman's eyes widened at the mention of her daughter's name. 'You knew Melanie?'

The question was directed at Hannah, and to admit the deceit would most likely result in the door being closed. 'That's right,' Hannah said through gritted teeth, unhappy about stringing along this vulnerable woman.

'Come in, come in,' Mrs Fowler said, stepping away from the door and ushering them through.

The scent of lavender dominated the hallway, even though there wasn't a single flower in sight. The short hallway, led to a large open plan kitchen-diner at the far end, and off to the right they arrived in a large living room, with a television in one corner, two armchairs directly in front of it. There was a third armchair close to the bay window, where a bag of wool rested against the small wooden leg of the chair.

'Please sit,' Mrs Fowler said, waving towards the two chairs, while she reclaimed her seat by the window, so they could all see each other. Mrs Fowler delicately lowered herself into the chair, and took a deep breath to compose herself. 'How is it I can help you?'

Hannah didn't know where to start. How could she ask whether or not Mrs Fowler had heard from her daughter in the five years?

'You have a lovely home,' Hannah offered, hoping to establish some rapport before hitting her with the killer line.

'Oh, thank you,' Mrs Fowler said, smiling from ear-to-ear. 'We like it.'

'Is Mr Fowler home as well?'

'Not at the moment, I'm afraid. He's gone to the shop to buy his newspaper. Do you need to speak to him as well?'

'No, not necessarily,' Hannah said, smiling back, but feeling horrid for invading this woman's life. Taking a deep breath, she said, 'We were trying to get hold of Melanie because we're organising a school reunion.' What was one more lie on top of the rest?

'Oh, I see,' Mrs Fowler replied the smile disappearing, replaced by disappointment.

'We were hoping you might be able to provide us with her latest contact information – email address, phone number – so we can get in touch with her.'

'I see,' Mrs Fowler repeated, staring down at her hands, no longer able to meet their stares.

'Or you could pass her our details if you prefer,' Hannah continued, 'and then she can get in touch when she's ready.'

Mrs Fowler didn't reply, head still bowed.

Hannah glanced over to Bea who simply shrugged.

'Mrs Fowler?' Hannah said, guilt overwhelming her. 'Is everything okay?'

'I guess you didn't hear,' the older woman whimpered. 'Melanie went missing in 2015, and we haven't heard from her since.' She still hadn't re-established eye contact with either of them.

Standing, Hannah made her way over to the bay window, and crouched down at Mrs Fowler's feet, forcing their eyes to meet. 'I'm sorry to hear that, Mrs Fowler. Is there anything I can get for you? A cup of tea, maybe?'

The older woman nodded silently, and Hannah indicated to Bea to take care of it, while she remained where she was. 'Are you able to tell me about that time? Did the police investigate her disappearance?'

As Mrs Fowler nodded, a tear splashed against the cracked skin of her hands. 'They said the case would remain unsolved and would be reviewed again if any new evidence came to light, but we haven't had any update on it in over a year.'

'Do you have any idea where she might have gone, or why?'

Mrs Fowler's eyes focused for the first time. 'None. She was happy – or at least we thought she was – and the police searched all the places we suggested she might have gone to. How does someone just disappear like that? Her bank accounts haven't been used in all that time, and she's never tried to make contact with us, even though we were always such a close-knit family. She used to come and visit us at least once a week, and if she couldn't come over because of work or whatever, she'd phone instead. The last time I spoke to her, she was excited about a possible promotion at work. There was no hint or sign that she would just up and leave without saying goodbye. She wasn't like that.'

Hannah could hear the kettle boiling in the kitchen, and felt a growing urgency to leave and stop interfering in something that didn't concern her, but Mrs Fowler suddenly grabbed Hannah's wrist. 'I have no doubt that Melanie died, but there was no sign of a struggle and no body, so the police couldn't pursue it. If she was still alive, she would have made contact, or found some way to let us know that she is safe.'

Hannah extracted her wrist, and quickly stood. 'I am so sorry for your loss, Mrs Fowler, but I think it's best if we were on our way. I really am truly sorry.'

Finding Bea in the kitchen, Hannah grabbed her arm, dragging her out through the front door and back to the car.

'Hey, hey what's going on?' Bea demanded when she'd closed her door.

'This was a terrible idea,' Hannah chastised. 'We've just made that woman relive a horrendous memory, and for what? Just because we find Nigel a bit creepy. It isn't right, Bea. We need to stop this before we cause any more hurt.'

Bea didn't respond, but her mouth dropped as something through the windscreen caught her eye. Turning her head, Hannah was shocked to see Mrs Fowler with her hands pressed against the bonnet. 'Please don't go,' she called out. 'Please? There's something else you need to hear: I know who killed my daughter.'

TEN

Hannah blew ripples in the tea before daring to take a sip, and grimaced as the hot liquid scalded her lip. With Mrs Fowler blocking their escape, they had reluctantly agreed to return to the large bungalow where she had made them sit, while she prepared the tea. Hannah couldn't ignore the possibility that the scalding tea was karma's punishment for stirring up a hornet's nest.

'I'd never seen her so happy,' Mrs Fowler said, when she'd returned to the armchair by the window. Despite the vast cloud coverage, the light coming through the window was more than enough to brighten the room. 'That's why her disappearance was so out of character. Melanie had always been such a good girl, never in trouble for truancy from school, or anything like that. We were aware she'd had boyfriends, but she was just so sensible that, when the police suggested she may have just uprooted and gone, it set off alarm bells for us.'

Hannah lowered her cup to the carpet, away from her feet so she couldn't accidentally knock it over. She felt like an intruder, but it wouldn't benefit anyone to reveal she'd never actually met Melanie. Ultimately Bea had known her and from the way Mrs Fowler was now talking, the disappearance remained unexplained.

'She'd told us that someone in her block of flats had invited her out for dinner,' Mrs Fowler continued. 'She'd always let us know of any romantic interludes she was planning to go on; as I said she was sensible. She knew that for her own safety it was better that we know where she was going, and who with; at least until she got to know them better. We never met Nigel – not until after she'd disappeared – but she'd spoken to me about him. He was very keen on her, but I was surprised by his appearance when we came face-to-face; certainly not her usual type. It's not my place to judge, but he was more plain-looking than I'd expected. As you know, Melanie was a very pretty girl, and her previous boyfriends had all been athletically built with traditionally-handsome faces. Nigel was just not what I expected her to be dating. I'm sorry, I probably sound like such a snob right now.'

'He's no looker,' Bea chipped in. 'I never understood the attraction either.'

Mrs Fowler's head snapped up. 'Oh, you know Nigel then, do you?'

Bea's eyes widened at the slip-up, and she turned to Hannah in panic.

'Bea lives in the same road as Melanie did,' Hannah quickly covered. 'She was there when the police arrested Melanie's neighbour Nigel.'

It was better to mix some truth in with the deception. Mrs Fowler nodded in acceptance of the explanation, and Hannah choked down the urge to sigh with relief.

'Do you remember how long Melanie was seeing Nigel for?' Hannah continued, keen to move matters on.

'Now, let me think,' Mrs Fowler said, looking upwards as she tried to recall the answer. 'She went missing in the December of that year, and I'm sure she first went out with him a couple of weeks after her birthday, which was in July of course. So, I suppose four to five months.'

'Did the police tell you why they arrested him, or what it was that led them to suspect he may have been involved in her sudden disappearance?'

'They mostly dealt with Colin – that's my husband, Melanie's father – more so than me. I found it too difficult to concentrate, you see. I was in shock and fearing the worst that I just shut down from the real world. I was just so frantic with worry that I wasn't eating or sleeping properly, and in the end the doctor had to prescribe some pills just to help me get through the day. Melanie and I were always so close, and… I found it very difficult not having her there to talk to.'

Hannah understood exactly what she meant, and wanted to ask her how she had managed to overcome the worst of it, but to do so would be to reveal her own recent loss, and she wasn't prepared to divulge any of that.

'Colin will be back soon enough, but he doesn't like to talk about what happened. He's always been very pragmatic has Colin, and after the first year had passed with no resolution, I think he grew to accept the worst, and stopped clinging to hope. To be fair as the years have passed, my grasp has gradually diminished too. The two of you showing up today is the first time I have openly talked about that period in quite some time.'

'We're sorry to have made you relive it,' Hannah added with an empathetic frown.

'Don't be sorry. I'm actually glad that you did come. So many of our friends find discussing Melanie taboo. I think they are worried about upsetting us, and so the subject is off-limits, and because they find it awkward, we don't raise it either. Funny how we're all so polite in this country, isn't it? Anywhere else, and we'd be banging on the local MP's door demanding answers. I'm afraid I will go to my grave never knowing what happened to my little girl.'

'You reckon he did it though, right?' Bea challenged. 'Nigel, I mean.'

Mrs Fowler sipped from her cup, before looking back at them both. 'The moment I met him, I just sensed there was something not quite right about him. Call it women's intuition or a mother's base instinct if you will, but he just struck me as… odd, I suppose. I couldn't tell you exactly what it was about him, but I just couldn't trust a word he said. After the police released him, he came round here to offer his support. He said it's what she would have wanted: for the three of us to be there for each other. I had to have Colin throw him out, before I told him what I really thought.'

'Did you tell the cops how you felt?' Bea pressed.

'Colin kept reminding me that the police couldn't act without evidence, but yes he did pass on our concerns. I don't think Colin trusted him either, but neither of us could quite say why.'

The front door opening distracted the three of them, as a man in a flat cap entered the bungalow, removing his hat and coat, hanging both on a hook behind the front door. A look of confusion gripped his features, as his eyes fell on the three of them.

'These ladies are old friends of Melanie's, Colin,' Mrs Fowler told him. 'I was just telling them about that Nigel the police arrested.'

He considered Hannah and Bea for a moment, before tucking the newspaper under his arm and excusing himself, moving through to the kitchen.

'I think he finds hope too painful to deal with,' Mrs Fowler explained. 'Melanie was his world, a real Daddy's girl, and coming to terms with her disappearance was heartbreaking for him. It was his idea to have the memorial placed in the graveyard, giving us somewhere special we could go when we wanted to be with her. Silly, I know, but it was that which helped me come to terms with things. One day, it would be a relief to have her buried there. You see that's the worst part of all of this: the not knowing where she is or what happened to her. At least if we could bury her, we could progress with the grieving process, rather than being stuck in this cruel kind of limbo.'

Hannah picked up her cup and took another tentative sip of the drink. At least that was something she had: the certainty that she'd never see John again. It was a pain she wouldn't wish on her worst enemy, but there was some merit to what Mrs Fowler was saying.

'I still catch glimpses of her every now and again,' Mrs Fowler added. 'When I'm at the supermarket, or when I go into her old bedroom, just for the briefest of milliseconds I'm sure I see her. At first I thought it was just my mind playing tricks on me, but now I live for those moments, as I like to think it's her spirit returning to keep an eye on us.'

Hannah thought back to the moment she'd briefly mistaken Steve for John in the park. Maybe it had been his spirit coming back to check on her. It was an idea that filled her with warmth, even if there was no logic to it.

'Would you like to have a look at her room?' Mrs Fowler suddenly said. 'We've kept it exactly as it was when she left. I still wash the bedding once a month to keep it fresh, but sometimes I like to just go in there and look at her things. My memory isn't what it once was, and it helps to have visual aids to boost recall.'

'Oh no, we couldn't…' Hannah began to say, but Bea was already on her feet and followed Mrs Fowler out of the living room and along the hallway to the two bedrooms at the other side of the property. Hannah remained where she was, refusing to intrude any more than she already had, and was relieved when Bea and Mrs Fowler returned a few minutes later.

'We've taken up enough of your time already,' Hannah said, standing before Bea could get comfortable in the armchair again.

Mrs Fowler showed them to the door. 'Thank you for thinking of Melanie for your reunion, but I'm afraid without some kind of miracle, she won't be able to attend.'

Hannah wanted to hug the woman and to tell her that her bravery was an inspiration, but instead she settled for a reassuring nod, following Bea back to the car.

ELEVEN

It was like the wind had been kicked out of her. There he was, in the middle of the street, his handsome face not looking at her, but distracted by something off to the side.

John.

She would recognise those cheeks, that smile and his piercing blue eyes anywhere. It was impossible, and yet…

Hannah just about managed to grab onto a row of stacked trollies, as her legs went from under her. She'd only popped to the supermarket to pick up her dinner.

It couldn't be John, yet as her vision blurred at the edges, all she could see were the snapshots of memory: the large shadow of red spread across the bed, soaking through the sheets and leaving a permanent stain on the mattress; his lifeless eyes staring up at her, at peace, but a picture of lost innocence.

'You alright, luv?' a stranger's voice asked, and as she looked up she saw the kind eyes of a wrinkled face buried beneath a flat cap. He was one of the supermarket's customers, trying to add his trolley to the stack she was leaned against. 'Do you want me to call you a doctor?' he asked.

Shaking her head, and clamping her eyes shut to stop the tears falling, Hannah took a deep breath, willing the strength back into her legs. 'I'll be fine,' she whispered. 'I just had a shock.'

He was moving awkwardly from one foot to the other.

'Should I speak to one of the shop staff? Maybe they have somewhere you could sit.'

He was trying to be kind, and his uneven movement suggested he needed to be somewhere else but wasn't prepared to abandon her until he was certain she wouldn't collapse again.

'I'll be fine,' she repeated, trying to sound more assertive this time. In truth, she had no idea whether she would ever truly feel fine again.

'I think I should get someone,' he continued, the anxiety still gripping the crow's feet around his eyes. He was wearing a beige anorak, and plaid trousers, and his pale brown shoes creaked as he continued to shift his weight.

'It's very kind of you, but I promise you I will be okay. Thank you for helping me, but I'm sure you have better things to be doing.'

The older man helped her to her feet, and checked she was stable before taking his leave. Steadying herself, she looked back to where John had been standing, but now she could no longer see him. Straightening, she pushed herself away from the trolleys scanning the immediate vicinity for him.

Although she was telling herself her mind had played a cruel trick, she wasn't prepared to accept it without confirming once and for all that it had all been a mirage. It was impossible for John to have been there in the market square outside the supermarket. She'd seen his bloodstained body on the bed, and had been at the hospital when his brother Patrick had confirmed death at the mortuary, and yet his face had looked so real. If it wasn't John, then it was certainly his doppelganger.

Stumbling further towards the market, stalls lining the square perimeter, she continued to look from face-to-face, striving to find him. There had to be hundreds of people milling about, some with bags, others with shopping trollies. She continued to look from face-to-face, striving to find him. Nearing the far side of the square, she spotted the yellow and navy coat he'd been wearing. He was a good twenty metres further ahead, but there had to be at least a dozen other people between them.

From behind, he looked the right height, and although his hairline was thinner and a fraction lighter than she remembered, a lot could have changed in the last twelve months.

She stopped still. What was she thinking? That John faked his death, and had been living out someone else's life for the past year? That his brother had helped him cover the ruse, and that the police had been willing to go along with it. To what end? They'd had a happy marriage – not perfect – but happy.

'Get a grip!' she told herself.

The figure in the jacket was still ahead of her, and despite her reservations, she had to know for certain, and continued onwards, pushing past other shoppers, and out of the market square. He'd continued onto the town's main high street, and was now about fifteen metres ahead. As she followed, her view of him was no longer blocked. Now she could see he wasn't alone.

Beside the figure in the yellow and navy jacket was an overweight woman in a brown and pink velour tracksuit, her greasy orange hair tied in a scraggly pony tail; enormous hooped earrings hanging down. In her hands the handle of a double pushchair. A third child was bouncing around, tightly clutching the man's hand. The boy couldn't have been much older than three, his head a mop of blonde curls.

Crossing the road, so that she could get ahead of them without the figure noticing, Hannah was relieved and saddened in equal measure as she caught a glimpse of the man's face, finally confirming that the figure in the yellow and navy jacket was definitely not John. As she now looked upon him, she could see his belly protruding from the jacket, and facially he really wasn't all that similar to John at all. This man's nose was bent like a boxer's, and he lacked any of John's poise nor rugged good looks.

Watching the three of them, and the two other boys in the pushchair, it was impossible to understand how she ever could have mistaken him for John. Perhaps the guilt of trying to move on with her life had taken a toll.

Maybe Dr Yenny was right. Moving to a new area, buying an apartment, decorating it, *and* hunting for a new job were massive lifestyle changes, and taking on all four at the same time would be a lot of pressure for any normal person, let alone someone in her situation. She hadn't wanted to admit that she was feeling the strain of it all, determined to bury her head and battle on, but wasn't that naïve? Was she in danger of a backwards step if she continued to ignore the warning signs?

Promising herself she would take a proper look at the list of psychiatrists Dr Yenny had recommended, Hannah stopped walking, and turned to head back towards home. But with each step she couldn't ignore the feeling that she was being watched. Looking around her, she couldn't see anyone paying her undue attention, and yet the feeling remained. Increasing her pace, she was now just desperate to get back to Barney and the safety of home.

TWELVE

The salad she'd bought for dinner at the supermarket had done little to satisfy her appetite, and Hannah's stomach grumbled as she threw the plastic packet into the bin, dropping her fork into the sink.

Barney padded into the kitchen behind her, and pressed his head against her leg until she yielded and filled his bowl from the bag of dried food in the cupboard. The cul-de-sac beyond the kitchen window looked so peaceful, but that didn't stop her quickly lowering the blind. With Barney racing to finish his food, she left him to it, moving into the living room, turning on the main light, and closing the curtains. She repeated the process in the back and spare rooms, before returning to the living room and sitting at the table.

The loft felt so cold that she wouldn't have been surprised to see her breath waft out in clouds of condensation. Leaning over and touching the radiator, she was surprised at how icy cold it felt. The central heating was timed to come on from five until nine to counter the chilly October evenings, but the radiator felt like it hadn't been on all day.

Returning to the kitchen, she was surprised to find both the heating and hot water switched to the off position. They definitely hadn't been that way this morning when she'd woken and showered. She had no recollection of adjusting them, but nobody else had been in the loft apart from Bea, and she hadn't been out of Hannah's sight the whole time she'd been there. What was the alternative: that someone had broken in and adjusted the dials?

An image of Nigel flashed into her head, but she quickly dismissed it. Bea and Mrs Fowler's judgemental suppositions were starting to rub off.

Flicking both switches on, she grabbed a thick woollen sweater from the bedroom, just as Barney finished his dinner and joined her on the sofa. His loyalty and unflinching love never failed to amaze her. Given it had been barely a month since she'd adopted him from the shelter, it was difficult to remember a time when he wasn't a part of her life.

The answer machine next to the phone on the coffee table was flashing, and as she pressed play, she heard a welcome voice.

'Hi Hannah, it's Patrick, sorry to call so late, but can you give me a call back when you get this? Just want to see how you're doing and to find out when you're going to pop back and visit your nephews and niece. They ask about you every day. Anyway, give me a call please.'

It had been an hour since Patrick had called, and she doubted he'd still be in the office. Picking up the phone, she called his home, and waited for the line to connect.

'Hi Patrick, sorry I missed your call. Everything okay?'

'Finally,' he said jovially, 'been out burning the midnight oil have you?'

'Hardly! It's barely eight o'clock. I bet you haven't long been home from work.'

'You don't know the half of it! How is my favourite sister-in-law? You settling into that flat okay?'

She knew he was teasing. 'I'm your *only* sister-in-law, and it's an apartment, rather than a flat.'

'You say tomato.'

She caught her smile in the reflection of the photo frame

on the sideboard across the room. The still of Patrick and his children was a gentle reminder of the life she'd once had.

'How are the kids?'

'Missing their Auntie Hannah, especially Daisy. I don't think she understands that you moved away. She still expects you to drop round at any minute. In fact, whenever she hears a car door closing outside her first question is whether that's you and John arriving.'

Hannah's smile evaporated. 'Have you still not explained that he's gone?'

Patrick sighed. 'She's not even three yet, and I don't have the heart to break hers. The boys are older, and have a better understanding of how the world works. I know I'll have to tell her one day, but right now I just want her to hold onto her innocence for as long as possible. We all know how hard life is, but I'm in no hurry for her to learn it.'

'How are Ben and James coping?'

'Just when I think it's getting better, something seems to come unstuck. I went into James's room last night and found him crying. He'd had a dream about John and when he'd woken and remembered he was gone… it just breaks my heart. He's seven, but he's always been more sensitive than Ben.'

'Is Ben still playing football?'

'Yep, every Sunday morning Wendy has to transport him to one muddy sports field or another. He's in the under-10s now, and really enjoying it. There were a couple of scouts from United at one of the tournaments the other day apparently, but I've told him I'll never forgive him if he signs for them.'

Hannah had never understood how territorial football fans could be for what was essentially ninety minutes of kicking a bag of wind around. John and Patrick were avid City fans who would go to matches whenever they could get tickets, which wasn't as often as either would have wanted.

'How is Wendy?' she asked.

'Tired and stressed out, but otherwise okay. She's gone out with some friends tonight, but I know she's keen to catch up with you too. So, any idea when we can expect to see you again? I know you want to get settled, but it would be great to see you back here, even if just for a weekend. The kids would especially love it. I know there are a lot of painful memories -'

'Okay, okay,' she interrupted, knowing he wouldn't let up until she agreed to a date. 'I'll check my calendar and I'll let Wendy know. I promise.'

'Good, good. How's the new place looking? I remember you saying there was a bit of work to do.'

Hannah surveyed the bare walls, knowing she would need to increase her efforts if she was to get it finished. 'It's really coming along.'

'Wendy mentioned you'd adopted a dog too?'

Hannah rubbed Barney's ears, grateful that he was dozing with his warm head on her socked feet. 'That's right. You'd love him.'

'John wouldn't; not with his allergies.'

Neither responded for a moment.

'Work okay?' Hannah eventually asked.

Patrick sighed again. 'We're still coming to terms with things since… since John… well, since what happened.' He paused, and when he spoke again, his voice was strained, like he was willing himself to ask her. 'I don't suppose John ever told you about any of the other companies he was investing in, did he?'

Hannah frowned, trying to recall any conversations they'd ever had about work, but her mind was blank. 'He never used to share any of that with me. You know what he was like: work was work, and personal was personal. He compartmentalised everything. He used to say it was to shield me, but in truth I think he just didn't want to bore me.

Numbers and business were never my forte; I was always the creative one. What is it you want to know??'

'It's nothing,' he grumbled, but she could sense he was holding back.

'No, go on, Patrick, you can tell me. Is there something wrong?'

'Yes, no, not exactly. Don't worry about it. It's nothing I can't solve, I just wondered whether he'd ever mentioned anything specific to you. Forget I asked.'

She was pretty certain she wouldn't forget, but if he didn't want to discuss it, she wasn't about to pressure him.

'It's the anniversary next week,' Patrick continued, changing the subject. 'Have you planned anything specific for the day?'

Hannah thought about the square on the calendar she'd put a big red mark over. 'Nothing specific. I know it's going to be hard, and figured I'd just take it one second at a time.'

'I understand. If you feel like you need someone to talk to, or vent at, please don't hesitate to call me. Promise me that?'

'I promise. Listen, Patrick, I'd better go as I need to walk Barney. Is there anything else?'

'No, you go on. Thanks for calling me back. Take care.'

Barney sat bolt upright at the mention of a walk, and as she returned the phone to the table, she nodded at him. 'Come on then.'

THIRTEEN

The bright lights of Eastleigh town centre beckoned ahead, but Barney seemed to be enjoying the new smells, stopping to sniff lampposts and small tufts of grass along the way. She hadn't really considered where she was going, but on some subconscious level she'd decided against going towards the grass park where they usually went, because with no street light, it would be as black as the night sky above them.

The lead became taut in her hand. Turning she saw Barney smiling at her as he cocked his leg against a thin tree trunk. A loud group emerged from a bar just up ahead. Their conversation was indiscernible, but the shrieking and whooping suggested they were having a good time. Wearing short dresses, and their hair-dos held firmly in place by a shower of hairspray, the three women at the front were wearing sashes. Three more girls emerged from behind them, their faces plastered in glossy lipstick and thick eyeliner, tottering on ridiculously high heels, and not one of them looking anywhere near sober.

'Come on, ladies,' the one at the front shouted, her arm shaking as she tried to point towards another brightly-lit venue. 'We'll hit The Station next, and then get a taxi into Southampton.'

The statement was met with more cheering as the six of them wobbled onwards, their alcohol intake not aiding movement in the inappropriate footwear.

Hannah couldn't remember the last time she'd been on a proper night out with a group of likeminded individuals. Things had changed – she had changed – after marrying John. It hadn't been a conscious choice, but she'd become less interested in wasting money on getting drunk. It wasn't that she was envious of the group up ahead, but she did miss that level of companionship; a best friend she could discuss anything with. After marrying John, she'd grown apart from her usual rabble of friends – none of whom had been ready to marry and settle down. Even her best friend, Lucy had drifted away. Regular calls had become irregular messages, and even those had stopped a couple of years ago.

A grey-haired couple emerged from a small Tandoori restaurant as she was passing. The gentleman, maybe in his late sixties, nodded and smiled in her direction as he held onto his wife's hand. She was too busy fastening up her coat to notice Hannah or the dog. Barney pulled over towards another lamppost, his nose working feverishly as the couple walked around them and continued on their journey, arms linked. For a moment Hannah remained where she was, watching them, wondering whether she would ever meet someone to hold hands with as she entered her twilight years.

John would be a tough act to follow for anyone. It wasn't like she felt ready to even consider dating anybody new, but she was too young to declare a life of chastity. She hoped one day at some point in the undetermined future, a handsome stranger would cross her path and sweep her off her feet; John wouldn't be happy with her settling.

Reaching the end of the high street, Hannah pulled Barney to the right and headed into a residential area. She'd walked this way home once before, after she'd handed her application form in at the supermarket. About two hundred yards up on the right there was another street which ran parallel to the high street, culminating in an alley way that would bring her out not far from home.

It was important to learn how each of the streets connected around the town centre, and she planned to take Barney on plenty of longer walks to help map those streets in her mind. The wind was stronger and bitter here, whipping against her cheeks, and reminding her that autumn had arrived. The noise and bustle of the town centre suddenly felt miles away. There was no sound other than the crunch of browning leaves underfoot, interspersed with the clip-clop of her boots on the pavement. With limited lighting ahead, the feeling of isolation grew stronger with every step.

'Come on, Barney,' she said, for her sake as much as his.

The road up to the alleyway wasn't much further, but she quickened her pace, suddenly keen to be back in the loft where it was safe and warm. Barney pulled towards every lamppost, but she wasn't prepared to hang around any longer. Semi-detached properties lined the streets, but with curtains closed and blinds drawn, there was little additional light to put her at ease.

The sound of approaching footsteps from behind quickened her pulse. Tugging at Barney's lead, she broke into a jog, spotting the sign for the public footpath up ahead. As she strained to hear the other footsteps fading into the background, her heart skipped a beat as the person behind also quickened their steps. Reaching into her pocket, she fumbled for her door keys, the only thing nearing a weapon should she have to defend herself. With so many houses close by, surely an attacker wouldn't be stupid enough to make a move here.

Slowing, she allowed Barney to sniff at a garden fence, tightening her grip on the keys, and daring to look up as the darkened figure came closer.

'Evening,' the man in the baseball cap offered, as he moved past, pulling a terrier of some kind away from

Barney.

Hannah's throat was dry, and although she opened her mouth to return the greeting, no sound came out. Remaining where she was, she looked back along the street, to check for anyone else. Waiting until the guy in the baseball cap had turned into one of the properties further up, she moved onwards again, taking deep breaths to settle her nerves.

As they finally reached the alleyway, she was surprised by just how dark it was. When she'd used it a couple of weeks before, it had been the middle of the day, and she hadn't even considered how dark it would look this late at night. It was only a couple of hundred yards long, and then she'd be back to the main road and a couple of minutes from the loft. The alternative was to head back down the road, turn onto the street that led back to the town centre and then head back the way she'd come. That would add a good twenty-five minutes more to her journey, and as the wind continued to whip at her face, the thought of spending any more time out here was more daunting than heading into the darkened footpath.

It had been a bad idea coming this way without being better prepared. She had a large torch at home that would have been far more effective than her phone. Making a mental note for next time, she stepped into the darkness, trying to imagine anything other than the potential attackers waiting to leap at her from the shadows.

Barney didn't seem concerned by the engulfing shadow, and when they'd been walking for about a minute, she dared to turn back and look to see what distance they'd covered. The dense abyss had now cut off her path. With another deep breath, she continued forwards, breaking into a jog once more, overwhelmed with relief as the main road beckoned, the lights of passing cars confirming she was nearly there.

Bursting out of the darkness, she found herself on the

main street, exhaling, and delighted when she spotted the corner shop across the street and to the right. Heading to the crossing, she waited for a gap in the passing traffic, and the two of them hurried across the road, past the shop and into the cul-de-sac. She could just about make out the loft as she hurried along the road, the light peeking out from the edges of the kitchen blind. Suddenly she was at the entrance to her building, and her breath was escaping in clouds of steam, highlighted by the security light overhead. Just as she was once again reaching for her keys, she heard the clatter of a car door being closed from the street. Turning, her eyes widened when they met with Nigel's.

Bea's warnings about him flooded her mind: *nobody knows where she is or why she suddenly disappeared.*

It was all Hannah could do to get the door open before he came and tried to engage in conversation. Pushing it closed, she headed for the staircase, but as she reached the first floor, she could hear his feet on the stairs behind her.

'Excuse me, excuse me,' he was calling. 'Hello? It's Hannah isn't it? Can you just stop for a second, there's something I want to talk to you about.'

Hannah didn't slow, instead, racing past the second floor, and only stopping when she reached her own front door. Barney was panting next to her, as she opened the door, just as Nigel reached the top step. Their eyes met, but that didn't stop Hannah closing the door, breathless.

She jumped as he knocked against the door.

'Hannah? It's Nigel from downstairs. Sorry if I frightened you. I've been meaning to introduce myself.'

She couldn't just stand there in silence. He'd seen her go into the loft, and to ignore him would be suspicious. 'Sorry, Nigel, I was desperate for a wee.' She cringed at the lie. 'Listen, it's a bit late, maybe we can catch up tomorrow instead? I need to get some sleep now.'

There was a pause. 'Sure, sure, of course. I understand.

I'll just leave you with something and then we can talk at some point over the next couple of days.'

The sound of a leaflet being pushed under the door frame was followed by his footsteps heading back down the stairs. She took one glance at the leaflet and decided she didn't have the energy to read it now. Entering the kitchen, her trembling fingers pulled the carving knife from the block. If he came back, she'd be ready.

FOURTEEN

Hannah hummed along to the radio, as she pressed the peeler into the potato, and scraped off the skin. White droplets of starch sprayed up as she ran the peeler along the skin again and again, until she was satisfied it was clear. Chopping it, she dropped the cubes into the pan of salted water on the hob. The blue flame flickered beneath the pan's base, casting eerie shadows on the tiled wall behind the hob.

The chicken had been roasting for an hour, and the smell of the lemon and garlic was now filling the room. Pressing a hand against her abdomen, she was certain she could feel movement. John would be surprised by the news, but she had no doubt he would be thrilled too. A child to carry on the family name, one day take over the business, and someone they could mould in their own image. She was bursting with joy and excitement. Pregnancy wouldn't be easy – she'd read the books – but it would be worth it to hold her son's or daughter's hand and know that they were part of her.

A loud thud on the ceiling caught her attention.

Funny, John wasn't home yet. She was sure he wasn't. She hadn't heard him come through the door, and he hadn't come in to greet her.

Untying her apron, she switched off the radio, and stepped into the hallway, straining to hear any other noise. Had she left a window open? Perhaps the wind had caused something heavy to fall over, though she had no idea what.

She heard a second thud, the ceiling light shade shaking with the vibration. If it was John, what was he doing to cause all the noise?

Slowly creeping up the stairs she could hear muffled voices arguing from beyond the door to the master bedroom: a man and a woman's voice. Curiosity got the better of her, and she approached the door, straining to make out what was being said.

Was that Patrick's voice? It was too difficult to tell. The deep baritone sounded similar, but she didn't recognise the higher pitched voice challenging it.

Pressing her ear against the cool pine of the door, she desperately tried to make out any of the words, something to give her a clue as to who the two of them were, and why their voices were raised, but it was no good.

'Hello?' she tentatively said into the door. 'Hello? Is everything okay?'

There was no break in the argument, the deep voice booming, and the other voice practically shrieking.

Tapping on the door with her knuckle, Hannah tried again. 'Hello? Um, is there anything I can help with?'

It was as if they couldn't hear her, and so she thumped on the door with the palm of her hand, surprised at how loud it echoed around the hallway, but still the muffled argument continued unabated.

Coiling her fingers around the handle she forced it down, leaning into the door, but still it didn't budge.

Funny, the bedroom door didn't have a lock on it, yet it was stuck firm. Keeping the handle lowered, she pressed her shoulder firmer into the door, driving her feet into the carpet, trying to put her full weight behind the push, but the door remained closed.

Her anger rose, and she hammered the door with the sides of her clenched fists. 'Let me in,' she yelled in time with the banging.

An agonised scream came from inside. It was the male voice, and now she had no doubt it was Patrick inside the room.

'Patrick? Patrick? Are you okay? Let me in.'

Another anguished growl. He was in pain, she knew instinctively.

Lowering the handle again, she pressed into the door, but it still didn't budge.

'Let me in!' she screamed, thumping the door until her hands ached. 'Let me in!'

Patrick's anguished cry continued to chill her blood. Taking several steps back, Hannah launched forwards, butting the door with her shoulder, desperate to get in to him. The door remained shut. Racing backwards again, she launched forward, over and over again, until the wood of the frame splintered, and suddenly she was falling forwards, as the door crashed open.

Pushing herself up from the carpet, she grabbed the side of the bed for support, and squealed as her eyes fell on John's bloody body, rather than Patrick's. Lying on the bed, his head between their two sets of pillows, his chest a pool of shredded shirt and thick dark blood. Beside him the large knife, stained the same colour, the blood blotting into the bed sheet beneath it.

The tears burned in her eyes, and splashed against her cheeks. 'John?' she tried to whisper, but his chest was still. A deathly silence gripped the room.

Yet they were alone. Whomever he'd been arguing with was gone, leaving no trace.

She couldn't lose him again. Flashes of the trips to the police station, the counsellor's office, antidepressants being dropped into the palm of her hand; none of it would happen if she could just get him to live through it this time. Climbing onto the bed on her knees, she stared down at his rapidly paling face.

'I can't lose you,' she declared to the room, and pinching his nose between her thumb and forefinger, she lowered his chin with her other hand. Pressing her lips against his she blew into his mouth. His chest rose and fell in time with the large breaths, but as she pulled away, her own clothes now splashed with his blood, his eyes remained lifeless.

Heavy footsteps approached on the stairs. The intruder was coming back up, and this time he would finish her off as well, and as she opened her mouth to scream, she felt a warm hand on her face.

Looking down she saw the hand was attached to John's arm, and it was he who was holding her cheek. 'I'm sorry,' he said, before his eyes rolled back into his head, and his hand went limp against her cheek, leaving the warm blood like death's sign on her face. She let out a deep guttural scream of anguish, waking herself in the process.

FIFTEEN

Hannah hadn't returned to sleep after waking from the nightmare. She'd remained in bed for almost an hour, not daring to head out into the eerie shadows of the living room. Eventually, her full bladder had won, and making sure to switch on every light as she went, she stumbled to the bathroom, Barney at her side, and the carving knife thrust forward to catch any unwanted visitors.

That had been three hours ago, and now, as the morning news programme started up on the television, all she wanted was a few hours peaceful rest, but it was too late. Switching on the kettle in the kitchen, she let out a yawn as she opened the blind and stared out at the street, bathed in fresh morning light.

No strangers lurking in dark corners this morning. The leaflet Nigel had slid under the door was staring up at her from the counter, and as she now studied the black ink of the hand-drawn lettering, she couldn't help but think of Bea's summary of Nigel: *a religious nut.*

Hannah liked to think she was open-minded when it came to peoples' choices of religion. Her own faith had been tested and failed in the last year, but she didn't want to question what others chose to rely on. The leaflet was advertising church services every other night for those craving spiritual guidance. How she could do with some guidance right now, but she wasn't ready to dip her toe into something she knew nothing about and organised by a neighbour who intimidated her. Folding the leaflet in half, she dropped it to the countertop.

Outside the window, she could hear voices, and staring down, she saw Bea, dressed in a short kimono, hugging a man at least six or seven years younger than her. It was barely seven o'clock, and already she was welcoming young men into her boudoir.

Hannah frowned at her own prudishness. Who was she to judge what others did on a Saturday? She should be pleased for her neighbour, and the person she'd spent most time with since moving to the area.

Bea must have felt the burn of Hannah's gaze, as she turned and waved up at the loft window. Hannah's cheeks reddened for getting caught watching, and offered an awkward wave back. The young man covered his eyes against the sunlight and looked up too. Early twenties at most, but clean-shaven, hair sculpted into a Mohawk, and as skinny as a rake; handsome face too, Hannah noted.

Bea and the young man hurried inside, as the kettle reached boiling point. Barney was waiting by the fridge, clearly sensing that she was about to reach for the milk, hopeful some food morsel would come his way.

Opening the breadbin, she removed two slices of wholemeal from the packet, dropping one into Barney's metal food bowl, and nibbling on the other, watching as he devoured his meal in seconds. His hopeful eyes looked up at her in expectation, but despite her lack of appetite, she wasn't going to share hers. Filling her mug with water, she swished the tea bag around, and was adding the milk when banging on the front door startled her.

Bea and her young man were waiting in the hallway as Hannah stared though the peephole, before opening the door.

'Hannah, this is my brother Chris,' Bea said.' Chris, this beautiful lady is my neighbour Hannah.'

Chris smiled warmly as he extended his hand. 'Nice to meet you.'

'Can we come in?' Bea asked, already pushing through, the kimono doing little to cover her modesty.

Hannah closed and locked the door behind them, offering tea. Both accepted and waited for her to carry the mugs through to the lounge table.

'I'm glad you're up,' Bea said, a mischievous look in her eyes. 'I have news.'

Already sensing that she wouldn't share Bea's enthusiasm for whatever the news was, Hannah tried not to frown.

Bea clapped her hands together. 'Don't be mad… I know you said you weren't interested in setting up a Facebook account, but I kind of did it for you anyway.' Bea wrinkled her nose. 'It'll be worth it, I promise. I set up a dummy email account in your name, and then built the profile. There's no need for you to be worried about your identity being stolen, I made up a date of birth for you, and there's nothing else listed on the profile. I added myself as a friend, so Nigel will be able to find you if he looks.'

Hannah bit her tongue to keep from berating Bea in front of her brother.

'Relax,' Bea continued, sensing Hannah's disapproval. 'Nothing bad is going to happen. *If* he adds you as a friend, I think we go to the police and see if we can speak to somebody who was working on the original investigation and express our concerns. At the very least they might warn him off for us. I'm pretty sure if he sees the police sniffing around us, he'll stay well clear.'

Chris hadn't batted an eyelid, suggesting he already knew exactly what his sister was talking about.

Hannah forced herself to smile through her annoyance, accepting that Bea's motivation for ignoring her request was well-intentioned.

'Anyway,' Bea continued, sipping her tea, 'you've had a friend request.'

Hannah's eyes widened, as she thought back to him chasing her up the stairs last night. 'From Nigel?'

'No,' Bea laughed. 'Do you think I'd be this calm and relaxed if it was from him? No, the request was from someone called Lucy Davison?'

Flashes from her hen do fizzed through Hannah's mind; Lucy the ringleader for mischief always. It had been so long since they'd last spoken, both drifting apart as their new lives had started.

'Looks about your age from what I could see on her profile,' Bea added. 'Name mean anything to you?'

'She was a friend from school,' Hannah admitted, amazed at how quickly her old friend had found the profile.

'Do you want me to accept the request then?'

Hannah wasn't sure how the whole process worked, and felt silly for allowing the technological world to pass her by. That sort of thing had always been John's remit; she looked after the home, and he took care of everything else. He'd tell her stories of client companies being hacked by cyber terrorists, and fraudsters stealing people's information through emails and viruses. It had all sounded so scary, yet Bea seemed totally unfazed by it all. Maybe her neighbour was just oblivious to the risks of putting her life online, or maybe things weren't quite as bad as John had suggested.

'Do I have to accept the request?' Hannah said after a moment.

'You don't have to. Right now, all she can see is your name, and the picture I uploaded of you.'

'Picture?'

Bea pulled out her phone, and presented it to Hannah. 'I snapped it on my phone yesterday when we were at

Mrs Fowler's house. You're not mad are you? I think I captured your best side, but what would I know? You're the professional photographer, what do you think?'

Hannah studied the image, surprised at how calm and serene she looked in it.

'I applied a filter,' Bea added. 'Anyway, that's all she can see at the minute. You can block her request if you want, and that will stop her seeing you online anymore, or you can accept it, and she will be able to see anything you post, or any images you upload. Up to you really.'

It would be good to catch up with Lucy and find out what she'd been up to in the last few years; whether she was married, and whether she'd qualified as a doctor.

'I'll think about it,' Hannah said. 'If I was to accept it, I don't have any means to engage with her.'

'You can use the laptop I saw the other day. Or download an app on your mobile.'

'I can't access the internet on my phone.'

Bea raised her eyebrows. 'That's why Chris is here. He works part-time at the phone shop in the town centre, and although today is his day off, he's said he's happy to go there with you and help you get a good deal. I tell you what, I'll accept Lucy's request for now, and then once Chris has set you up, you'll be able to send her a message and swap numbers or whatever. It'll be fine. Trust me.'

Chris smiled warmly. 'Bea mentioned something about a camera you might be thinking about selling? If you show me where it is, I can give you a valuation if you want?'

Hannah looked questioningly at Bea. 'I never said I wanted to sell my camera.'

'Not in so many words, but I got the impression that you weren't planning on using it again. Seems silly to leave it lying around gathering dust.'

Hannah glanced over at the camera on the sideboard.

'I'm sorry, but I'm not ready to sell it yet.'

Chris raised his hands in a pacifying gesture. 'No worries, but if you change your mind, I'll be happy to get you a good price. Any friend of Bea's is a friend of mine.'

Bea clapped her hands together again. 'Right, come on then. Town awaits. Let's see if we can't drag you into the modern age.'

Hannah finished her tea, and agreed to meet them downstairs once she was properly dressed. John would be proud to see her standing on her own two feet, wouldn't he? Ignoring the sobering thought, she carried the cups through to the kitchen, gasping when she saw Nigel down on the street staring up at the window. He waved when their eyes met, but she didn't respond, choosing to draw the blind instead.

SIXTEEN

The trip to the phone shop had been less painful than she'd anticipated, and with Chris explaining each of her options, and reassuring her about the ways she could stay protected online, she returned home feeling braver than she'd been in years. She'd learned that Chris was studying law at the university, and planned to train to become a solicitor once he'd graduated. Bea referred to him as "the brains of the family," and it was clear she was proud of the life he was carving for himself.

Now armed with a touchscreen phone and a monthly data allowance, Hannah had promised Chris she would call him if she had any issues with it. The phone remained sealed in the box, and as she stared at the bare walls of the living room, she knew exactly what she needed to do.

She was just opening the paint can when the sound of the outside doorbell shattered the silence, and Barney trotted to the loft's front door, where the intercom phone was flashing to indicate someone outside had summoned her.

Leaving the paint tin on the lounge table, Hannah put the intercom phone to her ear. 'Hello?'

'Hannah, it's Mum, darling. Can you buzz me in?'

Opening the front door, she heard footsteps on the stairs, and a moment later her breathless mother appeared at the top. Hannah stepped back, allowing her to enter, and was about to close the door, when her dad's hand appeared in the gap, the skin looking weathered and cracked.

'Hello, sweetheart,' he said, as she opened the door wider and he leaned in and pecked her cheek. 'Hope you don't mind us dropping round unannounced.'

'It's lovely to see you both,' Hannah said, wishing they'd telephoned ahead so she could have straightened the place a bit.

'We were just passing, and I thought we might be able to take you out for lunch,' her dad added.

'Sorry, I've already eaten,' Hannah fibbed. 'I can fix you a sandwich if you want, but I can only offer cheese.'

Hannah's mum disappeared off to the kitchen, as the two of them headed through to the living room.

Without a word, he moved across to the furthest wall, raising his glasses, his nose barely an inch from the plaster. 'You about to put on a first coat?' he asked. 'I wish you'd told me you were doing this today, I'd have come to lend a hand.'

Smiling, she said, 'I didn't want to put you out.'

Lowering his glasses he moved away from the wall, and gave Barney a gentle pat on the back. 'How's this one getting on?'

'Really well. We've not had any accidents, and although he barks when there's someone at the door, he's otherwise quiet.'

Hannah's mum reappeared in the doorway a moment later. 'I worry about you, Hannah, dear. There's no fruit or vegetables in the fridge, and you look thinner than the last time we saw you. Are you eating properly?'

Hannah ground her back teeth at the thought of her mother going through the fridge and looking for flaws. 'I'm well, Mum, you don't need to worry about me. I'm due to pick up a few bits and pieces from the supermarket this afternoon, which is why the shelves are empty. I'm taking good care of myself, I promise.'

The parents exchanged a look, before her father came

closer and put an arm around his daughter's shoulders. 'We understand that you're an adult with your own life now, but we'll never stop worrying about you. Why don't we hang about for a bit? That way I can give you a hand with the painting, and your mother can fix us a nice meal for dinner. You know she loves to cook, and the decorating will definitely be quicker with two pairs of hands. What do you say?'

She knew they both meant well, and as much as it pained her to relent, she nodded gratefully. 'Thank you.'

Watching her father delicately running the brush against the corner of masking tape, Hannah had to admit the room was looking better than she'd ever imagined. Because he'd insisted, he'd even managed to put a fresh coat of paint on the ceiling with a roller.

'You should have been a professional decorator, Dad,' she said, not for the first time since he'd arrived.

'I used to dabble back in the day,' he added, pulling his brush from the wall. 'In fact, my first ever job was as a handyman's assistant. I was sixteen, and living in Bristol, and it was the summer holidays, so my dad got me a job with a mate of his. It was the sixties, so any money I earned used to be wasted on girls and records. Anyway, he was the one who showed me how to paint. He used to say it was a mug's game. Back then, I don't think it was as well paid as it is these days.'

He had a wistful look in his eyes, like he was watching memories unfold before him. She'd seen the odd photograph of him as a younger man, with hair down to his shoulders, but she couldn't picture him as a teenager.

'You could always try taking it up now,' Hannah said, lowering her own brush into the paint tray. 'I'd recommend you.'

He smiled warmly at her. 'Thanks, love, but it's a young man's game. Besides, I wouldn't lend my services to just anybody, you know. Seems I must have a soft spot for you.'

Closing the distance between them, she wrapped her arms around his neck and held him tightly. 'I, for one, appreciate your help. Thank you.'

They parted, and she was sure she saw his eyes tearing up as he turned his back on her. She'd never seen him cry; not the done thing, he used to say. He'd dabbed his eyes during her wedding ceremony, and from what her mum had told her he'd sobbed like a baby when they were alone in their room together, but he wouldn't allow Hannah to see his emotions get the better of him.

'Right,' he sniffed, 'just need to do around the edge of the windowsill and then we should be done. I don't suppose you'd mind making an old man a cup of tea, would you? I'm parched.'

She didn't need telling twice, and providing refreshments was the least she could do.

'Something smells good,' Hannah said, as she opened the door to the kitchen and entered, finding her mother leaning over the stove, the aroma of tomatoes and garlic wafting around the room.

'The ragu is nearly complete, and then I just need to make up the roux, and construct the dish.'

Hannah stifled a laugh. To anyone else, ragu was bolognaise, and roux was the cheesy sauce that interspersed the layers of lasagne. Her mother insisted on using the traditional words, having spent three weeks travelling around Italy a decade ago. In the weeks after John's death, her mum had insisted on showing Hannah how to cook some of her favourite dishes, and stories from Italy had been frequently referenced.

'Cup of tea, Mum?' she asked, reaching for the kettle

and carrying it over to the sink.

'Lovely, darling, thank you. How are you and your dad getting on?'

'All but finished,' Hannah said, returning the kettle to its stand and switching it on.

'That's good. Is that where you're planning to stop for today? I know he likes to help out, but he does tire easily these days.'

'I understand,' Hannah nodded. 'I'm not ready to attack the spare room yet. Now my bedroom and the living room are complete, the place feels a bit more like my own. Once I've hung up some pictures, it'll feel more homely.'

Her mother was still stirring the pot absently, but suddenly looked up as a thought struck her. Turning, she reached for something on the counter before handing it over. 'What's this?' she asked.

Hannah looked at the leaflet in her mother's hand. It was what Nigel had squeezed under the door last night.

'Oh it's nothing. Just something one of my neighbours gave me.'

'You're not actually thinking of going along to it, are you?'

Hannah pulled a face and shook her head. 'No, of course not.'

Her mother's expression was still deeply focused. 'You're sure? Because I do worry about you, Hannah. After everything you've been through you're vulnerable, and you hear such stories about these modern churches.'

Hannah frowned. 'Stories?'

'Brainwashing, darling. They prey on the vulnerable, offering dreams of life improvement while defrauding their victims.'

Hannah snatched the leaflet and tore it into several pieces, before dropping them into the dustbin. 'Do you really think I'm that stupid?'

Her mother forced a sympathetic smile. 'I'm sorry, darling, but I can't help worrying. You know that I think you moved out too quickly. It's not even a year since... well, since *it* happened. I know you need to restart your life, but I worry that all of this is too soon. You've done well to climb out of the hole you were in, and I'm terrified you'll slip and fall. All I'm asking is, if you do start to feel like things are getting on top of you, you'll pick up the phone to me before you go running off to some new age church.'

'I'll go and check on dad,' Hannah said, finding an excuse to leave the room before she reacted.

Closing the door behind her, she found her dad tugging at a piece of tape. The painting finished, he had started to remove the protective coverings from each surface.

'Everything alright, love?' he asked as he saw the angry expression on her face.

'Yes,' she sighed. 'I just wish Mum wouldn't keep treating me like a child.'

Raising his eyebrows in empathy, he stopped tugging at the tape and moved across to her. 'I know she worries about you – we both do – and I know she's not always very good at expressing what she wants to say. In fact, she can sometimes be a bit of a bull in a china shop; the two of you are more similar than either of you would ever admit. Don't be too hard on her, though. This hasn't been easy for her either.'

'What do you mean? What hasn't?'

Glancing towards the closed kitchen door, he pulled Hannah away from it, lowering his voice. 'Did she tell you she's been seeing a counsellor as well? After what happened... it was really tough for both of us seeing the state you'd been left in. We nearly lost you that night, and I think she was relieved when you moved back in with us. I think you forget that you're our only daughter, and you mean the world to us. That night... it had more of an impact on us than you realise. So go easy on your mother. Please? She only wants what's best for you.'

Hannah couldn't keep the frown from her face, but nodded her understanding. She'd had no idea that John's murder had left such an impression on the two people she loved more than any other. Kissing him on the cheek, she returned to the kitchen and gave her mum a big hug.

'What's that for, dear?' her mother asked.

'Just wanted to say thank you for everything you do for me, and to tell you I love you.'

Her mother patted her on the back. 'You're very welcome. Kettle's boiling, but do you fancy a glass of wine instead? I know it's still early, but I picked up a bottle of white if you fancy?'

Hannah smiled and nodded, opening the cupboard and removing two glasses. Maybe her dad was right: they were more similar than she'd realised.

SEVENTEEN

The courtroom was far larger than she'd expected, and there was a bitter draft low down, making it feel like her feet were trapped in blocks of ice. Thank goodness she'd opted for a thick overcoat, which remained fastened.

She was the only one sitting in the public gallery, high above the court like stalls at a theatre. Below her the actors busied themselves with paper shuffling, whispered conversations and adjusting their ill-fitting clothes. The mustiness of the gallery, and the cracked leather cushions couldn't be ignored. It was like time had stopped in this place, and that if she sat still for too long, it would catch up with her too.

The indistinct hum of chatter continued below, but even if she could hear what was being said, she wasn't sure she would understand the cacophony of legal spiel. Word had reached her that the jury had decided on a verdict, and there was no way she was going to miss hearing it. She would have to be strong. John would want her to keep her emotion in check.

A sudden commotion at the far end of the court was followed by a dozen men and women entering and taking their seats in the juror's box. Seven women and five men who would determine the fate of the man on trial. Hannah couldn't help but hope he got exactly what he deserved. None of them looked up to where she was seated, and little did they realise the faith she had imparted on them. If they failed to find him guilty, it would feel like the floor had just dropped out of her world. They couldn't find him not guilty, could they? The prosecuting barrister had been so convinced he would win the case that he'd told her he'd work for free if he failed to deliver the outcome she longed for. He had his back to her now, but his shoulders looked relaxed.

A moment later a second door opened and all those below immediately terminated their conversations and stood in unison. The man in thick red robes who'd appeared made his way along the bench, before sitting behind the large microphone. The teams of legal professionals before the judge took their seats, and he told the defendant to stand and confirm his name. Hannah craned to see the defendant's dock, a wooden box with glass panels on two sides, but she couldn't see inside it. She hoped he was panicking.

One selfish and reckless act had had such an impact on so many: from the jurors who had been invited to listen to all the evidence; to the teams of barristers and solicitors working to prove or disprove the charges; to the judge; and the court clerks. Not to mention the pain and misery inflicted on Hannah her family's lives. Did he realise that this would happen when he'd called at their house that night? If he had would he still have called round?

The court clerk, wearing a black cloak as dark as his thinning hairline addressed the lead juror. 'Have you reached a verdict on the charges against the accused?'

An overweight woman in green, stood. 'We have.'

'By what majority were the verdicts reached?'

'Unanimous.'

'Very well. I will now address each charge and I require you to confirm the verdict for each individually. Do you understand?'

'Yes.'

The clerk consulted his notes. 'To the charge of illegal entry, how do you find the accused?'

The woman unfolded the piece of paper she was holding. 'Guilty.'

'To the charge of causing actual bodily harm, how do you find the accused?'

'Guilty.'

'To the charge of murder, how do you find the accused?'

'Guilty.'

Hannah exhaled in delight.

The court clerk collected the Issue Paper from the woman in green and carried it to the judge, who carefully unfolded it, before addressing the defendant. 'Please stand.'

'A jury of your peers has found you guilty of all the charges brought against you by the police. The manner with which you callously dispatched the victim has left me appalled. His blood was found on your clothes, and your footprints were found at the scene. A witness identified you as fleeing the property moments before the police arrived. Yet you had the gall to deny what you had done, forcing one of the victims to sit through a lengthy and painful trial process. You have shown no remorse for your actions, and it is now my responsibility to pass sentence.

'To the charge of illegal entry, I sentence you to three years imprisonment. To the charge of causing actual bodily harm, I sentence you to a further three years in prison. To the charge of murder, I sentence you to life imprisonment, of which a minimum of eighteen years must be served before parole will be considered.'

Hannah resisted the urge to punch the air, but moved to the end of the row of seats so she would be able to see his face, but as her eyes fell upon the figure behind the glass, the breath caught in her throat.

There had to be some kind of mistake.

It wasn't Seamus Fahey in the dock. Instead the frail face and warm eyes of her father greeted her, and he mouthed the word, 'Sorry.'

Hannah's eyes flew open, and she felt tears on her cheeks. The room was in complete darkness, save for the glow from the alarm clock beside the bed. Her heart thundered in her chest, and it took several moments for her to calm down and convince herself it had been just another cruel dream.

It had felt so real.

Even though she hadn't attended Fahey's trial, she'd been convinced it was his face she would have seen behind the glass.

Pushing the duvet back, she wiped her face with the sleeve of her pyjama top, before standing and reaching into the darkness for the door handle. Opening the door, she shuffled towards the bathroom, and turned on the light, blinking against the pain of the bright intrusion.

Her reflection in the mirror looked tired, eyes red raw and puffy. Her hair straggled, with flecks of paint on her neck where she'd failed to clean them earlier.

Hannah's parents had stayed until eight, consuming the lasagne and finishing the bottle of wine she'd shared with her mum. The conversation had been light as they'd recalled memories from her childhood; holidays abroad, school trips and a long list of unsuitable boyfriends. She'd felt more relaxed than she had done in a long time.

Clearly her father's presence in her new home, and the fact that he'd helped her with the decorating had inspired him to appear in her dream. Or maybe it was the toxic combination of wine and cheese that had led to the nightmare. Whatever the cause, it was the first time she'd experienced that courtroom scene before.

Running the tap, she pushed her mouth beneath the flow and gulped water, before squatting on the toilet, and washing her hands afterwards. What she needed was a proper night's sleep, not interrupted by strange dreams.

Heading back through the living room, she stopped when she saw the edge of the digital camera glinting beneath the light. Had she been silly to turn down Chris's offer of a valuation? Was there any point in keeping something which she hadn't used properly for some years? Technology was always improving, so wasn't she better off selling it now while it was still worth something?

Picking it up, she turned it over in her hands, doubting whether it would still hold any charge. She had no idea when it had last been charged. Pressing the on switch, she was pleasantly surprised when it whirred and flashed to life. Putting her eye to the viewing window, she adjusted the lens focus between her index finger and thumb. The view of the dining table blurred in and out of focus.

It felt good holding it again. For a time she had grown to resent the device, but this now felt like seeing an old friend. Maybe it hadn't been silly to hold onto it. Hampshire as a county was packed with picturesque spots, and she was only a stone's through from the National Forest. A trip to an area of natural beauty could be the break she needed.

Adjusting the setting switch to view the contents of the memory card inside the camera, she gasped at the picture of John that filled the panel. He was topless, perched on the end of their old bed in their house in Salford, but she didn't recognise the image. Surely she would have remembered taking such a picture, but her mind was blank. John looked like he was trying to reach up and stop the picture, or take the camera from her, his face in playful angst.

Flicking to the next image, she immediately recalled the moment she'd first captured the robin pulling the worm out of the wet mud of the lawn. It had been breakfast time when she'd seen the robin scavenging and had immediately picked up the camera to capture it. At the time she'd thought it would look good blown up on the wall in the kitchen, but had never got round to doing anything with it. The remaining dozen images were of other garden creatures: squirrels, sparrows, and a fox she'd snapped late one night during the height of the summer three years before.

Returning to the image of John, she studied it, but still no flash of memory triggered, but the panel was only three inches wide. Making a mental note to have the image developed, she returned the camera to its spot on the dusty sideboard, and headed back to bed.

Barney was lying in the warm spot she'd vacated in the bed, and as she stepped into the room, he looked up at her with hopeful eyes.

'Okay, okay,' she said. 'Just for tonight. Tomorrow you're back in your own bed.'

Climbing in at the other side, she pulled him close and kissed the top of his head. At least he would protect her.

EIGHTEEN

Pressing a hand to her nose, Hannah tried to block out the mustiness of the waiting room; like a damp cloud hanging just beneath the ceiling's strip lighting. A laminated sign on the reception desk apologised for the broken air conditioning, and advised that an engineer had been called. Even Hannah knew the NHS wouldn't spring for an emergency electrical engineer on a Sunday. It wouldn't be so bad if someone would open a window or two, but the only breeze able to penetrate the smog was when the automated door occasionally opened to welcome or bid farewell to another patient.

She'd only been waiting for ten minutes, and from the queue of seven people also sitting in the waiting room, she sensed her appointment wouldn't run to time. The one patient who'd been called in since she arrived had yet to emerge from the corridor of offices at the far side of the waiting room, meaning the average appointment time so far was approximately eight minutes and counting. Quick mental arithmetic told her it would probably be another hour until she could emerge, hopefully with the answer she needed.

Last night's dream had been both intense and cruel, but it was just one in a string of nightmares terrorising her sleep. It was time to take control, and hopefully the emergency GP would take pity on her and prescribe something to calm her sleeping pattern.

'Is it a medical emergency?' the woman on the emergency NHS referral line had asked.

'Probably not,' had been Hannah's unwitting reply, but then she'd burst into tears before the woman could ask another question.

After gentle cajoling, Hannah had managed to compose herself long enough to try and explain that she was struggling to cope with the pressures of daily life. It had felt easier to admit it to a faceless stranger, and as the woman had then asked questions about Hannah's treatments in the past year, she had allowed herself to tell the unabridged version of events, and a little of the weight had eased from her shoulders.

'Are you experiencing suicidal tendencies?' the woman had asked next.

That had almost set the tears flowing again, but Hannah had managed to choke them back. With all that had happened from the moment she'd woken in the kitchen, to burying John in the ground, and then learning that she'd suffered a miscarriage, at no point had she ever felt the desire to end her own life. She'd wanted it to end – no doubt about that – but she didn't have the patience nor imagination to inflict it upon herself. Had death's angel come for her on any of those lonely and gut-wrenching nights, she would have willingly gone, but he never had.

'I think it's best if you come and speak with the on-call GP,' the NHS woman had finally concluded.

Hannah's phone sprang to life in her bag on the floor, and she quickly scooped it up, pressing the phone to her ear. 'Sandra?'

'Hi, sweets, sorry to ring so early, but I've got a client due at half past, and then I'm back-to-back until lunchtime.'

'Business still going well?' Hannah asked.

'Well, yes, it's improving. I never told you, but after… you know, after what happened, things did drop off for a bit.

I don't know, maybe people were just scared to be near your old house, or something. All of that's forgotten about now though, I think.'

Hannah hadn't even considered that the attack could have impacted Sandra's business, but it would help to explain the lack of contact she'd had from other former neighbours in the street.

'Anyway,' Sandra continued. 'How are *you* doing? How's the house?'

'It's an apartment, well, more of a loft space. Plenty of room for me and Barney.'

'Ooh, who's Barney?'

'He's a bearded collie. I adopted him from a dog rescue centre. I'm telling you, Sandra, you'd love him. Looks just like the one they used to use in the paint commercials'

'Sounds cute.' A pause. 'Listen, the real reason I phoned is to let you know some girl was here the other day, asking about you.'

'Some girl? Who is she?'

'I don't know. I spotted her out of my window yesterday afternoon while I was washing up. She was going door-to-door, and I thought she must have been a salesperson, or a Jehova's Witness or something. I wasn't going to answer, but when she knocked, my dog went ballistic, so it was obvious I was home. She said she was an old friend of yours, but didn't give me a name.'

A feeling of dread crept along Hannah's spine. 'Describe her for me.'

'That's the weird thing... she didn't look like someone you would have been friends with. She was about your height, but can't have been much older than eighteen, if that. Caramel-coloured hair, straightened to within an inch of its life, padded bra, knee-length boots and a skirt that left little to the imagination.'

Hannah frowned. 'She mentioned me by name?'

'Not at first. Initially she asked whether I knew the couple that had lived next-door. She said one of the other residents had steered her in my direction, so I reluctantly nodded. She said she was an old friend and had lost touch with you. Given her age, I just couldn't see how the two of you would have been friends. She looked like a student, but one trying to look older than she really is; do you know what I mean? Do you remember being sixteen and putting on makeup to look old enough to get past bouncers and into pubs? That's what she reminded me of.'

'Did she leave any contact details? A name or number?'

'When I said I did know you, she started asking where you are now, and when I'd last spoken to you. It put me on edge, so I told her I didn't have time to speak because I was about to go out. I told her we weren't close, and that I hadn't heard from you since you'd sold up and moved. I thought you should know, and wondered whether you wanted me to pass on your number if she comes back?'

'No,' Hannah said after consideration. 'If she comes back, take a name and number and tell her you'll pass it on to me. I'm reluctant to give out my number, particularly to strangers.'

'Which is what I figured. Forgive me if I'm speaking out of turn, but is everything okay with you? You're not in any kind of trouble are you?'

'No, of course not. Why?'

Sandra sighed as if she'd been debating with herself whether or not to continue. 'After she left the street, I went and spoke to Marcus across the road. He was out washing his car when she'd spoken to him, and I asked him what she'd wanted. She told him she was from a debt-collection agency and was trying to locate the woman who used to live in the property. That's why I wanted to phone you this morning. Are you in financial trouble?'

Hannah pictured her last bank statement, and all the

zeroes that had followed her balance. 'Believe me, money isn't an issue. If she is from a debt-collection agency, they must have the wrong end of the stick. Leave it with me, I'll chat to John's brother about her and see if he can dig anything up. He's good with things like that.'

Another pause. 'Are you sure you're okay?'

Hannah crossed her fingers. 'I promise I'm fine. Thanks for letting me know about the woman; I'll keep my eyes peeled for her.'

The sound of feet in the corridor was followed by the first patient emerging, and disappearing out through the automatic door.

'Hannah Davenport?' a voice called.

Looking up, Hannah was surprised to see the young man with a close-cropped dark beard staring at her.

'Yes,' she said, standing, and picking up her handbag, trying to ignore the dirty stares emanating from the others in the waiting room who'd all hoped they would be next in.

Hannah followed the doctor down the corridor and through the third door on the left. He closed the door behind them, and encouraged her to sit in the chair to the side of the desk.

'How can I help today?' he said, turning to face her, and resting his palms on his legs.

'I need something to help me sleep,' she said, nibbling on a fingernail.

His brow furrowed. 'You're not sleeping?'

'Well, yes, I am, but I keep having nightmares.'

'Okay. What kind of nightmares? Can you describe them to me?'

Hannah looked away, her eyes misting. 'They're about what happened to my husband last year. He... he was murdered in our home.'

'I'm sorry to hear that. How long have you been having these nightmares for?'

'I used to have them a lot, and then months passed without a single one, but in the last week they've started again.' She paused to blow her nose with a tissue. 'They're so... so real.'

'Has anything changed in your personal life, which might be acting as a trigger for the new dreams? Anything new you've taken on, or anything that might be adding stress?'

'New town, new home, new dog, new job.'

He raised both eyebrows. 'Oh, wow, that's a lot of change. I believe you told the agent on the phone that you'd suffered mild depression and PTSD?'

She nodded, flashes of the psychiatric ward briefly popping into her memory before she banished them. 'I was in a bad way following my husband's death.'

'The last thing I want is to force you to relive it, but can you fill me in on the treatment you received post your husband's passing?'

'My GP referred me for counselling, and prescribed paroxetine.'

'Paroxetine is a sedating antidepressant. Things must have been pretty bad then?'

She looked away again. 'I was briefly sectioned in a psychiatric ward. I wasn't a danger, but my mum was concerned that I wasn't looking after myself properly. It was only for a week, and it was a real wake-up call, and that's what led me to see the GP.'

'Are you still taking the paroxetine?'

She shook her head.

'Are you currently taking any other prescribed medications?'

Another shake of the head.

'Are you taking any other forms of non-prescribed medication, including alcohol?'

'I have the occasional glass of wine, but little more than that.'

'Are you still seeing your counsellor?'

'Not exactly. She was really pleased with my progress when I was seeing her in Manchester, but apart from a brief chat the other day, I haven't spoken with her.'

The doctor scribbled something on a pad. 'How are you otherwise? Diet?'

'I eat regularly, probably not as many vegetables as I should, but who does, right?'

'Any pains or aches, particularly in your head, shoulders, or neck?'

She frowned. 'No, not that I'm aware of.'

More scribbles on his pad. 'I'm sure you don't need me to tell you that sudden changes to routine – no matter how minor – can be enough to upset the equilibrium in the brain. From what you've said, you've made some significant changes to your lifestyle, and what you're experiencing at night is probably just your body's coping mechanism. I know that's not particularly helpful. What I suggest is making an emergency appointment with your GP in the morning –'

'I'm not registered,' she blurted. 'What I mean is, not down here. My GP is still technically in Manchester.'

His brow furrowed again. 'I can't prescribe you anything that's going to help you sleep, but your GP may be able to. What I would suggest is arranging a provisional telephone appointment with your old GP, and asking them to reach out to a surgery closer to your home so any treatment can start sooner rather than later. Registering you at the new surgery will take time, and for any medical notes to be sent across, but if your old GP speaks to them on the phone, it might be a bit less painful.'

'So there's nothing you can do?' She hadn't meant it to sound so blunt, but having poured her heart out she'd expected some kind of resolution.

'The best thing I can suggest is visiting a pharmacist today and asking what kind of herbal sleep aids they can recommend over the counter. There are plenty of things on the market that can help calm the mind and body in the build up to sleep. I'm sorry, I know it's not what you were hoping for, but that's the best thing I can suggest for now.'

Standing, Hannah left the room with a shake of her head. She was on her own.

NINETEEN

Hannah was pulling the house keys out of her handbag when she heard a car door slam behind her, and a familiar voice calling her name. Turning, she raised a hand to shield her eyes as she watched the blurred figure approaching.

'Patrick? Goodness, what are you doing here?' She embraced him, surprised by how thin his frame was. He'd never been overweight – neither brother had – but the blazer and shirt were hanging from his body. Pulling away from him she noticed how his face was dripping with sweat.

'Let's get you inside,' she said, opening the door and leading him up the stairs.

Barney went crazy when the two of them walked through the door, bouncing up and trying to sniff and introduce himself to Patrick. The man she'd known who previously would have gone crazy to meet a new dog, brushed Barney away and headed through to the living room, dropping into the sofa and burying his face in his hands.

Hannah removed her coat and hurried through, perching down next to him. 'What's going on, Patrick? What's wrong?'

His head remained where it was, his shoulders gently rocking, and as she put an arm around him and pulled him closer, she could hear the sound of him crying.

Twenty minutes later and with a mug of steaming tea each, Patrick had composed himself enough to ease her fears.

'As lovely as it is to see,' she began, 'what brings you here?'

Removing his blazer, he rolled up the sleeves of his shirt, and tried to smile, failing to convince her everything was okay. 'I'm in big trouble; what I mean is, the business is in big trouble. I've been trying to keep a lid on it, and I didn't want to burden you, but there it is.'

'I don't understand, Patrick, when I last spoke to you, you said business was booming and that you'd never had so much interest in the company.'

He nodded as he sipped his tea. 'We were all set to blaze ahead, and I was even looking at opening a second office, closer to Deansgate, but then our accountant got in touch and told me there is a massive black hole in our books. Close to a quarter of a million pounds is missing from our accounts.'

Hannah frowned. 'Missing? How does that amount of money go *missing*?'

He shrugged. 'It's disappeared into thin air. All we can tell is that it happened in the six months leading up to John's death.'

Hannah's eyes widened. 'You think John took the money?'

Patrick's cheeks blazed. 'No, that's not what I'm saying, but... I don't know how else to explain it. We were partners: I was the salesman and he did the books. That's what made us so strong. I've really struggled with that side of things since he passed. All I can hope is that there's some secret account, or investment I know nothing about that will explain where it's all gone.'

'What do the company's bank statements say? Surely the accountant can track where the money goes?'

Patrick took another sip of tea. 'We'd been investigating the prospect of branching out into Europe. John was in charge of all of that. In fact, it had been his idea. He reckoned if we could buy up a couple of cheap businesses – undertaking similar work to our own – we could slowly build a global brand. It required major investment, and so we set up an account for him to pursue that activity, enabling him to travel to countries and investigate the market. He had full reign over that account, but that's where the black hole is. I can't access the account because he was the only signatory on it, and the bank are making us jump through hoops to allow me access to it.'

'I'm so sorry, Patrick. Is this what you wanted to tell me on the phone on Friday night? I sensed there was something you were keeping from me.'

He nodded. 'I'm sorry to call around unannounced, but I didn't know where else to turn. I've been working all hours trying to figure it all out; I've not been sleeping properly, barely eating, I'm a mess.'

'Does anyone else know? Have you confided in Wendy?'

He shook his head. 'She has enough on her plate looking after the kids. There's nothing she can do to help us.'

She paused. 'Why are you telling me all this? I mean, I don't mind you unburdening – a problem shared is a problem halved – but I'm not sure I can help you out. I never had a head for numbers, and it was John who always took care of our finances and insurance policies.'

Patrick stood and moved across to the window staring out at the street below. 'I know you boxed up some of John's stuff when you moved… I was hoping you might let me take a look through his stuff, to see whether I can find any clues about what might have been going on.'

'Of course, you're more than welcome to look if you think it will help, but I don't understand what you're hoping to find. John wasn't stealing from the company; he wouldn't do that.'

Patrick span on his heel and opened his mouth to speak,

but no words came out. He looked like he wanted to say something, but either didn't have the courage or couldn't find the right words. 'I don't want to believe that my brother was up to no good, but right now that's the only answer I have.' He moved closer to her, lowering his voice. 'The thing is: if we can't find out what's happened to that money, I could be in big trouble.'

'What sort of trouble?'

'You really don't want to know, and I don't want to worry you any more than I already have. Just let me search through the boxes and maybe I'll find what I'm looking for and the long journey down will have been worth it.'

Hannah nodded towards the spare room. 'Everything's in there. Be my guest. In the meantime I'll fix us some lunch. God knows, you look like you need a decent meal.'

TWENTY

Hannah could hear Patrick swearing in the spare room, as she carried the sandwiches through to the living room. Could he be right? Had John been siphoning money from the business? She didn't want to believe it for a second. The two brothers had created the company from scratch, first starting on their own, advertising their services online and wherever they could leave stacks of business cards. Gradually, they'd been forced to take on support staff to help manage the workload, until they'd finally officially registered at Companies House and with HMRC.

She'd watched with great pride as they'd worked tirelessly to build the business from the ground up. She'd even joked with John that he loved that company more than he loved her. If he had been helping himself, what had happened to the money? She hadn't noticed any additional income, or him splashing out on luxurious goods. There had to be some other explanation, although what it might be she had no idea.

The image of John naked in their bedroom flashed into her mind, and she stared down at the camera on the sideboard, before dismissing the idea. John didn't have the time for a second life. His world was Hannah and the business; that was it.

Patrick emerged from the room a moment later. 'Are there any more boxes? Is this all you've got?'

Hannah could see the room over his shoulder was in an

even worse state than she'd left it. At least the boxes had been neatly stacked, even if they hadn't been in any kind of order. Now they were all down on the floor, some with flaps left open, and one of the boxes lying on its side, the contents spilling out.

'There's still a couple of boxes in my mum and dad's garage, but I think they're just my clothes. I wanted to keep John's stuff nearby until I'm ready to go through it. By the way if there's anything you'd like me to hang on to for you, let me know and I'll be sure not to donate it to charity.'

John had been grumpier in the weeks prior to his death. He'd said things had been stressful at work, but she hadn't liked to ask him exactly what was wrong, as she'd assumed he would tell her when he was ready. She'd suggested they get away for a holiday, but he'd reacted angrily, telling her that was the last thing he needed. He'd apologised for his outburst, but if it was related to what Patrick was suggesting, then maybe it made sense.

Patrick stalked along the hall and into the room. 'You're sure there's no other boxes here? You're certain none of his stuff could have become mixed up with what's in the garage?'

'I'm pretty sure, yeah. What exactly is it you're looking for? If you could describe what it is I can keep a look out.'

A single bead of sweat ran the length of his face, but he made no effort to wipe it away. Large dark patches of on his shirt revealed it wasn't just his face that was suffering. The loft wasn't overly warm, and Hannah was wearing a cardigan over her top without any sign of overheating.

'That's just it: I don't know what I'm looking for. I guess I thought he might have kept some kind of ledger, or notebook with details of his actions. What about his computer? Where's that?'

'I assumed his work laptop would have been at the office, and our shared laptop is in my bedroom, but he rarely ever used it. I had it when I was running the photography business, but it's so slow and old now.'

'Can I have a look anyway? Maybe he's got a spreadsheet set up or something.'

'Of course you can, but why don't you sit down and have something to eat first? I only had cheese in, so it's cheese sandwiches, but I have sandwich pickle if you want to liven it up.'

'I'm not hungry.'

Hannah folded her arms, recognising the stubborn nature of the Davenport men. 'I won't take no for an answer. Eat first, and then I'll fetch my laptop. After the long drive you've had this morning, you must be exhausted. You're not going to figure out what's going on if your mind isn't taken care of.'

'Fine,' he snarled, reaching for one of the plates.

'Do you want some pickle?'

'Can you get me a glass of water?'

Placing her own plate on the dining table, she returned to the kitchen, filling a glass and reappearing a moment later. Only, Patrick wasn't where she'd left him. He'd put his plate down next to hers and she didn't need to ponder hard to work out where he'd gone. Heading towards her room, she found him bent over the far side of the bed.

His cheeks reddened as he straightened with the laptop in his hands. 'What? I thought I could check the laptop and eat at the same time. Kill two birds, and all that.'

Stepping aside, she allowed him to pass back into the main room, before he dropped onto the sofa, and flipped open the lid.

'What's the password?'

She opened her mouth to respond, before thinking better of it, and scooping it up, quickly typing it in before passing the laptop back. She then handed him the sandwich, leaving the glass of water on the table.

'I'm pretty sure he wouldn't have left any notes on that,' she warned. 'I don't think it even has any spreadsheet software on it. Have you checked his work computer?'

Patrick took a bite of the sandwich. 'The beauty of working in the IT industry is having specialists who can bypass passwords. It was the first place we checked, but nothing stuck out. He'd have been stupid to leave evidence on his work system anyway, as they're all linked when they come back into the office, to protect and back-up all documents. He'd have known I'd be able to see what he was up to.' He took a second bite, and swallowed. 'He definitely didn't have a personal laptop, or tablet?'

Hannah sat down at the table and nibbled at her own sandwich. 'No. He didn't do social media, and he spent so much time with computers at work that I think he detested seeing them at home. You know how obstinate he could be about things like that.'

'What about his mobile?'

'I still have it, but cancelled the contract. I don't know what his PIN is, but you're welcome to take it back with you and see if one of your experts can crack it.'

He nodded, without smiling, his gaze wandering around the room. 'I like what you've done with the place. Somewhere this size in this area can't have been cheap, nor would hiring a decorator.'

Anger coursed through her veins as she realised the implication. 'When John died, his life assurance paid off the mortgage, and when I sold the house it left a large sum of money that I used to buy this place. As a matter of fact, I decorated this room with my dad's help, so just mind your tongue. I'm willing to be supportive, but not if you're going to start lumping me in with your crazy suspicions about John.'

He looked shocked by her outburst. 'I'm sorry, it's just... oh Jesus, I'm shit-scared I'll end up in prison for fraud or something. As the remaining company director, if the shit hits the fan, it's me who'll suffer the consequences.'

'Prison?'

He shrugged. 'It's one potential outcome. That's why I need to find this bloody money. I can't concentrate on anything else.'

'I'm sure it won't come to that, Patrick,' she said, calmer now. 'You said yourself you know nothing about it.'

His plate suddenly flew across the room, smashing into pieces as it connected with the wall, the remains of the bread and fragments of plate landing on the wooden flooring.

'You think that'll make a blind bit of difference? You hear about company directors being lynched for misappropriation of funds all the time. They won't give a shit whether it was his or my name on the accounts. They'll just assume we were in it together and I'm blaming him because he isn't around to defend himself.'

Hannah swallowed loudly, her breaths coming in short bursts. She'd never seen Patrick so animated before. She'd heard him swear plenty of times, and she'd overheard the brothers arguing in the past, but she'd never witnessed such a violent rage.

Throwing the laptop to the spare cushion, he quickly stood and made his way back towards the spare room, before stopping and slamming his fist into the wall.

Hannah subconsciously eyed her route back to the front door. 'You can't carry on like this,' she warned. 'You can't carry this burden on your own. Maybe the best thing would be to approach HMRC or whoever and explain what has happened. They'll probably be more lenient if you bring it to their attention. My gut tells me John wouldn't do something like this – he definitely wouldn't risk prison for a bit of flash cash – and he wouldn't do something to hurt you. You were his big brother and he'd have crawled over hot coals if it would help you out. You know that!'

'So where is the bloody money?' he sobbed.

'I don't know, but promise me you'll talk this over with someone. Maybe speak to your accountant or informally to a solicitor. If you don't, you'll run yourself into the ground and you won't be the only brother I end up burying.'

TWENTY-ONE

Standing by the living room window, Hannah waved at the departing vehicle, hoping Patrick would remain calm as he hit inevitable traffic on his return to Manchester. Moving away, she shuddered as her eyes fell on the smashed plate and remains of sandwich on the laminate floor near the wall. Spots of grease shone on the surface of the paintwork.

His outburst had frightened her. Clearly the stress of this accounting problem was getting to him, but she couldn't help thinking there was something else he had kept from her, but exactly what was beyond her imagination. Picking up the plate fragments, she carried them out to the kitchen, dropping them into the bin, before reaching for the kitchen roll, and returning to clear up the sandwich. Dabbing at the spots of grease with the tissue did nothing to reduce the stain, and she wasn't sure water would help. She made a mental note to call her father later and see what he suggested; hopefully not another coat of paint.

Although Patrick had offered to tidy the boxes in the spare room, she'd told him she would do it, keen to keep him from damaging anything else. Yet, as she looked into the spare room, the stacks of boxes now unevenly scattered across the worn carpet, she couldn't quite bring herself to make a start.

Barney padded over, and gazed into the room to see what had captured her attention, before looking up at her.

'I know you're right,' she said, staring into his soft,

questioning eyes. 'I should grow a backbone and just sort through John's stuff.' She sighed. 'I know, I know. It's been long enough, and if I don't do it soon, I'll keep putting it off.'

The flaps of the small box nearest to her were open. Inside she could see a mug with the title "World's Greatest Husband". She'd bought it for him on their first wedding anniversary, but he'd never used it for a drink. He hadn't wanted to spoil it, he'd said, and instead it had sat in his office at work as a pen and pencil tidy on the corner of his desk. This had to be the box that had been sent from the office, and it was the one Patrick had seemingly spent most time checking.

Hannah blinked back the sting of tears, refusing to cave. The reason all the stuff had remained boxed for so long is that she feared the rush of cherished memories that would flow with each familiar item. It wasn't the memories she was anxious about, but the feelings of loss and emptiness that would follow, knowing she'd never be able to create new memories with him.

Her mother had passed comment on the room yesterday, offering to help sort through the boxes, but Hannah knew it was something she wanted – *needed* – to do on her own.

Taking a deep breath, she exhaled through her mouth. 'Right, okay,' she told Barney. 'If we're going to do this, I'm going to need some black sacks, and a strong cup of tea.'

Barney rubbed his head against her leg affectionately, until she ran her hand through his fur, stooping and planting a kiss on the top of his head.

'You'd tell me if I was being ridiculous, wouldn't you?'

He didn't respond, and she took it as her cue to fetch what she needed. Two minutes later, and armed with a pair of rubber gloves, a roll of bin liners and a large mug, she entered the room, and lifted the small box onto one of the taller ones, and pushed the flaps wider.

There was no point in keeping the "World's Greatest Husband" mug other than for sentimental value. She knew there would doubtless be dozens more items that would also hold sentimental value, and she didn't have the room in the loft to keep it all. The mug was still in good condition and it seemed a waste to throw it away when someone else could find it of benefit.

Lifting the small box down to the threadbare carpet, she carefully emptied it, before returning the mug. That box would be reserved for charitable donations. Tearing off one of the sacks, she opened it, and put it just outside the door of the small room; that would be for rubbish.

The next item that had been in the small box was a mouse mat she'd bought him for Christmas a couple of years ago bearing the crest and images of his beloved Manchester City Football Club. She'd bought it in a pound shop, as a cheap stocking filler, but he'd loved it, and promised to use it every day. As far as she knew, he'd lived up to the promise. She couldn't see how anyone in the area would want to purchase it, but it was also in good condition, and so it ended up in the charity box too.

Taking a sip of the tea, her eyes met Barney's, up on the sofa in the living room. She'd known it was going to be tough to go through the boxes in this room, but she'd only looked at two items and was already choking back the tears. There were at least another six much larger boxes for her to tackle, and the thought of going through them was overwhelming. Maybe she should have taken up her mum's offer of help. What she needed was someone objective enough to slap some sense into her.

The remaining items from the little box included an engraved biro she'd bought him when they'd moved into the office, a hole punch, and a Newton's Cradle toy. Putting the pen on the small book case for safe-keeping, she put the other items back into the box.

'One down,' she declared proudly, before reaching for a larger box, and sliding it across.

Raising the flaps, this was one of the clothes boxes, which had been packed by the professional removals team she'd hired. Although the jumpers, shirts and trousers had been neatly packed originally, the contents of the box were now a mangled heap of materials, where Patrick had callously rummaged.

Pulling out a large woollen, navy cardigan, she pressed the edge to her nose, breathing in John's scent, and for a moment the world around her disappeared and it was like he was there with her. She hadn't realised how much she'd missed that potion of aftershave, testosterone and body odour. She couldn't prevent the tears escaping her eyes. What would he think if he could see her now? Would he think her callous for dividing his belongings into piles? Or would he tell her she was being ridiculous for getting so emotional over material possessions?

Her heart ached, and it was like being back in Sandra's house last year as the police had confirmed his passing. She hadn't wanted to believe it then, and she wished it wasn't true now.

Opening the cardigan, she slid her arms into the sleeves and pulled it tightly around her middle. It swallowed her whole, but she didn't care. Just having his aroma so close felt like he was hugging her tight, giving her the strength she needed to continue.

Reaching for the next item, a superhero t-shirt one of his nephew's had bought him for Christmas, which she'd never seen him wear, she battled on. Refolding the t-shirt, she dropped it onto the charity box, and systematically withdrew each remaining item of clothing, folding tops that could be reused, and bagging up pants and socks.

Reaching for the next item, she was surprised when her

fingers brushed against something small and soft. Gripping it tighter, she removed the small pink teddy bear, and frowned at it. The toy was six inches tall, the colour of candyfloss, with the word Torquay embroidered into one of the bear's feet.

He had to have bought it on one of his business trips to Devon and Cornwall, but she was certain she'd never seen it before. Perhaps it was something he'd bought and forgotten to give to her. Or maybe it was something he'd planned to give to her before that night. Either way, it wasn't what she'd expected to find.

She was about to place the bear in the charity box, when her thumb felt something hard inside the toy. Rotating it in her hands, to see if it was supposed to be musical, she couldn't explain why there appeared to be a box of some kind inside the toy. She squeezed each of the bear's feet in turn, but none seemed to contain a switch to set off a song.

Turning it over, she studied the back of the bear, finding a loose stitch and opening at the base of the toy's spine. Pulling on the thread, the join separated enough for her to pinch the box and pull it out. She gasped as the small black Nokia phone dropped into her lap. It was only a couple of inches long, and several years old, lacking any of the touchscreen functionality of the phones Bea's brother Chris had shown her; practically an antique in the current market.

Why would John have a second phone, and why would it be hidden in a stuffed toy she'd never seen before? Pressing the power button, she was disappointed when the display didn't illuminate; the battery was dead.

Standing, she left the room and headed to the kitchen. The phone Chris had encouraged her to buy was still in its box on the side. Opening the lid, she removed the phone's charger, and compared it to the slot in the Nokia, but it didn't match.

Patrick had asked whether John had any other devices,

and now she couldn't help thinking that this phone was what he'd been so desperately searching for. But why? What could such an old device hold? One thing was certain: she would need to get the battery charged if she was going to find out.

TWENTY-TWO

The supermarket was busier than Hannah had anticipated. Pushing her trolley up one aisle and down the next, she scanned the shelves for any sign of a mobile phone charger, without success. She'd driven to the large Asda in Chandlers Ford, hoping it would stock what she needed, but after ten minutes searching, she was regretting not phoning Bea's brother Chris and asking for his help, but that might have required her to explain why she desperately wanted to charge the old Nokia. She was out of her depth.

Wheeling the trolley back to the front of the store, she decided to start her search again. Passing an in-store photography lab, she remembered the small memory card she'd found in the digital camera, and how she'd planned to get the image of John printed. Opening her purse, she fished out the memory card, and carried it over to the lab. The girl behind the counter had large glasses and a brace, and didn't look old enough to have a job.

'Excuse me,' Hannah said, 'I'm wondering if you can help me? I want to print an image from this memory card, is that something you can do here?'

The girl took the memory card and turned it over in her fingers, as if she expected it to reveal its secrets there and then. She handed it back. 'It should fit in our machines,' she said nodding at a bank of screens by the wall. 'Stick it in the slot and then you can choose which images, how many and the size. Print the receipt and bring it back here to pay, and the pictures should be ready by tomorrow.'

Hannah turned to look at the screens. 'Is there any chance it could be done sooner? It's just one specific picture that I'm looking to print.'

The girl glanced at her wrist watch, and pulled a face. 'Just the one image?'

Hannah nodded hopefully. 'I need it urgently.'

The girl looked around conspiratorially. 'Okay. You're lucky that it's quite quiet today. Bring me the receipt as soon as you have it, and I'll bump your order to the front of the queue.'

Hannah thanked her and moved across to the screens. Things had certainly changed a lot since she'd run her photography business. When she'd first started out, her camera had a roll of film that had to be carefully handled when extracting images; a craft she'd learned to do in a darkened room at home when she was still at school. These days all anyone needed was a computer and a printer.

Pushing the memory card into the slot, she waited for the screen to process it, before a folder of images opened on the screen. John's face filled the screen as she tapped on the picture, suddenly conscious that any passing stranger would now be able to see her naked husband. Looking around her, nobody was showing any interest though.

Returning her gaze to the screen, she clicked through to the next window. The largest size available was A4, and so that would have to do. Pressing on the printer icon, the machine whirred, before spitting out the memory card and a small paper receipt. Grabbing both, she returned to the counter, and handed the receipt to the girl.

'What time will it be ready?' Hannah asked, handing over the cash.

'Come back in an hour, and it should be done,' the girl said with a friendly smile.

Hannah thanked her, collected her empty trolley, and

headed back into the shop in search of cables and electrical equipment. Along the back wall of the store were a range of flat screen televisions, and it was while she was browsing the items in this area, that she located cables of all varieties, but nothing resembling the port on the phone.

'It's Hannah, isn't it?' a voice said over her shoulder.

Turning, Hannah blinked twice, recognising the man who had helped her catch Barney when he'd run off on Thursday.

'Steve,' he said, offering his hand to shake. 'It's okay if you don't remember me.'

'Steve, of course,' she said, her cheeks reddening. 'I remember. What are you doing here?'

He raised the basket in his hands. 'Just picking up supplies. Dog food and a dinner for one. How about you?'

'Getting a picture developed.'

'How's that dog of yours? Bearded Collie, right?'

'He's well, thank you. And your dogs?'

The awkwardness of the exchange had Hannah racking her brain for anything to say that didn't sound as pathetic as trying to discover what her husband had been up to before his death.

'They're fine. Will we see you tonight?'

Hannah was taken aback by the directness of the question. 'Um…'

'Dog training,' he quickly added, blushing. 'Sorry, I didn't mean –'

'No, of course you didn't,' Hannah interrupted, wishing the ground would open up and swallow her whole.

'I think your Collie would really benefit from socialising with some other dogs, and the first night's free of charge, so there really isn't anything to lose.'

What would John say if he could see her now? He hated the thought of anyone else showing an interest in her.

'There will be loads of other dogs there for him to meet,'

Steve continued. 'I promise it really is a good class. What do you say?'

Would John think she was flirting with Steve? She wasn't trying to, but it was hard not to mirror the kind smile he was projecting.

Steve reached into his pocket and handed her a leaflet. 'In case you lost the other one,' he said, smiling again, revealing his dimple. 'The address is on the front, and the class starts at seven. Please say you'll at least think about it?'

It wasn't like Barney couldn't do with some behavioural training. She hadn't forgotten the panic she'd experienced when he'd shot off on Thursday, and if she was to be able to trust him off the lead, then proper training wasn't a bad idea. She accepted the leaflet, trying to ignore the voice in her head. 'If you think it will help.'

'Brilliant. I hope to see you then.'

He was just moving away when she remembered her reason for coming to the supermarket. 'You can't help me find something can you?'

He turned back, nodding.

Hannah reached for the Nokia from her handbag. 'I'm looking for something that will charge a phone like this, but none of these seem to fit.'

He took the phone and studied the port, before scanning the variety of cable packets hanging from the stand. Selecting one, he handed it to her. 'This ought to do the trick. You really should think about getting a newer phone. This one's an antique.'

'It's not mine,' she said, before she could stop herself. 'What I mean is… it belongs to a friend of mine. I said I'd find her a charger.'

She couldn't tell from his face whether he'd believed her or not, but he didn't question her reason.

'Okay, well I hope to see you and your Collie tonight.'

And with that he moved away, disappearing at the end of the aisle.

Hannah's cheeks still felt warm, and she unzipped her jacket for some air. Spotting a sign for the café, she pushed her trolley towards it. Tea and a slice of cake would help kill the time until the photograph was developed.

Forty-five minutes later, Hannah had finished her tea and scone, and read the store magazine from cover to cover. Paying for the charging cable, she made her way back to the photo lab, nodding at the girl with the brace and glasses.

'I'm early,' Hannah apologised. 'Is it ready yet?'

The girl avoided eye contact, taking Hannah's voucher and moving across to a pile of envelopes, flicking through them until she found the one she was looking for, sliding it across the counter. Hannah couldn't understand the reaction at first, until she remembered the image was of a naked man, and suddenly became self-conscious. God only knew what the girl was thinking about her.

Hannah picked up the envelope without another word, placing it in her carrier bag, and with her head bent low she left the store, and returned to her car. Once behind the wheel, she opened the envelope and slid out the A4 glossy photograph.

No doubt in her mind now that the room was definitely theirs; she recognised the navy pattern on the cream bedspread, and the angle of the television on the wall just over John's shoulder. They had thrown out that bedding eighteen months ago, so it had to have been taken before that.

Why couldn't she remember taking it though?

Both of John's arms were by his side, so that ruled out it being a selfie. Had he arranged for someone else to take the picture of him? If so, why, and more importantly whom? And why was he undressed?

Nothing about the picture made any sense. And then something in the top left corner of the photograph caught her eye. She hadn't noticed it in the small viewing window of the camera, but it was impossible to miss in the enlarged version. To the left of John was the reflection of something long and crimson in the floor-to-ceiling mirror. Studying the reflection closer she had no doubt that it was part of a dress, wrapped around a shapely figure she knew wasn't her own.

Hannah didn't own any clothes that colour, and whoever it belonged to, she had clearly been the one holding the camera, capturing John's perfect smile.

Another woman in Hannah's bedroom, taking a picture of her naked husband, it was all Hannah could do to stop herself throwing up.

TWENTY-THREE

Bursting through the front door, Hannah tore at the packaging, pulling out the plug and cable, and thrusting it into the nearest available socket in the kitchen. With her free hand she reached into her coat pocket, grasped the Nokia phone and pulled it out, almost dropping it on the counter as she did. The loft felt overly warm as her clammy fingers tried to grip around the tiny cable end. She finally had it between her thumb and fingers, but dropped it twice as she tried to connect it to the phone's port. It finally clicked into place and she let out a relieved sigh.

Stepping back, she waited for the tiny LED at the top of the phone to glow, before removing her jacket, and finally allowing her breathing to return to a steadier rate. Staring at the thermostat, she was surprised to find the heating switch set to on, instead of operating on the timer. She was about to switch it back, when she stopped. That was the second time in as many days that the thermostat wasn't as she'd expected to find it. Either the system was playing up, or…

She didn't want to finish the thought. Barney stretched his legs as he came padding into the room. He must have been asleep when she'd first come home, as he hadn't raced to greet her like he usually did. Stooping, she massaged his furry ears, before he moved across to his bowl of water and taking a satisfying drink.

Hannah straightened and picked up the Nokia phone, jamming her thumb against the 'On' button and waiting for it to light up. Nothing happened. The screen remained dark, and apart from the small power LED there were no other signs of life.

It was possible that in the year since John's death, with no charge in the phone, it had simply given up the ghost and would not work again. That would be hugely frustrating. She'd tried putting the SIM card into the phone Chris had made her buy, but it was too large. If she wanted to find out what was on the SIM, she needed this or a similar phone to work.

She thought again about phoning Chris to help, but something deep inside didn't want her to become so dependent on another man. Without John, it was time for her to stand on her own two feet.

She was about to try switching the phone on again, when she heard the landline phone ringing in the other room. Resting the Nokia to the counter, she headed into the living room, and put the phone to her ear.

'Hello?'

'Oh thank heavens,' DI Jeanette Chandler's broad Yorkshire voice answered. 'I've been trying to get hold of you all morning, where have you been?'

The directness of the question caught Hannah off-guard. 'I had to go to the supermarket for a few bits and pieces. Why? What is it?'

'You haven't watched the TV news yet then?'

'News? No not yet, why?'

Chandler took an audible breath. 'Seamus Fahey tried to top himself last night. I found out this morning. Silly old duffer tried to make some kind of noose out of his bed sheets, but he was spotted within a couple of minutes, and brought around.'

Hannah gasped, uncertain whether to feel any sympathy towards the man who had stolen everything from her.

'He's been transferred to a local hospital so they can

monitor his vital signs. His body was starved of oxygen for a couple of minutes so they need to make sure no lasting damage has occurred. Anyway, somehow the local media got wind of the story and reported it nationally. I didn't want you to hear it from anybody but me.'

Hannah quickly sat, as her legs weakened. 'What does this mean?'

'For him it'll mean closer scrutiny on his movements and actions for the remainder of his sentence.'

'And for me?'

Chandler paused. 'In my view, it's a sure sign of him not being able to deal with the guilt of his actions. Throughout the trial he maintained that he couldn't remember being inside your home, despite the overwhelming volume of DNA evidence and the presence of John's blood on his clothes and shoes. I would imagine, after his appeal was overturned this week that the reality of the future has finally hit him, and he couldn't live with the guilt.'

'You don't think this suicide attempt is a means of him trying to escape?'

'Ha!' Chandler snorted. 'At his age? He's no spring chicken, and after decades of living rough, he's hardly in peak physical condition. Besides, he has prison officers and some of my boys and girls in blue at the hospital with him. There's a chance he'll be back inside before the sun sets tonight, but worst case scenario they'll transport him back in the morning. Don't worry, he's not going anywhere.'

Hannah took a modicum of comfort from that, but her heart still raced as she pictured his face.

'There's something else,' Chandler said awkwardly. 'I wasn't going to tell you, but somehow the press got hold of it too.' She paused. 'Fahey wants to meet you.'

Hannah couldn't breathe. 'Meet me? Why?'

'If I had to guess it's so he can make his peace with you.'

'How do you… I mean…'

'How do we know? Fahey's been adding your name to his list of approved visitors.'

Hannah choked down bile in the back of her throat. 'I don't want to be on the same planet as him, let alone in the same room.'

'I know, I know, but that doesn't stop him recording your name on the list. Doesn't mean you have to go.'

'How would I know my name was on this list?'

Another pause as Chandler summoned courage. 'He's been writing to you. Every week since he was sentenced.'

Hannah gasped again. 'What? I've not received any letters.'

'We've been intercepting them,' Chandler explained. 'Well at least the prison service has and passing them on to me.' She sighed. 'We've had a number of offenders who try to contact their victims to taunt them. It's all about power and control. At first I thought that's what he was trying to do, and I figured you'd been through enough already.'

'So why tell me now?'

'As I said, the press have found out he's been writing to you, and I thought it right you hear it from me, so I could explain why I've stopped the letters getting to you.'

Hannah took a moment to settle the thoughts and questions racing around her head. 'What do the letters say?'

'They're not exactly Shakespeare,' Chandler scoffed. 'He doesn't say a lot, just asks if you'll come and visit him.'

'Why is he so keen to see *me*?'

Chandler sighed again. 'It could be so he can confess what he did and seek your forgiveness. In light of what happened this morning that would be my best guess.'

'Never going to happen,' Hannah said firmly.

'I thought that'd be your reaction, and I can't blame you for that. But…' the words hung in the air menacingly.

'But what?'

'I think you should consider it.'

'No way –' Hannah began before Chandler cut her off.

'I meant a *supervised* visit. I'd be right there with you to keep things in check and to stop him if he tries to say anything upsetting.'

'You know I can't bear to be in the same room as him.'

'I know, sweetheart, and I wouldn't ask you to think about it if I didn't think it could help. Him as well as you. I think he wants to apologise and if you let him that may bring him some inner peace and stop him trying to top himself again, which is a waste of a lot of people's time and energy. For you it might help bring some closure on things.'

'*I will never forgive him for what he took from me,*' Hannah growled.

Chandler didn't offer a challenge. 'Don't make a decision now. I'll give you another call tomorrow or Tuesday, and then whatever you decide, we'll leave it at that. Please do think about it though, Hannah. I genuinely think it could benefit the both of you, and I wouldn't ask if I didn't think you were strong enough to cope. By God, you're one of the strongest women I've ever met. Most of the rest of us would have crumpled after what happened to you.'

Hannah didn't respond, disappointed that Chandler would even consider asking her to allow Fahey to apologise. If he was feeling guilty about what he'd done, then he deserved to suffer too.

'I need to go, sweetheart,' Chandler finally said. 'I'll call you in a day or so. You take care.'

Hannah disconnected the line, and stomped to the kitchen, reaching for the kettle, but stopping as her eyes fell on the Nokia. An animated battery symbol had now appeared on the screen. The phone was charging.

TWENTY-FOUR

Staring at the phone, the single bar flashing in the battery icon on the screen suggested a full charge would take some time. At least it was working.

Filling the kettle, she resisted the urge to try and switch on the phone, concerned that it would fail mid-operation and she'd be back to square one. The kettle boiled and she made a cup of tea, every glance at the phone's display bringing nothing but disappointment. As much as she tried to ignore the voice jabbering away in the back of her mind, her attention kept returning to what the Nokia might hold.

There was a good chance she would learn nothing new about John. It could easily be an old phone that he'd forgotten to throw out. It was equally possible that it wasn't even his. Just because she'd found it in a box of his things from work, didn't necessarily mean that it had belonged to him. Accidents could happen, mistakes could be made.

But what if…?

That was the question that kept leaping to the forefront of her mind. What if it explained what had happened to the money Patrick was so desperate to find? What if it revealed a second life John had been living and keeping secret from everyone, *including* her?

Hannah was allowing her imagination to run away with her again, but having had no contact with John in almost a year, this gave her something to cling onto: a link to the past. Wasn't that worth grabbing hold of with both hands?

Sipping from the mug, she turned her back on the phone, hoping out of sight would be out of mind. What she needed to do was busy herself with something else, and hope that the distraction lasted long enough for the battery to charge sufficiently.

After twenty minutes of trying to read a book, she took Barney out for a walk, the entire time her mind constantly returning to one question: what if?

Checking the Nokia's display again, the single bar of battery life continued to flash. Did that mean the charger wasn't working properly? Or did it just mean that battery degradation would mean a longer charging time? Regardless, she jammed her thumb against the 'On' button and held her breath as the screen flickered and the battery icon was replaced by a welcome message. This was followed by a spinning hourglass as the device searched for a network. Just as suddenly, the hourglass vanished, replaced by a bright turquoise screen, the network provider's name in the top left corner. The smaller battery icon in the top right corner was flashing red to indicate the lack of life.

Opening the phone's menu, a table of nine images appeared. Scrolling to the icon resembling a brown notebook, she opened the contacts list. The message on screen told her 'No Contacts Stored'. Cursing under her breath, she returned to the main menu and scrolled to the envelope icon to open any messages, but again, the folder was empty.

Her heart sank. Although the phone was now working, her worst fears had been confirmed: it didn't bridge that gap to the past. It was as if the phone had never been used. The only thing of interest was the fact it had still managed to connect to a network, meaning the SIM card was still live. If it was John's phone, she was certain she hadn't seen a monthly bill for it. If it wasn't his phone, why hadn't the owner stopped the contract?

She was about to switch it off and unplug the charger when another thought crossed her mind. Scrolling to the image of a phone, her heart skipped a beat as she opened the call history list and one number stared back at her. It wasn't a number she immediately recognised, but what had her gasping for breath was the date and time of the last call. According to the phone, John had called the number an hour before he'd died.

Highlighting the number her trembling finger pressed redial and then she put the phone to her ear. Silence greeted her before a recorded message advised the number was no longer in service. Disconnecting, she returned the phone to the counter.

It shouldn't have been so surprising. It was commonplace for people to regularly change mobile contracts, and discarding their previous number. That didn't help explain who John had phoned so close to the end, nor why. She was about to phone DI Chandler to see whether the police could trace the phone's owner when she thought better of it. What was she going to say?

'Hi Jeanette. Listen, I found this old phone and I think it must have been John's, and it turns out he phoned someone on it less than an hour before he died. Could you trace it for me?'

Chandler would probably laugh at her down the line. The number probably meant nothing. For all she knew it could have been some business contact that he happened to call in order to place an order, or arrange a meeting, or even cancel a meeting. The timing was purely coincidental. Again, it highlighted to Hannah just how much she needed some kind of closure. She couldn't spend the rest of her life inventing conspiracy theories about that night. The killer was behind bars; justice had been served.

The Nokia beeped in her hand as it received a message

advising her that eleven pounds credit remained on the phone. At least that explained why she'd never seen any mobile bills. As a Pay As You Go phone, John would have added credit to use it. Did that mean this was a business phone then? She could remember Patrick saying they were thinking of ordering work mobiles so they didn't keep using their personal allowances on work matters. Yet she was sure John had been against the idea; worried that he'd lose one of the phones. It didn't explain why the phone would have been hidden in a stuffed toy.

The best thing would be to call Patrick, explain what she'd discovered and ask him if she should have it couriered up so he could check it, yet something stopped her placing the call.

'Right, I've run some searches on this other number,' Bea's brother Chris said, removing his glasses and resting them on the table next to his laptop, 'but the most I can tell you is it was an unregistered Pay As You Go phone.'

The Nokia was still plugged into the charger in the kitchen, but had still yet to reach full charge. Hannah had finally relented and called someone with greater expertise in technological terms, but he hadn't brought her any closer to resolving who John had phoned an hour before his death.

'Thanks for trying,' she said.

'Commonly known in the business as a burner phone,' Chris added. 'Popular amongst drug dealers and those trying to hide other criminal activities. How did you say you came across it?'

'I found it in the park,' she said, carefully reciting the lie she'd sold him on the phone. 'Just thought someone might have lost it and would want it returned.'

'Judging by the age of the phone, I wouldn't have

thought it would hold much value, other than to an enthusiast. You're better off leaving it switched on and maybe the owner will phone it and you can arrange an exchange. Otherwise, there's nothing more I can tell you about it or the number it called almost a year ago.'

As disappointing as the news was, she wasn't surprised.

He stood and snapped the laptop closed. 'How are you getting on with your new phone?'

'Fine,' she lied, hoping he didn't happen to glance into the kitchen and see it still sitting in its packaging.

'Good, good. You know I was pleased when you called me,' he added sheepishly.

'You were?'

'Yeah. Bea told me you're not seeing anyone at the moment, and I wondered if you maybe fancied going out for a drink some time.'

Hannah blinked at him in rapid succession. 'A drink? You and me?'

'Only if you want to.'

He had to be at least six or seven years younger than her, which wasn't an unreasonable gap, though she couldn't imagine a single thing they might have in common.

Her cheeks were burning as she tried to think of a way to let him down gently. 'Um, listen, it's sweet of you to ask, Chris, but I'm not sure.'

'I'm a lot more mature than I look,' he said, not willing to be so easily rebuffed. 'My sister said you're new to the area, and I just thought… never mind. Listen, I can see you're not interested and that's okay. Forget I asked.'

He was doing a lousy job of hiding his disappointment.

Hannah grimaced, as she failed to stop herself speaking. 'Okay, you're right, I don't really know anyone down here yet, and I owe you a drink after all the help you've been this week.'

He smiled. 'Great, how about tonight?'

Hannah hadn't expected him to be so keen. 'Um, I can't do tonight. I... um, I'm taking my dog to a training class,' she said, trying to find any reasonable excuse. I've got your number. How about I give you a call in a few days?'

His smile widened. 'Sure, no worries.'

Showing him to the door, she started when she saw Bea emerging at the top of the staircase.

Bea gave the pair of them a quizzical look until Hannah explained why she'd called Chris.

'He's a good boy,' Bea said, once Chris had said goodbye and the two neighbours were inside the loft. 'You could do a lot worse than date someone like him, you know.'

Hannah couldn't ignore the feeling that Chris's willingness to be so helpful wasn't some plan of Bea's to play matchmaker.

'Anyway,' Bea continued, I'm glad I caught you; there's something I need to show you.

Hannah raised a sceptical eyebrow, until Bea presented an A5-sized notebook and handed it over.

Opening it, Hannah was horrified to read, "Diary of Melanie Fowler June to December 2013."

TWENTY-FIVE

Hannah looked from the diary to Bea. 'Where on earth did you get this?'

Bea pulled an awkward face. 'I took it from Melanie's room when we called round to visit her parents the other day.'

Hannah couldn't keep the incredulity from her voice. 'You stole her diary?'

'Not stole, *borrowed*,' Bea corrected. 'I'll give it back when we're done.'

'Did Mrs Fowler see you take it?'

'Of course not. She was the one who showed it to me, and then when she turned her back, I shoved it into my handbag.' Bea raised her eyebrows expectantly. 'We need to know more about her if we're going to figure out what Nigel did.'

'And when Mrs Fowler returns to the room and discovers it missing? Then what?'

'Relax, will you? The police won't be round here banging on our doors over something little like a diary. Plus, imagine her face when we prove what Nigel did, and she can have the satisfaction of seeing him put away for the rest of his life.'

Bea had a point, not that Hannah was prepared to concede so easily. It was one thing to help bring solace to a grieving woman, and quite another to steal a treasured memento.

'We need to take it back,' Hannah concluded. 'No, correction: *you* need to take it back.'

'How? She lives miles away and I don't drive. Anyway, you're missing the point. The reason I told you I have it is I think I've found something.'

Hannah looked at her sceptically, before curiosity got the better of her. 'What did you find?'

Bea placed a protective arm around the notebook, holding it against the multi-coloured t-shirt she was wearing. 'First, I want you to admit that it was a good idea for me to take it, and stop all this talk about going back to Mrs Fowler's. I will take it back, but only once that madman is behind bars.'

'Fine,' Hannah exhaled loudly. 'I don't think it was right to steal the diary, and you should probably at least phone Mrs Fowler and let her know that we have it, just in case she goes to find it later.'

Bea rolled her eyes, before opening the notebook and reading aloud.

Monday 13 May 2015

Today I met Nigel. He's just moved in upstairs, and although not traditionally handsome, he has deep, brooding eyes, and I'm sure I sensed him watching me after we'd passed on the stairs. He was carrying large boxes into the flat for hours, stacked with books, which means he must be an avid reader like me. He's not the usual guy I would fancy, but after Billy, maybe I'd be better off going for someone different. All I long for is someone who wants to take care of me. Good-looking guys come with baggage. Nigel is no model, but there's something about him that makes me want to learn more.

Hannah gave Bea a confused look. 'Is that it? Doesn't sound that sinister to me. Who's Billy?'

'From what I can tell, Billy is an ex-boyfriend who cheated on her, I think. I skimmed the first half of the diary until I came across Nigel's name. There is the occasional reference to Billy, but usually just to confirm how different Nigel is to him. I did go back to the January entries, but I think the relationship with Billy preceded 2013. Whatever happened, I don't think it ended well.'

'Well there was nothing there about Nigel that screams he's a killer.'

'You don't think it's a bit creepy that she felt him watching her? Didn't you feel the same way the other night when he was stalking you on the stairs?'

Hannah thought back to the incident on Friday night that had resulted in Nigel chasing her up the stairs.

'And you have to admit him sending me a friend request when we've barely exchanged two words is freaky,' Bea continued.

'She didn't sound freaked out,' Hannah countered, 'more hopeful that he'd been interested in her.'

'It gets worse,' Bea promised.

Wednesday 05 June 2013

Tonight was not quite what I expected. Nigel collected me at seven, as we'd agreed, but rather than taking me to dinner and a movie as I'd anticipated, he took me to church! It wasn't just any church; it was *his* church. Picture the scene: I'm dressed in the new skinny jeans I bought at the weekend, the top I'd got in the sale and my favourite boots. To say I stood out like a sore thumb would be an understatement, yet I couldn't tell you whether I was overdressed, or underdressed. The other people there were all very welcoming, and at least ten of them came over to tell me how wonderful Nigel is, and how meeting him has changed their lives for the better. I was sceptical when we entered, and my instinct was to turn and run; I haven't been to any kind of church since leaving home – hope Mum never reads this! – but he looked so excited that he was sharing a part of him that he holds so dear that I didn't feel I could do anything but stay. I didn't want to embarrass him in front of his friends.

We sat in a circle, and he sat down right next to me, because I think he sensed I was nervous, and at first it felt a bit like some kind of Alcoholics Anonymous support group. Everyone was invited to share something that they were really happy with, and something that was troubling them. I was amazed at the level of support and guidance everyone offered each other.

Then it came to my turn. I didn't want to speak, and had hoped Nigel would allow me to just watch, but he insisted. So, I told them I am really happy to be moving on with my life away from Billy, and that I am nervous about the rounds of interviews coming up for that promotion at work. One of the women sitting nearby said she is a recruitment specialist and offered to meet with me and provide some guidance and smart interview techniques. Despite my reticence to speak, I left the hall with a warm buzz.

Nigel escorted me home, and was a perfect

> gentleman. He said they meet once a week, and understands if I don't want to go again, he just wanted me to see his passion for helping others. I told him I would think about it, but the weird thing is, I'm not against the idea of going back.
> What is wrong with me!

Hannah hated herself for the twinges of jealousy coursing through her veins. What she would give to have that warm, fuzzy feeling again.

'Told you he was one of those new age religious nuts!' Bea declared proudly.

Hannah frowned. 'I'm still not seeing it the way you are. Okay, it's a bit odd to take someone to church for a first date, but she clearly enjoyed herself. When you said you'd found something, I thought you had something more concrete.'

'He was brainwashing her!' Bea declared.

Hannah pulled a scornful face. 'Hey?'

'That's how they do it; I saw it on a documentary on BBC2. They select vulnerable members of society, offer them a sense of acceptance in a community-environment, and then get their hooks in. It's all in here. At first her diary entries are a few times a week, with no obvious pattern of days or dates, but consistently three to four times a week. Then she goes to this church in June, and the entries reduce. They drop to a couple of times per week, and then once a fortnight, and then once a month.'

'That doesn't prove anything! Maybe she was using the diary to share her fears, and find resolution, but after she started going to the church they helped her overcome them. If the group was as she described, it sounds a bit like group-counselling.'

'Oh yeah? Well how do you explain this?' Bea turned

the notebook over, pressing out the inside spine. 'See these tufts of paper? This means pages were ripped out of this book.'

'And?'

'*And* maybe he did it because those entries revealed what a psychopath he is!'

'Or maybe she made a mistake and tore the page out herself. Come on, Bea, you're seeing things you *want* to see. Presumably the police examined this notebook during their investigation, and if they returned it to Mrs Fowler, then they didn't see any evidential value in it.'

Bea closed the diary. 'I see I'm wasting my time with you on this. No matter what I say, you shoot it down.'

Hannah's cheeks flushed slightly, seeing the hurt in Bea's eyes. 'Look, I'm sorry. I know you want to find out what happened to Melanie, and that's commendable, but I don't think you should jump to unrealistic conclusions just because Nigel comes from a different walk of life. The last thing you want is to start making wild accusations that you can't prove.'

'But –' Bea began to say, before Hannah cut her off by raising her hand.

'I will help you do some more digging into Melanie's background, just so you don't go doing something we'll both regret, but I think for now we need to stop focusing on Nigel. If things point us back in his direction at some point then so be it, but I don't think he should be the only consideration. For one thing, we need to know more about her ex Billy: what happened between them; was he ever considered a suspect?'

Bea nodded. 'I don't know. I vaguely remember different men visiting her, but she never introduced me to anyone called Billy. I'll ask Chris though; he and Melanie were at school together. Maybe Billy was someone they both knew.' She paused. 'That reminds me; that friend of yours – Lucy Davison – sent you a message on Facebook. I didn't mean to read it, but you should probably respond to her. Did Chris put the app on your phone yet?'

Hannah shook her head, subconsciously looking towards the kitchen. Bea took the cue and marched into the room, pulling the phone from the box and switching it on. 'Right, I'm going to get you set up. It's for your own good. I need to be able to get hold of you so I can make sure Nigel doesn't come for you too.'

TWENTY-SIX

Still reeling from Bea's admission to taking the diary, Hannah pulled Barney's lead closer as they battled against the strong wind. She'd thought about driving the two of them to the class, but how would that look? Turning up at a dog-training class having driven the animal, especially when it was only a mile from home.

She shouldn't have worried, as the public car park adjacent to the rundown church hall was overflowing, dogs of all sizes being harnessed up and dragged from their vehicles. She'd had no idea Steve's class would be so popular, and she was now regretting not phoning ahead to reserve a place.

Light blue paint was peeling away from the wooden doors into the building; the glass panels covered in grime. A damp sheet of A4 stuck to one of the windows indicated registration for Williams' Woofers would occur in the main hall. Hannah stepped back to allow another woman walk a miniature ball of fluff through the door. Was that even a dog? It was about the length of a rat, but the mass of fur covering the body made it look like the animal had just completed two cycles in a spin dryer. The dog's owner, wearing skinny jeggings, knee-length boots and a carefully-sculpted hive of hair looked like she was here for more than just education.

Hannah followed her through, nodding politely as the woman held the door for her, with a cursory glance at

Hannah's jeans and woollen jumper combo.

'First time?' the woman commented, her voice faux-posh.

'Yes,' Hannah said, feeling the urge to pull Barney's lead across her middle. 'Could you show me where I need to register?'

The woman nodded, and without another word proceeded through the next set of double doors and into the much warmer corridor. A closed shutter to their right protected the hall's makeshift kitchen, and then up ahead the corridor widened into the large expanse of square hall. The air here was musty and stale, like the windows hadn't been opened in decades, and by the look of the décor, it probably hadn't. Strips of dried tape remained stuck to the faded walls where pictures had once hung. It was a good space, but the laminated floor was pocked with scratches and scuffs, and the woman's booted footsteps seemed to echo around the room.

As Hannah stepped into the hall – wearing far more sensible and quieter trainers – she soon realised the woman with the beehive wasn't the only one to have made an effort with hair and makeup. Left and right, it was like they were waiting back stage at some kind of pageant, only the dogs and Hannah looking out of place. One redheaded woman dressed in a long fur coat, was flanked by two Dalmatians, like she had come to a fancy dress party as Cruella De Vil. Another, clad in spandex with a doll-like figure, was holding tightly to the lead of a whippet that had taken an uncomfortable interest in a poodle, immaculately groomed with a pink bow around one ear.

Hannah was about to turn and leave when she spotted Steve at the far side of the hall. He smiled and waved as their eyes met, and before she could head for the door he was cutting through the room like a hot knife through butter. The crowd of women parting like the Red Sea, each curious to see what had captured his attention.

'You made it,' he said as he drew close, looking pleased.

'I just wanted to come and see what all the fuss was about,' Hannah replied casually. 'I didn't book a place, and you look overcrowded.'

'Nonsense,' he quickly fired back. 'Always room for one more.' He stooped and rubbed Barney's ears. Barney responded by straining to get closer. Steve straightened. 'It usually costs ten pounds per dog per session, but your first is free. That way you can see whether you think you can keep up with what's required without spending a penny. So now you kind of have to stay.'

That smile; Hannah wondered whether Steve always got his own way. As he continued to look at her, she couldn't help smiling back at him. 'Okay, I'll stay. Where should I wait?'

He turned and pointed at the back of the hall, opposite to the side he'd come from. 'Everyone starts at the back so we can do some recall training, but then you'll split into smaller groups for other drills and use the hall's full space. For now, you can stick with me, or you can wait at the back. We'll start in five minutes or so.'

'I'll wait at the back,' she said, noticing the wall of stares in their direction.

'Great,' he said, gently rubbing her arm. 'Don't look so worried, my bark is much worse than my bite.' He added a wink for good measure, before heading back to the table he'd been at earlier, where a small locked cash box stood.

Hannah moved to the back of the hall where he'd indicated and positioned herself next to a much older lady with white hair, who was talking to a very obedient King Charles spaniel, whose name appeared to be Missy. The dog danced around in a circle before coming to heel, and then raising a paw, at which point the white-haired woman stooped and fed her a small treat.

'That's very impressive,' Hannah offered, unconvinced Barney would ever be so submissive.

'Thank you,' the woman said, a waft of strong perfume emanating from her lilac cardigan, secured by a large emerald brooch. 'All it takes is practise.'

'Have you been coming here long?' Hannah asked.

'Oh yes, we're regulars. Missy is very well behaved, but this gives her an opportunity to socialise with other dogs, and it gets us out of the flat. Steve is a very good teacher. Missy loves him to bits.'

The large gathering around Steve suggested Missy wasn't the only one hoping to catch his eye.

'I feel a bit underdressed,' Hannah said.

The woman considered her for a moment. 'I'm hardly in a position to comment on the latest fashion trends, dear. If you're here to train your dog, then I'd say you're more than adequately dressed. What's his name by the way?'

Hannah ruffled his ears as he panted, his eyes darting from one dog to another. 'He's called Barney. He's a rescue; I've only had him for a few weeks, so I thought I should try and teach him a few basic commands.'

The woman beamed. 'Well, you've come to the right place.'

A clap of hands a moment later was followed by the rest of the dogs and their owners lining up at the back of the hall. It was amazing they all managed to fit in one line. There had to be at least twenty dogs. Steve stepped forward, his two German Shepherds trotting either side of him, and sitting as soon as he stopped. He patted them both on the head.

'Welcome to everyone, especially any new members here for the first time,' he said, staring directly at Hannah.

Her cheeks flushed involuntarily.

'We're going to start today's class as we always do with a simple recall command. One by one I want you to tell your dog to wait, move ten paces forward, turn, make eye contact, count to ten and then call them over to you, making sure they sit to your right-hand side, before you give them a treat or make a big fuss of them. To demonstrate, I'll ask Hannah to step forward and show you how it should be done.'

Hannah's eyes widened at the mention of her name, and she awkwardly looked along the line to see if another Hannah was going to come forward. Nobody moved.

'Hannah?' Steve said, looking at her. 'Don't be shy. I know it's your first time here, which is why you'll be best to act as my guinea pig. Barney, come.'

Barney was already racing towards Steve before Hannah had time to tighten her grip on his lead, and so she bounded forwards with him, the room temperature seeming to go up a couple of degrees.

'Relax,' Steve whispered, his face only inches from her ear. 'Most of the dogs here will be far worse than Barney. Trust me.'

Telling Barney to wait, she counted ten paces, before turning to look at him. He was no longer sitting, but he made no move forward until she called him. At which point his claws scraped against the hard floor as he tried to grip and make up the distance in the shortest time possible.

'Move your hand around your body so he knows he needs to come to your side,' Steve instructed.

Hannah obeyed, and was amazed when Barney did as directed, resting at her right side. She gave him a treat from her pocket.

'Let's have a round of applause for Hannah and Barney. That was perfect! Now let's start from Gabby at the end. One by one tell your dogs to wait, move forwards, count to ten and call them. If they don't wait where you've left them, return them to the line and start again.' He moved across to Hannah. 'See, that wasn't so bad was it?'

She didn't like the fact that he'd singled her out, but it

did feel good to have done so well. Maybe teaching Barney wouldn't be so difficult after all.

The class continued, and Hannah was disappointed when the hour had passed so quickly.

'Well done, everyone,' Steve declared, back in the middle of the room. 'Same time next week, and for those who feel they need extra practise, there will be another class on Thursday night.'

Hannah bent down and played with Barney's ears. He'd mastered the recall examination, but had been less skilled when they'd been broken off into smaller groups, preferring to stray and sniff the bottoms of those dogs nearby rather than staying in place.

'He'll get over that,' the woman in the lilac cardigan had promised. 'Once he's been coming for a few weeks and knows to expect to see so many other dogs, he'll get bored of the novelty. Give it time.'

Hannah reattached his lead, and was heading for the door, when Steve came bounding over. 'So how was it?' he asked, reaching for her arm and inviting her back inside the hall, away from the other women and their disapproving scowls.

'I enjoyed it, thank you. I think Barney needs a few more lessons though,' she said.

'Good, then that means I'll get to see you again – the two of you I mean,' Steve said. 'In fact, I was hoping you might be free tonight? I thought you might like to go for a drink somewhere quiet?'

Hannah's right hand instinctively shot down to her ring finger, and was alarmed to find the wedding band missing. She must have taken it off when washing up earlier.

'It's kind of you to offer,' she began, genuinely flattered, but already feeling guilty about abandoning John.

'I know a quiet little bar, not far from here. Give me twenty minutes to drop the dogs at home, and then I can meet you there. Come on, what do you say?'

She was certain the look he was giving had been learned from all the puppies he must have trained down the years.

'I promise to have you home before ten,' he added.

With no reason not to, she reluctantly agreed, giving him her number so he could text her the address of the pub. Fighting down the wave of guilt sweeping through her, she held her head high as she left the hall, much to the envy of the woman in the skinny jeggings and knee-length boots.

TWENTY-SEVEN

Applying the handbrake, Hannah dared to look up at her reflection in the rear-view mirror. The morose woman staring back at her told her everything she needed to know about the guilt gripping her every sinew.

John had once told her that he wouldn't be able to go on if something bad ever happened to her. That was on their wedding night, and she'd known then just how much he loved her. And for the first few years he would call her from work every day just to check how she was; sometimes returning with surprise flowers when she'd had a bad day. After she gave up her business, he'd even suggested she come and work for the family firm. She'd argued she knew next to nothing about IT, but he'd said she had lots of other skills she could use. She'd tried it for a week, and it had been nice driving to the office with him each day, and meeting for lunch, before driving home together. But then she'd inadvertently overheard John telling Patrick that he'd only offered her the job to boost her low self-esteem. After that, it hadn't been the same, and she'd eventually given it up. She never told John what she'd overheard, as she hadn't wanted to embarrass him.

Why were her eyes in the mirror watering?

'It's just a drink,' she snarled at her reflection. 'After all, Dr Yenny said you need to widen your circle of friends.'

Twelve months didn't feel long enough though, and she didn't want to do anything that would betray his memory.

She was about to restart the engine and pull away when she saw Steve's lumbering figure pass the windscreen. He paused, doing a double-take, and then smiled and waved as he saw her.

'Too late,' she muttered under her breath, pushing the door open and climbing out, the breeze bitter.

'You found it okay then?' he said, as she joined him at the front of the vehicle. 'Shall we head in?'

She nodded, ploughing forward, the nervous energy in the pit of her stomach contrasting with the memory of the guilty stare that she sensed following her as they stepped into the building. A blast of warm air hit them as the door closed. The pub had a welcoming atmosphere, the bar immediately to their right dominated by wooden beams, and the smell of aged casks. In the distance, the quiet hum of music from the jukebox could just about be heard above the flurry of conversations at each of the small round tables across the carpeted floor. It was busier than she'd anticipated for the day of the week.

Steve took her hand, sending a bolt of shock up her arm, but before she could pull it away he led them towards a free table a few metres into the venue.

'Is this okay?' he asked, nodding at the two vacant chairs and releasing her hand.

'Uh, yeah, sure,' she stuttered.

He pulled out one of the chairs, tucking it in as she sat, before sitting in the chair opposite. 'Are you hungry? They do good food here if you are.'

She smiled awkwardly. 'Let's start with a drink and see how things progress.'

He held his hands up in surrender. 'Of course. I'm sorry, I didn't want to be pushy.'

A waitress in a white blouse and dark apron appeared beside the table to take their orders. Steve ordered a draught beer, and Hannah requested a latte.

'Is the dog class always that busy?' Hannah asked. She'd never been good at small talk, and was out of practise in starting conversations with strangers. She'd never had to force conversation with John. He'd pursued her, and his naturally confident charm had swept her off her feet. This situation was quite alien.

'I've been running the classes for about six months,' Steve replied, and the first few classes were quiet, but then things picked up around Easter; word of mouth I suppose. My agreement with the parish council is that I'll allow no more than thirty people in, but we haven't hit close to that number yet.'

'Are all the attendees women?' She blushed at the bluntness of her question. 'I'm sorry, I didn't mean that to sound –'

'It's okay,' he chuckled. 'My friends rib me about that too! We do have the occasional male dog owner turn up, but it does seem to be a largely female audience for some reason.' His cheeks reddened this time.

The drinks arrived much to Hannah's relief and she blew on the bubbles of warmed milk, before sipping. 'What do you do besides running the class?'

'I'm a plumber by trade,' he said, 'but I'd like to focus more on the dog training. I adore dogs, and it's great to see those that come to the class improving each week. You said you adopted Barney, right?'

Hannah nodded. 'That's right.'

Another awkward silence fell.

'Have you lived in Southampton long?' she tried again.

'Born and raised,' he said, the dimple in his cheek returning.

'You live locally?'

'Not far.'

Hannah sipped her coffee again, as he took a long drink of his beer.

'I'm sorry,' he finally offered. 'I'm not very good at this kind of thing. It's been a while since I've asked a girl out, and I think I'm out of practise. I was in a long-term relationship until a couple of months ago.'

'Oh, what happened?'

He grimaced. 'Didn't end well. She was carrying on with my best mate behind my back for almost a year, and then I walked in and caught them at it in our bed.'

It was Hannah's turn to grimace. 'Ouch.'

He nodded. 'I moved my stuff out the same day, took the dogs with me and decided to start again. What about you? I'm surprised some handsome man hasn't won your heart yet.'

'My husband passed away last year,' she said, choking down the urge to gush.

'Oh, I'm so sorry,' Steve said, the smile vanishing. 'Is that why you've moved back?'

She nodded.

'What a pair we are, eh?' he said. 'I hope I haven't said anything to upset you?'

She blinked back the tears in her eyes. 'No you haven't, it's still just a bit raw.'

'I won't be offended if you want to knock tonight on the head,' he continued.

Hannah shook her head. 'We're not doing anything wrong. Just two people having a drink. No reason for either of us to feel guilty or awkward.'

He raised his glass. 'Shall we start again? Hi, I'm Steve Williams, I'm a plumber and run a local dog training class.'

She clinked her cup against his glass. 'Hi, I'm Hannah Davenport, and when I'm not ruining conversations by mentioning my dead husband, I work in a supermarket; at least I will do as of tomorrow.'

They both lowered their drinks.

'It's nice to meet you, Hannah. Which supermarket are

you joining?'

'The one at the top end of the town, near the market square.'

'Sure, I know where. Perhaps I'll see you in there sometime.'

'Maybe.'

He nodded at a framed painting on the wall nearest their table, depicting an old ship crashing through the waves of a rough sea. 'Stormy waters,' he said. 'Feels apt for our evening so far.'

'Are you in to art?'

He shook his head. 'Not really. You?'

'I used to be. I was a photographer before... well, once upon a time. I would spend hours waiting for the right light balance to capture the perfect shot. These days anyone thinks they can do it with all the filters and options on modern camera phones.'

'Is that why you stopped doing it? Too much competition?'

'No, I just... lost my passion for it.'

'I'd love to see some of your work some time.'

She smiled, her shoulders relaxing for the first time that evening. 'Well, if you're lucky maybe I'll let you some time.'

'I was really nervous about inviting you out,' he said, 'but I'm glad I did.'

She smiled back at him. 'I'm glad you did as well. What made you ask? I mean, I'm sure any of the other class attendees would have bitten your hand off if you'd asked them. It can't have escaped your attention, them fawning over you.'

He raised his eyebrows in a false show of humility. 'I don't know what you mean.'

She wasn't buying it though. 'Seriously, why me?'

'Honestly? I don't know. There's something about you.

I can't put my finger on it, but I knew I would regret *not* asking you out.'

He excused himself to go to the toilet, leaving Hannah glancing at one of the menus, her stomach starting to grumble. Steve had seemed so self-assured when she'd met him in the park on Thursday, and then at the class earlier, but without his dogs he seemed so much more vulnerable.

'Hannah?' a voice said catching her attention.

Looking up, Chris's youthful face was flecked with confusion.

'I thought it was you. Small world. You here with my sister?'

They both looked at Steve's pint glass at the same time, and then his gaze returned to her, a look of resignation on his face.

'Oh, I see.'

'It isn't what you're thinking,' Hannah quickly said, feeling guilty but unsure why.

Chris backed away from the table. 'You don't need to explain.'

'I'm just here with a friend,' she tried again, but Chris simply turned his back and moved away, leaving her watching after him, until Steve then reappeared at the table.

'Everything okay?' Steve asked, reclaiming his seat.

'I need to go,' she said suddenly. 'I'm sorry, it isn't you… I just… I need to go.'

She stood, pulling on her coat, and apologised again, before racing from the pub, Chris nowhere in sight.

Hannah hammered her hand against Bea's door. It was eventually opened, Bea dressed in a kaftan reading glasses perched on the end of her nose.

'Is Chris here? Have you spoken to him tonight?'

Bea's brow furrowed. 'Chris? No, why. Has something happened?'

'Yes, no, I don't know,' Hannah replied, the guilt of him catching her out with another man when she'd said she wasn't ready to date, overwhelming.

Bea invited her into the flat, much smaller than the loft space upstairs, but the layout otherwise identical. A settee was against the window where Hannah's dining table lived, and a futon occupied the opposite wall. Melanie Fowler's diary rested on the arm of the sofa where Bea now sat.

'I was at the pub with a guy when Chris came over,' Hannah explained. 'He looked quite upset, even though there's no reason for him to be so.'

Bea studied Hannah's face, before waving away the concern. 'Don't worry about Chris. I know he fancies you, but he gets plenty of attention. If anything, Chris seeing you with another guy will probably only make him more determined to win you over.'

'He's sweet, but I just think the age gap is too great; he's still at university.'

'As I said, don't worry about it. I warned him that you were still in a vulnerable state after your husband died, and that he shouldn't get his hopes up. I'll give him a call if you like?'

'Would you? I just don't want him thinking that I've led him on. He's been so supportive, and I don't want him to think that I used him.'

'No worries. While I try and get hold of him, have a read of this,' Bea said, handing the diary to her. 'You remember what I told you earlier about Nigel taking Melanie on a date to that church of his? The next couple of entries don't mention it or him. They talk about work stuff, there's a brief reference to her ex Billy, but that's about it. Two weeks after the date at the church, she wrote this.'

Hannah stared at the page, and silently read.

Wednesday 19 June 2015

I wasn't going to go. I debated it all day at work with Sally and Rachel, and they both said I was crazy for even considering it. I guess curiosity just got the better of me. I waited until I heard him arrive home, and then I went and knocked on his door. I've never asked a guy out before, and it gave me a real insight into what they must go through when they do it. I was terrified! He looked nervous when he opened the door, and I quickly explained that I wanted to know whether his invitation was still open.

What must he have thought of me? I've barely seen him since that first date, and then I just turn up unannounced and proposition him. He said yes of course – too polite not to – and I told him we should go for a bite to eat afterwards. I still felt nervous going into the church, and although I recognised a couple of the faces from last time, I couldn't remember any names. That didn't matter as we all had to wear labels with our names on. Nigel sat me next to him again, and made a real show of welcoming me back. It was a little embarrassing, but a kind gesture all the same.

Then an hour into the meeting, there was a sudden commotion at the back of the hall. Nigel was in the middle of reciting a prayer, but the disturbance was so loud that he had to stop. Everyone's heads snapped round and there was this man with long, straggly hair, wearing a denim jacket and faded jeans.

One of his shoulders hung lower than the other, like he was injured or something, and in his other hand he was holding an open can of lager. He looked such a state, and although I should have sympathised with him, I was too scared.

Nigel wasn't. He calmly stood, told the congregation not to be alarmed and approached the man, explaining why we were meeting and that he was welcome to stay if he calmed down and felt God's calling. There was something not right about the guy. He was slurring – a result of all-day drinking I would imagine – and then he suddenly punched Nigel, catching him square on the jaw. I don't know why, but I leapt up and raced to Nigel's side to check he was okay. The guy in denim stank, a cocktail of stale beer and urine. I told him I was going to phone the police if he didn't leave immediately, and he quickly skulked away, yelling obscenities at the group.

Nigel thanked me for my help, and led me back to the group so we could finish the prayer and end the meeting. That was that. He didn't mention the guy in denim, and nor did anyone else.

When everyone else had gone, and we'd stacked the chairs, I asked Nigel if he was okay, or whether he thought he should have his jaw checked at the hospital. He said he was fine and that he'd only fallen because the punch had caught him off-guard.

He apologised, telling me he knew the man: a former member of the church who had gone off the rails spectacularly and now blamed them for all his misfortune. Nigel said he had tried to help the guy, without success, and that he showed up every now and again to disturb the meeting as he had tonight. Nigel's eyes were sad as he spoke of the man, and I saw just how much he cares for his flock – that's what he calls them. I know now I was wrong to be so judgemental towards him.

As he walked me back to my flat, I pulled him inside and we made love.

TWENTY-EIGHT

Hannah was grateful that the entry stopped there, her stomach turning at the thought of intruding on someone else's private experiences. Bea returned to the room, phone in hand, saying she'd left a message for Chris, and that he was probably already out pulling someone else.

'Did you finish the passage?' Bea continued. 'What do you think?'

Hannah chose her words carefully. 'I think we should stop reading private entries from another woman's life. Nothing I read there suggested Nigel was anything but a kind and caring soul, and she clearly seems to be the one pursuing him, rather than the other way around. What I'm asking is for you to convince me of his guilt.'

Bea responded by flipping through the notebook's pages until she found what she was looking for, and read aloud.

> **Sunday 15 September 2015**
> What is wrong with some people? There we were eating dinner, minding our own business, when who should rock up but Billy – drunk again evidently – shouting the odds. I could have died from embarrassment. Bad enough discussing exes with a new partner, let alone the two of them coming face-to-face. Why did we have to choose that restaurant? There must be hundreds of pubs

or restaurants we could have chosen to eat in across the county, but no, we just happen to choose the place that Billy happened to be drinking at. If our mains hadn't just been brought to the table I would have suggested we cancel our order.

'You left me for this prick?' was his first challenge. Well, no, Billy, actually I left you because you seemed to think it was okay to get pissed with your mates and then get off with other women. I wish I'd had the courage to say that to your face tonight, but I didn't want Nigel thinking less of me. I hate that I put up with your philandering for as long as I did. The furtive glances between my friends when the two of us would turn up together. They all knew, and none of them told me what you were up to.

If I could have that year over again, I would boot you out, rather than support you for as long as I did. When I think of the time, money and energy I wasted on our relationship, I feel nothing but shame. Shame because I allowed you to use me like a doormat.

Your actions tonight just underline how different you are to Nigel; no, actually how much better Nigel is compared to you. He didn't sink to your petty level. He didn't throw his fists and shout and yell. Instead, he reached across the table for my hand to check I was okay. Then he – far more politely than I would have managed – asked you to leave us alone.

This is the kind of man I want to be around: someone who makes me his priority.

'From the sound of that, I'd say Billy is the one more likely to have done something to Melanie than Nigel. Do you know whether the police ever interviewed Billy after Melanie disappeared?'

'They had to,' Bea replied, 'after what happened between Billy and Nigel.'

Hannah frowned. 'Why? What happened?'

Thursday 19 September 2015

Every coin has two sides. Maybe I was tempting fate by thinking things were going so well with Nigel. His mask slipped tonight, and I'm now questioning whether everything I've seen until now is part of some façade.

He was in a foul mood before I got to the restaurant. I sensed something wasn't right by the way he half-heartedly kissed my cheek when I arrived. I was so excited to tell him that I got the promotion at work, but his first question ripped the rug from under my feet.

'How many men have you slept with?'

I know it shouldn't have been such a big deal. I've answered that question in relationships before, and most of my friends probably know the answer too. Hearing the question from his lips, and the disgusted sneer that accompanied it cut deep.

I never lied to Nigel about my past, so I can't understand why he was so angry about it. We've both been in previous relationships; at our age, who hasn't? What does it matter how many men I've slept with? I'm not sleeping with any of them now, so it shouldn't matter.

> After Billy's outburst the other night, I should have realised that Nigel would be his usual conscientious self and do some digging. I never expected him to log into my Facebook account and look at all my photographs. Nor did I expect him to print some and bring them to the restaurant with him.
>
> He lifted image after image, demanding to know whether I'd slept with this guy or that guy. My cheeks were on fire by the time the waitress came over to take our order.
>
> I can't believe I thought Nigel was so much better than Billy. In that moment – and even now as I write – I feel as much of a doormat as I ever did with Billy.
>
> Why should I apologise for my past? So I had sex with my ex-boyfriends, it isn't a crime. I was in relationships with each of them, and it isn't a sin to enjoy sex. What gives Nigel the right to judge me?
>
> I never asked how many women he'd slept with, and I don't want to know. We were both different people back then.
>
> It just makes me so angry. How do I manage to pick such arseholes all the time?

Bea closed the notebook. 'There's an entry the next day where she explains that Nigel found Billy and the two came to blows, ending with Nigel in A&E for a gash to the face. It seems he sought out Billy and confronted him, but Billy didn't respond kindly to the interruption and got handy with his fists.'

'Where's Billy now?' Hannah asked, unable to picture Nigel raising his fists to anyone.

'I think he's still listed as one of her friends on

Facebook,' Bea offered. 'His profile picture has him with a redhead, so I guess he moved on with his life. There's only one more entry after that. From the day before she disappeared. All it says is she had a good day at work and was looking forward to starting her new role. There's nothing to suggest she was planning to do a bunk, or that she was going to cut herself off from her friends and family.'

'You think Nigel killed her out of jealousy?' Hannah asked.

'Number one motive for murder from what I've heard,' Bea replied. 'A motive as old as time itself. That and revenge.'

Hannah sighed. 'It would help if we knew what had happened to her. You know, like if there was a body then we'd know whether she was strangled, or beaten, or shot, or whatever; something that might help point to the culprit.'

'Not that I want to be morbid,' Bea said, leaning closer, 'but I think we need to swear a pact to watch out for each other while he's still living in the block. If he catches wind of what we're up to, there's no telling what he might do. You're the one I worry about most,' Bea added, nodding at Hannah. 'Facially, you're similar to Melanie, and we know he's already taken a bit of a fancy to you.'

'Well I have no intention of dating him if that's what you're thinking. I have no intention of going to any church either.'

'Good.' Bea said, pausing. 'There's something else… I accepted his friend request on Facebook.'

Hannah gasped. 'What? Why?'

'I wanted to have a better look at his profile. There are a few photographs of him and Melanie, but he doesn't seem to ever post anything. If he hadn't sent me the request, I'd have said he doesn't even use his account. But now I think he just uses it to go on and watch other people.'

Hannah didn't like the risks Bea seemed so willing to take. 'Promise me you won't do anything silly, Bea. Maybe we should get in touch with the police, and just mention our concerns.'

Bea shook her head. 'Okay, let's go together, in the morning. I'll tell work I've got food poisoning or something and then we can go.'

Hannah pulled a face. 'I can't do tomorrow. It's my first day in my new job.'

'No worries, I'll go to the police station, and then we can get together when you finish work and I'll tell you what I learned.'

Hannah agreed, stifling a yawn as fatigue finally caught up with her. Saying good night, she left Bea's flat, and slowly climbed the stairs, eyeing Nigel's flat suspiciously as she passed it, certain she could see his feet moving in the light beneath the door. Hurrying upstairs, she locked her own door behind her, before sinking to the floor until her breath returned.

TWENTY-NINE

Hurrying along the road, Hannah couldn't help glancing at her watch every few seconds, willing time to slow down long enough for her to make it to the supermarket on time. Being late on her first day was not the lasting impression she'd hoped to create. After a restless night's sleep, her morning alarm hadn't woken her, and if it wasn't for the sound of Barney snoring in his bed, she might not have stirred until much later. She'd definitely set the alarm the night before, but then following a nightmare involving Nigel creeping around the loft, she'd woken screaming in the early hours. Somewhere between sleep and alertness she must have somehow turned off the alarm, though she had no idea how.

Running in through the door, her watch showed she'd arrived with five minutes to spare. Breathless, she stopped at the door leading out to the warehouse and administration offices and attempted to compose herself. Staring at her reflection in the door's glass panel; she ran a hand through her hair, trying to make it look less like she'd been running to work.

Before John her hair had been long and flowing, and then one day he'd bought her a voucher for a day's pampering at a local salon. She'd been so excited, picturing what she would have done, maybe a trim, maybe some lowlights, but when she'd arrived the stylist had already known exactly what to do. Hannah hadn't been too sure about the colour and the short length, but John had been so wowed by the outcome that it had grown on her.

John wouldn't be happy with the split ends and dark roots; maybe it was time for a change. If Bea's observation about her similarity to Melanie was right, then a different style might be exactly what she needed.

The mobile beeped in her pocket. Pulling it out she saw a notification advising her she'd received a second Facebook message from Lucy Davison.

> ***From: Lucy_Davison***
> *Hi Hannah, wasn't sure if you'd seen my last message yet or not. Hope you didn't mind me reaching out to you after all this time... I know I'm as much to blame for us drifting apart like we did, but I'm hoping we can put the past behind us and move forward.*
>
> *It would be really great to meet up with you soon, and catch up on everything you've been up to since we last spoke. Are you still living in Salford? Maybe we could meet at the Trafford Centre for coffee, or you can come to me if that would be easier?*
>
> *Miss you. Please call / message me back when you read this. Lucy xxx*

A minute ticked past on the clock in the top corner of the screen. Hannah had meant to reply to the message Lucy had sent yesterday, but it had slipped her mind with everything else that had been going on. Checking the clock again, she quickly ran her fingers over the screen's keyboard.

> ***From: Hannah Davenport***

Hi Lucy, I was so pleased to see your message. It really has been too long. Sorry I didn't message you yesterday, things here are a bit crazy. Would love to catch up with you too soon, but not living in Salford anymore. Long story short, I'm now in Southampton. Will give you a call soon. Hannah xxx

Hannah read the message back to herself before hitting send. She didn't want to explain the last year in an impersonal message, but she would have to broach the subject sooner or later. With two minutes until her shift was to start, now did not feel like the right time.

'Excuse me, dear,' a woman in a thick overcoat and fresh perm said, approaching. 'Would you mind helping me get something out of one of the freezer cabinets? I couldn't find anyone else.'

Hannah was about to say that she didn't work there, when she remembered the uniform she was wearing. 'Certainly, madam.'

Following the woman to the top of the aisle, and across two rows to the frozen section, here, tall glass doors lined the aisle, protecting frozen meats, fish, pizzas, and puddings.

'It's my granddaughter's birthday,' the woman explained, as they reached the door with tubs of ice cream visible through the glass. 'I said I'd buy pudding, so I thought I'd get a tub of vanilla ice cream, but it's on the top shelf.'

Hannah opened the freezer door, and reached up, identifying the tub and pulling it out, placing it in the customer's trolley.

'Oh, thank you, dear. I don't recognise you. Are you new here?'

'My first day,' Hannah smiled.

'I thought as much. I'm in here most days. Most of the staff know me. I'm always stopping by to say hello. What's your name, dear?'

'Hannah. Haven't got my name badge yet.'

'I'll try and remember that. I'm Daphne. Thanks again for the ice cream. Hope to see you around.'

With that the woman shuffled off, waving at the staff sitting behind the checkout terminals. Puffing out her cheeks, Hannah felt pleased that she'd aided her first customer, like it was some kind of rites of passage. Another check of her hair in the reflection of the freezer door, her shoulders tensed.

John's face was staring right back at her.

THIRTY

She had to be dreaming. That was the only possible explanation for his face being reflected in the glass panel of the freezer door. Her unblinking eyes had yet to leave his reflection, and the only sound she could hear was the thundering of her own heart.

It couldn't be John; he was dead. Of this she was certain, and yet there he was, still staring straight at her.

'John?' she whispered as she turned, the figure in the denim jacket slowly coming into view.

The breath caught in her throat, as her eyes fell on the dark-haired stranger who was no longer looking straight at her, but was busy reading from a shopping list in his hand. The young boy in the trolley in front of him playing with a dinosaur hand puppet.

It wasn't Jack.

Before she could grab something for support, her legs gave way, and she slumped against the freezer door, sliding down it to the cold floor in defeat.

How many more times was John's face going to haunt her? It seemed like every time she allowed her mind to drift from his memory, he popped up to remind her of what had happened. Was this how life was going to be forever? Constant reminders of the worst night of her existence? Why wouldn't life let her move on?

'Are you alright?' the dark-haired stranger offered.

She opened her mouth to respond, but no words would

emerge. How could she explain that her late husband was haunting her?

The public address system sounded and then she heard her name being announced. 'This is a colleague announcement. Would Hannah Davenport please go to the Personnel Manager's office?'

The man held out his arm, and helped her back to her feet. On closer inspection he looked nothing like her John. The jawline was all wrong and there were obvious wisps of grey above this man's ears.

'Look, are you sure you're alright?' he asked. 'You're white as a sheet. Did you slip? What happened?'

She took a deep breath. 'I'll be fine. Just had a shock. Thought I saw someone I knew. I'll be fine. Thank you for your help.'

The man fired another uncertain look in her direction, and she could feel him watching her, as she tottered unsteadily to the end of the aisle, turning towards the warehouse door.

By the time she had arrived at the Personnel Manager's door, the colour was returning to her cheeks. Knocking, she entered, offering her best attempt at a smile to the stick-thin woman sitting behind the desk.

She invited Hannah to sit down, a quizzical look on her face. 'I'm confused,' she said after a moment. 'We weren't expecting you until next Monday.'

Hannah mirrored the puzzled expression. 'No, we agreed I would start on the 19th, and today is the 19th.' Hannah was sure that was the date they'd agreed when she'd come in to collect her uniform after she'd accepted the role.

The Personnel Manager scrutinised the monitor in front of her. 'That was what we'd originally agreed, but then there was an issue with one of your references. I phoned yesterday and left you a message.'

Hannah pulled a face. 'Yesterday? Are you sure? There

wasn't any messages on my answer machine.'

'I didn't leave a message on your answerphone, I left it with your husband.'

Hannah froze. 'My husband?'

'Well I assumed it was your husband? Sorry, your boyfriend? Partner?'

'I don't have a boyfriend, husband or partner.'

The woman pointed at the screen on the edge of his desk. 'You're *Mrs* Davenport though?'

'Widowed. My husband died last year.'

The Personnel Manager shuffled awkwardly. 'Oh, I'm so sorry to hear that. Do you have a roommate then? Or a brother? I definitely spoke to someone on your number yesterday, and I definitely left a message with him, to advise we need to delay your start date by a week.'

Hannah's mind raced with anyone who could have been in the loft yesterday and answered the phone. Patrick and Chris were the only two men she'd seen yesterday, and she'd been with them the entire time. The phone hadn't rung.

'It was definitely yesterday?' Hannah tried again.

'I wasn't working on Saturday, and when I came in yesterday I saw the note from head office mentioning the issue with the reference. That's why I phoned.'

A growing sense of dread was slowly starting to creep across her spine. 'What time did you call?'

The woman considered the question. 'Quite early. Maybe ten o'clock? Half past at the latest.'

Her appointment with the on-call doctor had been at ten a.m. and she'd arrived there ten minutes before, meaning she'd left home not long after nine.

She studied the woman's face for any sign of deception, but all she found was confusion. If she was telling the truth that meant someone had been in Hannah's apartment when the call had been placed. Worse than that, they'd had the audacity to answer the phone.

A chill crept down her spine.

'What exactly is the issue with my references?' she asked, desperate to distract herself from contemplating exactly who had been in the loft.

'You gave us two referees to contact – both personal – but we have only received one response.'

It had to be disorganised Sandra who hadn't responded, and Hannah made a mental note to phone her as soon as she was out of the office.

'We received confirmation from a Sandra Kilpatrick,' the woman read from the screen, 'but have yet to receive a response from a Patrick Davenport. Hmm, funny, same surname. A relative?'

'Brother-in-law,' Hannah said quietly.

She'd seen how stressed Patrick had looked yesterday, but she was disappointed that he'd missed the deadline for returning the reference. He never mentioned it yesterday, and she hadn't thought to question it.

'I'll phone him,' Hannah said assertively. 'I am so sorry, this is so unlike him. I'll make sure he gets it over as soon as possible. This isn't going to affect anything is it? I mean, the job is still mine, right?'

'So long as the reference appears – and I mean in the next couple of days – then everything will be fine, and you'll be cleared to start next Monday.'

Hannah thanked her for her understanding, before excusing herself, and heading back through the warehouse, and onto the shop floor. Bea had helped her add the list of numbers from her phonebook to the new mobile's memory, and as she unlocked the screen with her thumbprint, she stopped and stared at the new Facebook notification.

> ***From: Lucy_Davison***
> *I heard about what happened to John.*

Now that he's gone, there's a lot we need to discuss. Please call me urgently. Lucy xxx

Hannah's confusion deepened. The message almost sounded sinister. What was so urgent, and why did she feel able to say it now John was gone?

It would have to wait, as sorting out her reference was her priority. Closing the app, she located Patrick's office number and dialled, but a recorded voice told her the number was no longer in service. Patrick hadn't mentioned changing his number. Dialling the company's main switchboard, the same message played again.

Frustrated, she decided she would go home and change before trying to reach him at his house. The wind was blowing stronger than it had been on the way to the store that morning, and the second she stepped outside, her fringe blew into her eyes. Shielding them, she kept her head low, as she headed for home, trying to ignore the voice in her head warning that her every move was being carefully observed.

THIRTY-ONE

Bea wasn't home when Hannah knocked on her door, and was relieved to find Nigel's car wasn't in its usual parking bay. Barney greeted her with his usual flurry of excitement as she entered the loft. Making a fuss of him for being so well-behaved while she'd been out, she dropped her handbag on the sofa, spotting the red flashing light on the answerphone.

Hitting play, she waited to hear the Personnel Manager's voice, hopeful that she'd just been confused earlier. Although she recognised the frantic voice on the recording, it wasn't one she was expecting.

'Auntie Hannah, you need to come and help us,' her nephew Ben said, sounding close to tears. 'It's Dad, he… he and Mum have been arguing all night, and… I don't know what to do. Please, we need you…'

The message ended, and Hannah had to play it back, to make sure she hadn't misheard what he had said.

Dialling Patrick's home number, it rang five times before the answer machine cut in. She redialled, but the outcome was the same.

The four of them – John, Patrick, Hannah and Wendy – had been a close-knit group for so many years. Regularly hosting each other for dinner, attending the works Christmas parties as a group, Wendy had been like the sister Hannah had never had. The arrival of Ben, James and Daisy had curtailed Wendy's social side, but that hadn't stopped

John and Hannah visiting the children at every opportunity. John was always so keen to entertain them, and Ben and James adored the attention.

After the murder, she'd seen them less; it had just been too hard to see Wendy, Patrick and the children, a constant reminder of who was missing from the group.

Ben wasn't the sort of boy who cried wolf. The fact that he'd reached out to her could only mean that something was seriously wrong. The message had been left last night while she was out, but she hadn't seen the answer machine flashing until now. Had she been home when he'd called, maybe she'd have a better idea of why he sounded so troubled. Dialling the number for a third time, she had to accept that nobody was home.

She couldn't just sit around and wait.

In hindsight, throwing a couple of days of clothes into a satchel, Barney's food and bowls into a carrier bag, and strapping him into the front of her car hadn't been her brightest idea. Traffic on the A34 towards Oxford was slow, and they still had at least another three hours of driving to complete before they'd be even get close to Manchester.

Barney was now curled up, gently snoring beside her. She'd hoped to make it to the M40 before stopping for a coffee and allowing Barney to stretch his legs, but that seemed like a pipe dream now, traffic far heavier than she would have anticipated for a Monday morning.

Ideally she wouldn't have dragged Barney along for such a long commute, but it had been such a rushed decision that she hadn't had time to look for a kennels. She was sure her parents would have willingly watched him for a couple of days, but that would have meant a detour via their place, and then they'd want to know why she was suddenly heading north, and she didn't want to get into that with them.

That only left Steve or Bea, and it wouldn't have been fair to take advantage. Besides, she had no doubt her nephews and niece would love to meet Barney. He was part of her family now, so why shouldn't he come along?

She jumped as a motorbike shot between her and the car in the outside lane. She wanted to blare her horn, but the rider was already out of earshot by the time she'd thought about it.

A message flashed up on the dashboard display advising her a call was inbound on her phone from Bea. She had no idea how the car could possibly know that, but accepted the call.

'You home yet?' Bea said, her voice filling the car.

'Not exactly,' Hannah shouted back, uncertain whether Bea would be able to hear her, with the phone in her bag on the back seat.

'Whoa, whoa,' Bea replied, 'you don't need to shout. Are you driving?'

'Yes,' Hannah said, quieter this time. 'There's been a family emergency, and I'm headed to Manchester. Everything okay with you?'

'I'm safe and sound, but wanted to update you on what I gathered from my trip to the police station this morning.'

It had totally slipped Hannah's mind. 'What did they say?'

'They refused to speak to me at first,' Bea huffed, 'but then I said I wouldn't leave until I spoke to someone connected with Melanie Fowler's disappearance, and then eventually this ginger guy with sweat patches beneath his arm pits appeared and took me into a room to take a statement. I told him about Nigel's friend request to me, and how we'd stumbled upon Melanie's diary, and how he had chased you up the stairs the other night. He thanked me for my time, and told me someone would follow it up, and that was that. He even had the nerve to point out that sending a friend request on Facebook isn't a crime; like I didn't know that already. I told him that I was scared for my life, and he said if Nigel tried anything I should dial 999, but otherwise there was nothing he could do. Can you believe that? I was going to point out that my taxes pay his salary, but I don't think it would have made any difference.'

Hannah didn't want to point out that the detective's response was what she'd expected, and that Bea's explanation could hardly be considered as proof of guilt.

'That's too bad,' Hannah said after a moment. 'At least they now have your concerns on record. Did he give you his number? I think I might need to give him a call when I get back.'

'How come?'

'I know it's going to sound crazy, but I have a feeling that someone has been snooping around my apartment. At first, I thought I was just being paranoid, but I'm sure someone has been messing about with my central heating system, and I can't find my red lipstick, oh and this morning my alarm didn't go off when I'm sure I set it. Oh, and another thing, apparently my new place of work called my home yesterday when I was out, and left a message for me with some unidentified man. Either I'm going crazy, or someone has been inside my apartment.

Hannah couldn't miss the sound of Bea gulping.

'Jeez, mate, that's so freaky. You think it's him don't you? Admit it.'

Hannah didn't want to think about the prospect of Nigel sneaking about in the loft, but who else was there? It's not like John's ghostly presence could answer a phone or mess about with the heating.

'I don't know what's going on,' Hannah eventually admitted. 'Just be careful, okay? I'll be away for a few days, but if you're worried, phone the police.'

'I will, believe me. Is Barney with you, or do you need me to keep an eye on him?'

Hannah stroked the top of his head. 'He's with me, but I would appreciate you keeping a watch on my apartment, in case you hear anyone heading up there. I'm not expecting any visitors while I'm away.'

Saying their goodbyes, Hannah spotted the sign for Services, and indicated to come off.

The traffic lights up ahead changed to green and she pulled forward. The Satnav was now advising her she was only minutes from arriving at Patrick and Wendy's house in Hulme, only a few miles from Hannah's former home in Salford.

Hulme was once a deprived and run-down area, a hub for high crime and unemployment rates, but had undergone massive redevelopment in the last fifteen years, and was now one of the city's brighter spots. Passing tall townhouses and purpose-built residential estates, it was unrecognisable from the place John and Patrick had been raised in. At Alexandra Park, Hannah indicated left and pulled into the estate.

'You have reached your destination,' the Satnav announced.

The four bedroom detached house stood proud, the wrought iron gates open and leading to a gravel driveway and the front door. Patrick had bought the house eight years ago, and had more than doubled his money on the property's value. Applying the handbrake she stared out at the front door, but immediately noticed the broken porch window. Without a second's thought, she clutched Barney's lead, and raced to the front door.

THIRTY-TWO

Although the glass panel was smashed, the pane had remained intact. Wendy's hatchback was parked on the driveway, which had to be a good sign. Banging her hand against the door, Hannah pressed her face as close to the broken glass to look for any signs of movement. A moment later, the door opened, revealing a flushed-looking Wendy, donning a confused expression.

'Hannah? Goodness what are you doing here?'

Wendy's usually neat, fair bob was on end in places, and the dashes of white flour on her cheeks and the dark apron tied around her waist suggested she was in the middle of baking.

Hannah leaned in and hugged her sister-in-law. 'Sorry to call round unannounced,' she replied. 'Ben phoned last night and left a message on my answer machine. He sounded really worried about you and Patrick.'

More composed now, Wendy gave a knowing nod. 'Ah, I see, he must have heard us arguing then. I'm so sorry if he alarmed you, and made you travel all this way. Please, please, come in. I was just baking some cupcakes, but you're more than welcome to stay.'

'Am I okay to bring Barney in? I'd prefer not to leave him in the car.'

'Of course, of course,' Wendy encouraged, already heading back through the hall and towards the kitchen at the rear of the property. 'Tea?'

'Please,' Hannah said, leading Barney in and closing the porch door behind them.

The warmth of the house was certainly in stark contrast to the chill that had hit her the second she'd stepped from the car.

'Daisy's in her playpen in the living room,' Wendy called out. 'Go in and see her if you like.'

Hannah poked her head into the lounge and her two year-old niece squealed and waved from within the octagonal-shaped playpen.

'Hello,' Hannah said, dropping to her knees and crawling across to where Daisy was standing.

The toddler, dressed in a pink floral dress was transfixed by the brightly-coloured cartoon on the large flat panel television hanging from the wall. Hannah could still remember the day Patrick had invited them around for dinner so he could show off its sheer size.

'Sixty inches,' he'd told them, much to John's annoyance.

As a result, John had gone out and bought a sixty-five inch screen to replace their year-old fifty inch model. Boys with toys, the brothers' rivalry was harmless, but expensive at times.

'What are you watching?' Hannah asked her niece, who was happily chewing on a plastic dummy.

Daisy looked at Hannah, and almost instantly the excitement evaporated, replaced by a balled up face and rapidly filling eyes. She let out an anguished cry a second later, until Wendy came hopping in to the room to see what was wrong.

'I don't know what happened,' Hannah said, standing as Wendy scooped Daisy out of the playpen. 'One minute she was fine, and then…'

'Don't worry about it,' Wendy said, pressing the toddler's face into her shoulder. 'She's probably just hungry. She's due a feed soon. You can give her the bottle if you like?'

Daisy's crying had reverted to a self-pitying sniffle, as Wendy carried her out to the kitchen, returning a moment later with a plastic bottle of milk in her hand. She waited for Hannah to be seated on the large leather sofa, before handing both child and bottle over.

Daisy found a soft spot on Hannah's leg, and lifted the bottle, pushing the teat between her lips.

'I'm sure she'll settle down in a bit,' Wendy said, returning with two mugs of tea, resting one on the table nearest Hannah. 'Have you been back in Manchester for a while, or just arrived today?'

'Just today,' Hannah said, sitting back slightly, and reaching for the tea. 'Are Ben and James at school?'

Wendy nodded. 'Yes. Ben's got football club after school, and I've got to collect James at quarter past three.' She paused, glancing at her watch. 'Which means I'll need to leave in half an hour. Are you going to stay for dinner?'

'I don't want to trouble you,' Hannah said too quickly.

'Don't be silly. You're family, it's no trouble at all, so long as you don't mind fish fingers, mash potato and peas?'

Hannah smiled. 'Sounds perfect!' She paused. 'What happened to the window in the porch? Is everything okay between you and Patrick?'

Wendy looked away, as a tear escaped, and was quickly wiped away with the back of a dusty hand. 'Aside from my marriage crumbling before my eyes, the threat of bailiffs, and having to explain to my children why Daddy won't be home for dinner… yeah, apart from that, I'm fine.' She tried to force a smile, but it did little to cover the dark bags beneath her eyes.

The last thing Hannah wanted to do was intrude on someone else's problems, but Wendy looked like she was eager to talk to someone.

'This time last week I was in blissful ignorance,' Wendy began. 'If you'd have asked how I was last Monday, I'd have told you everything was peachy. The boys are both doing well at school, Daisy's speech is developing by the day, and as far as I was aware the business was blossoming despite everything that happened last year. Now...' Her words trailed off.

'I had no idea you and Patrick were having difficulties. He never mentioned it yesterday.'

Thick crevices gathered in Wendy's forehead. 'Wait, you saw Patrick yesterday?'

'I was just as surprised to see him in Southampton as you were answering the door to me today. Did he not tell you he was going?'

The frown remained, but Wendy shook her head. 'What did he want?'

Hannah wasn't sure how much she should share about what Patrick had told her regarding the missing money, particularly considering how upset Wendy looked.

'He was looking for any notes John might have left.'

Wendy snorted. 'He wasn't asking you for a loan then?'

'A loan? No. Why?'

Wendy stood quickly, moved to the sideboard, and pulled out a sheet of paper before slamming the drawer closed. Handing the page to Hannah she folded her arms. 'I'd suspected things weren't as rosy at the company as he'd claimed because of the number of late nights he was putting in there, but when that then turned up on the doorstep, I realised just how cunning a liar my husband really is.'

Hannah studied the page, a warning letter from a bank advising that they'd been unable to collect the mortgage payment, and urging them to get in touch as quickly as possible.

'Turns out my beloved husband took out a second mortgage on this place without my knowledge, and then didn't have the funds to cover the first payment.'

Hannah's head shot up and her eyes widened. 'He took out a second mortgage?'

Wendy was nodding, her eyes venomous. 'At a crippling interest rate too. I can only assume he forged my signature on the paperwork as there is no way I would have agreed to do that, no matter how much trouble that bloody business is in.' She wiped away a fresh tear. 'I confronted him about it, and he could offer no explanation. That's when I booted him out so I could have peace and quiet to think about my next steps.'

Hannah took a deep breath. 'When he called round on Sunday he told me that there was a black hole in the company's accounts, and that he believes John had been stealing company funds. I told him John wouldn't have done that, but he was adamant. Kept asking whether I had any phones, tablets or computers of John's, which of course I don't. Then he left.'

'Christ, what a mess!' Wendy exclaimed.

'To make matters worse, he was supposed to complete a reference for me for a job I'd applied for, and they're now delaying my start date until they receive it. After I heard Ben's message, I just had to come back.'

'I'm sorry if Ben worried you. I had no idea he'd used the phone,' Wendy said sullenly. 'Patrick turned up here last night drunk, and started shouting the odds, saying this was his house, and that he had the right to come in. Woke the poor children up, and some of the language he was using was appalling. When I refused him entry, he threw a stone at the house, breaking the porch window. I imagine that's when Ben phoned you.'

'I wish you'd told me about all of this sooner. I'd have come up in a shot. It isn't fair that Patrick has left you to sort his mess out.'

Wendy tried to smile again in acknowledgement, but it

didn't stretch far. 'The last thing you need is our problems on top of the baggage you're already carrying. I have to admit though, it's good to see you back, Hannah. I can't help thinking that things would have been so different if John was still around. He was always the more level-headed of the two of them; Patrick's more of a bull in a China shop.'

Hannah glanced at her watch as Daisy finished the bottle, and returned the dummy to her mouth. 'I should let you get ready to collect James from school.'

'You don't have to leave on my account. You're welcome to stay here as long as you need. I can put James in Ben's room so you can have a bed to sleep in.'

Hannah stood, passing Daisy over. 'I appreciate the offer, but I'm already booked into a Travelodge. Would you mind if I left Barney here for a bit though?'

'Are you going to go looking for Patrick?'

Hannah nodded. 'I think I should.'

Wendy looked relieved. 'Tell him… oh I don't know. Will you tell him the kids miss him?'

'Of course.'

Wendy made goo-goo eyes at Barney. 'Would you mind if I walked him to the school with me and Daisy? I know James will be excited to see him. The kids are always banging on about wanting a dog. Maybe an evening with yours will get it out of their system.'

'He'll love the new sights and smells. Thank you.'

Wendy finished her tea, and nodded. 'You can collect him when you come back for dinner. I expect Patrick will be at the office. I'll aim to have dinner ready for seven, but just send me a message if you're running late.'

Hannah thanked her, and patted Barney before heading out to the car. Wendy was right: things would never have got this bad if John was still here.

THIRTY-THREE

It was never going to be easy to return to Manchester and *not* see constant reminders of her former life, but Hannah hadn't realised just how many buildings and landscapes would send her emotions into overload.

Driving out of Hulme, it seemed like a conveyor belt of memories, each touching her heart like a delicate rose petal, stirring hidden fragments buried deep beneath the immediate pain of the past year. The gym where John had spent countless hours getting in shape as he trained for the Manchester Half Marathon five years ago. At one point she'd feared he was having an affair such was his commitment to the tread mills, planking and weights. So she'd followed him one night when he'd phoned late to say he wouldn't be home for dinner.

'Just need to work on my glutes,' he'd told her on the phone, knowing she would have no idea what that meant. Wasn't it something to do with the bottom?

She'd driven to the gym, her eyes blinded by a fog of tears, and had been relieved to see his 4x4 in the car park. Of course that didn't necessarily mean the other times he'd claimed to be at the gym he had actually been there. So she'd parked up and entered, and while the athletic, pretty man behind the desk was busy on the phone, she snuck a glance at the sign-in book, easily spotting John's squiggled signature in several places on several pages. The relief had been palpable.

The gym looked like it was under new management again. It had certainly had a fresh lick of paint since she'd last seen it. John's gym-passion had died shortly after he'd completed the half marathon. Despite months of training to slim down and prepare for the gruelling ordeal, he'd struggled with the distance more than he'd anticipated, and it seemed like the race had got the urge to compete out of his system. Thereafter his attention had been consumed by driving the business forward.

At the next set of traffic lights, she jolted as she spotted the pharmacy – now boarded up and covered with graffiti – where she'd bought the three pregnancy testing kits the day before their home was invaded. She'd been feeling rough for more than a week, but had done well to keep her symptoms hidden from John. Finally determining it had to be more than a sickness bug, she'd pulled in when she'd spotted the glowing green cross and had purchased the three kits. She'd used all of them over the next twelve hours, each returning the two blue lines and telling her she was more than three weeks pregnant. That had spurred the trip to the GP, and the confirmation she'd been craving.

One of the hardest parts of the dark cloud of amnesia that continued to haunt her was the not knowing whether she'd managed to tell John about the baby. She'd played the possible scenario through in her mind countless times in an effort to trigger any kind of memory: John arriving home, her blurting the news out in wild excitement and him jumping for joy; John arriving home, and Hannah keeping her lips buttoned until after dinner, at which point she would have taken his hand, and placed it on her belly, him weeping with joy; John sitting down to eat dinner, lifting the napkin from his plate and finding the three tests with their blue lines staring back at him.

None of the imagined scenarios stirred anything but heartache. Had he died not knowing he was going to be a father? She would give anything to go back to that night and tell him. Even if she couldn't reverse the outcome of Fahey's attack, at least John would know the truth.

A horn blared from behind, and as she looked up, she saw the light had turned green. Putting the car into gear, she moved forward, holding her hand up to acknowledge the driver behind.

Other sites triggered memories as she continued the journey: the pub where she'd worked part-time while at university; the pawn shop where she'd had to temporarily dispense of some jewellery when student funds had got tight; the electricians where John had taken their toaster to be mended, and had returned with a new washing machine. So many memories of a life which no longer felt like her own. Even though she'd created each memory, it was now like she was watching some actor in a film, rather than living through the recollection.

By the time she arrived at the industrial estate, her face was puffy, her makeup washed down her face, and the pain in her heart greater than she could remember. Maybe it hadn't been such a good idea to head up here today. It was just after three according to the dashboard clock, and the sun was low in the sky.

The industrial estate was a large stretch of grey, with bespoke businesses and warehouses apportioned on either side of the road. It was the sort of place you didn't absently stumble into. There was nothing by way of shops or restaurants: either you worked here, or you needed something from one of the local businesses based here. Spotting the three storey building up ahead, she was surprised to see only Patrick's Land Rover in the car park.

Pulling into the space next to it, she had to assume Patrick had been lying when he'd said the business was doing well. Things were much worse.

The building lacked the usual vibrancy she'd been so

used to seeing. The large neon sign at the front was switched off, and there were no lights on inside either. Then she saw him: a shadowy figure standing on the top floor. It was impossible to tell whether he was looking down on her, or whether he had his back to the window.

Reaching into her handbag she removed the old Nokia phone and turned it over in her hands. Patrick had been so keen to know whether John had left any electronic devices that might point to where the money had gone, and even though the only information she'd found on the device was the call history to that unregistered number, maybe he could find more of a use for it. Yet something niggled at the back of her mind, and rather than returning the phone to her bag, she hid it inside the glove box. If Patrick had lied about the state of the business, what else had he been keeping from her?

Exiting the car, she locked it and walked quickly to the entrance, relieved when the front door opened as she pushed against it. The reception desk was vacant, and the thick layer of dust suggested it had been some time since it had been manned by anyone. Usually they had the radio playing throughout the building – John had always believed that workers were more productive with music playing – but now it was deathly silent. Calling the lift, she waited for three minutes but when it didn't arrive headed to the fire escape staircase, and climbed at a steady pace.

Arriving at the top floor, she pulled the door open, calling out Patrick's name as she went. He didn't answer, but she soon found him, slumped over the desk in his office, head buried in his hands. She couldn't escape how dark it seemed inside, despite the large floor to ceiling window dominating behind the desk.

'Patrick? Are you okay?' she asked, surprised by the anxiety in her voice.

He started, looking over to her, his face masked in

shadow. She now saw the almost empty bottle of cheap supermarket whisky beside him, and the shards of smashed glass on the carpet close to her feet. Fresh bruising and bloody scratches to his face and knuckles looked sore. Slowly taking in the rest of the room, it only now dawned on her how much of a mess it was. Filing cabinets hanging open, chairs knocked to the floor, and no computers or monitors in sight.

'Jesus, Patrick! What's happened?'

He didn't answer, but the tear rolling down his cheek glistened in the window's fading daylight.

THIRTY-FOUR

Reaching for the packet of tissues she always carried in her handbag, Hannah removed one and handed it to Patrick, who pressed it against one of the fresh welts on his cheek.

'You should get that looked at by a doctor,' she said, resetting one of the chairs, and dragging it closer to him.

'What's the point?' he replied absently, pressing the bottle of whisky to his lips, and draining the remaining few drops.

'Nursing yourself with that won't help. Where's your kettle? I'll make us a tea and then you can fill me in on exactly what's been going on.'

He grunted. 'What use is a kettle when the electric supply has been cut off? Why d'you think it's so dark in here?'

She couldn't keep the apprehension from her voice. 'You need to tell me what's going on, Patrick, and this time I want the truth. I saw Wendy.'

He glanced up at mention of his wife's name, and for the first time Hannah saw concern replace self-pity. 'Is she okay? Is she still pissed off?'

'She's really worried about you, and with good reason if you ask me. For goodness sake, Patrick, will you tell me why you look like you've been on the wrong end of a beating, why the office looks like a bomb has gone off, and why the power's been cut. This can't all be a result of John's passing away.'

He tried to return the whisky bottle to the desk, but he misjudged the edge, and it fell to the floor, rolling away. 'You sure you want to hear this?'

Forcing eye contact to steady her own nerves, she nodded firmly. 'Leave no stone unturned.'

Pushing his chair back, he stood, choosing to pace as he struggled to find the words. 'I probably came back to work too soon after what happened to John, but I didn't feel I had much choice. We had commitments to clients, and the team here needed direction, and so I buried myself in work, to keep grief at bay. Despite everything, we hit a real purple patch. I guess the company's name rode the shirttails of the stories surrounding John's murder and the subsequent investigation. Whenever they mentioned him he was referred to as Company Director. The publicity was priceless.

'A few months ago I was working late, when these three heavies turned up – you know the type: beefy, barrel-chested, five-o-clock shadow. I thought they'd taken a wrong turn, but then one of them – the ringleader I presume – sat down where you are now, and told me he'd invested a sizeable chunk of cash in the business with John, and now he'd come to collect on his investment. I almost laughed him out of the office. I thought they must have seen all the stories about John, thought we were worth a bit of cash and were just trying to hustle us. I told them to get lost, that my brother wouldn't be so stupid as to get mixed up with anyone like them. I told them to scram or I'd phone the police and report them for extortion.

'The guy simply smiled at me and clicked his fingers, and then one of his cohorts produced a brown envelope and handed it to him. Without a word he opened it and started pulling out photographs laying them on my desk, one after another. Must have been a dozen pictures. They were of the three of them, and John in some seedy-looking nightclub.

The background was dimly-lit, the girls topless, and a thick cloud of cigarette smoke hovering just below the ceiling.

'The guy tells me that not only had John convinced them to invest in our business, he'd promised them massive returns on that investment. The guy reckoned forty per cent on top of the original investment. It was ridiculous: no investor in the world would ever expect such a high return, particularly in a company as small as ours. I told him he was dreaming if he thought a few photographs of John in a lap dancing club would convince me. Then he pulls something else out of the envelope, and lays it on top of the photographs. It was on our company headed paper, dated last September and signed by John and whoever this bloke was.

'*A contract*, he tells me. *Makes it all legal*, he snarled. I read it carefully, and couldn't deny it did suggest that John had accepted a sizeable investment and promised the returns he'd quoted.'

'How much are we talking?' Hannah interrupted. 'How big is sizeable?'

'A quarter of a million, and given John's passing they'd decided now was the time to collect what they were owed. I told him I knew nothing about the deal and that I wasn't going to just accept some contract that could just as easily have been forged.'

Hannah continued to listen, fighting every urge in her body to shout and slap Patrick for spreading such lies about John. A strip club? Gangsters? Money laundering? It just wasn't her John. He wouldn't allow himself to get caught in such a mess.

'He wasn't happy,' Patrick continued. 'Left me in no doubt what he would do to me if I didn't cough up the money. I told him to leave me a copy of the contract so I could have it looked at by our solicitor. He agreed, and I sent a copy to the firm we use for negotiating third party contract terms. You can imagine my surprise *and* fear when they came back and confirmed it was legally binding. They told me any contract could be challenged in civil court, and that if we lost we would be liable to pay out the money along with court costs.

'I was so angry, livid in fact. And confused. Why would John take on such a risky investment, and what had happened to the cash? That was when I asked the accountants to look at the books, and when they told me about the black hole. Not only was there no record of the quarter of a million, but another quarter of a million was also unaccounted for. I made them check, and double-check, and triple-check, but they came back with the same response. Whatever he'd done with the money, there was no sign of it in our books or yield of company assets. The only conclusion the accountant could draw was that John must have stashed it in a non-company bank account, or spent it.'

Bile bubbled at the back of Hannah's throat, and it was all she could do to stop herself throwing up in the waste paper bin at her feet. 'John wouldn't do that,' she said, repeating it more assertively. 'He wouldn't do that. Not to you, not to me, and not to the business. You know him better than anyone Patrick, do you really think he would steal half a million pounds and leave us in shit?'

Patrick stopped pacing, pressing his hands on the opposite side of the desk, and leaning in. 'I didn't want to believe it either, but I've forensically examined everything he did in the months before his death, and there's no other explanation.'

'I hope you phoned the police.'

He shook his head, the sadness returning to his eyes. 'How could I? What could the police do?'

'If this investment was gained through illegal means, they can probably confiscate it.'

'There is no money,' he bellowed, startling her. 'Don't

you see? The police can't confiscate what isn't there! If the money was there I'd just pay them to make all of this go away, but it's gone. John fucked us over, and now I'm left to sort it. Look at my face, the state of this place, these people aren't the sort who worry about threats and legality.'

'There must be something the police can do. Or your solicitor?'

He was still shaking his head, once again pacing the floor. 'I tried. I sold everything I could; laid off staff, but it wasn't enough. I even took out a second mortgage on my home for a hundred grand. I thought if I gave them the forty per cent return it would buy me more time to find the rest, but they came back this afternoon and… well, you can see what they thought of that idea. I'm out of options and out of time. Unless I can find out where John put that money I'm fucked.'

'Then you need to go to the police!' Hannah practically yelled, the frustration getting the better of her.

Patrick's head snapped round with a venomous glare. 'They had a picture of Wendy collecting the children from school! If I go to the police, it won't just be my life I'm ruining, but theirs as well. Don't you see? If I don't pay them we're all dead. If I go to the police, we're all dead. There is no way out!'

Hannah thought back to the Nokia phone. 'After you left yesterday, I did find *something*.'

His eyes widened at the prospect. 'Found what? Money? Bank account details?'

'A phone,' she said, cringing as his face dropped.

'A phone?'

'It was in with his work things, only it was hidden inside a stuffed toy.'

'What sort of a phone? Did you manage to turn it on? What did it say? Did you bring it with you?'

Something about his sudden excitement troubled her,

and she shook her head. 'I don't have it with me right now. I don't know that it's much use either, as all it contained was the history of a call he'd made to a now unregistered phone number.'

'You have it with you in Manchester?'

'Yes,' she said reluctantly, now suddenly wishing she'd not mentioned it.

'Well where is it? Can we go and get it. Maybe it contains a message or email or account numbers, or something.'

'I'll drop it by, but I really don't think you should get your hopes up.'

'What was this phone number? Did you recognise it?'

She shook her head but recited it from memory. He didn't appear to recognise it either.

'John wouldn't hide the money and not leave a trail to it. He was always so careful. If he left the phone, it's because he wanted us to find it. Maybe he feared they would come after him and that's why he left it. You have to get that phone to me. Where are you staying? My house?'

'No at the Travelodge on the M62 services. I'll bring it by in the morning. Will you be here?'

He nodded at the rolled-up sleeping bag beneath his desk. 'Where else would I go?'

Hannah squeezed him tightly before heading out of the office, down the stairs and back to her car. Something Patrick had said was playing on her mind: *Maybe he feared they would come after him.*

What if he was right? What if these men had come after John that night? What if the real killer had escaped and was still out there? One thing was for sure: she'd never felt so uncertain about the man she loved.

THIRTY-FIVE

Dropping her bag of clothes on the floor, Hannah fell onto the bed, allowing herself a couple of minutes rest. Check-in at the Travelodge hadn't been as straight-forward as she'd hoped when she'd told them she would have a dog staying with her. Apparently dogs carried a surcharge, but in that moment she hadn't cared how much more they wanted to charge, and had freely handed over her credit card.

She hoped Barney wasn't too freaked out that she'd left him in a house full of strangers, though something told her he would be loving all the extra attention the children would be giving him. How she could have done with him here now though. Her head was filled with images of John in the seedy club with women dancing provocatively before him. He just wasn't like that; at least she hadn't thought he was. Then again, if he'd managed to lie about stealing money from the company so convincingly, how much of the rest of their life together had been a lie?

The snapshot of him in their room and that crimson dress leapt into her mind's eye.

What a mess!

With Patrick's life in danger, she had no choice but to notify the police. Yes, there might be repercussions for the company and Patrick himself, but surely that was better than the threat of violence. Or worse.

Hannah pulled out her smartphone and searched for DI Jeanette Chandler's number, before stopping herself. Was it fair to involve Jeanette? She probably had plenty of other work on her plate without becoming embroiled in this mess. Yet, if the thugs threatening Patrick had murdered John, didn't she need to know?

She tried the number, but it went straight to voicemail. She left a message asking Jeanette to call her back, but didn't say what it was regarding.

It was impossible to know what to do for the best. What she needed was a friend she could talk to. Selecting her former neighbour's number, she pressed dial.

'Hi, Sandra, it's Hannah Davenport, are you free right now? I'm in Manchester, and I really need someone to talk to. Can you meet me for a drink?'

The bar was situated midway along Deansgate, the near straight route through the western part of the city centre. It had been Sandra's choice, as she'd been desperate to go and check out their range of movie-inspired cocktails, despite the fact it wasn't even four yet. Hannah didn't care, so long as she didn't have to visit the old neighbourhood, certain she would spend the rest of the night blubbing if she saw her old house. Too many memories there.

The bar was well-lit and not yet too busy; the three barmen chatting amongst themselves behind the counter while Hannah and Sandra were sitting at one of the half dozen tall tables, tentatively perched on stools. Sandra had ordered a dirty martini, whereas Hannah had opted for tea to keep her head clear.

'I'll let you have first dibs,' Sandra said nodding towards the barmen, 'but I get the two that are left.'

Hannah looked over at them, and as well-groomed as they looked, she wasn't interested. 'Have all three. I won't judge.'

Sandra raised her eyebrows inquisitively. 'Don't tell me you've already hooked someone down south. You have, haven't you? Well who is he? What does he do? Is he any good in bed?'

Hannah almost spat out her tea. 'I didn't say I was seeing anyone.'

Sandra continued studying her face. 'Your lips are saying no, but that hint of a smile is telling me otherwise.'

Hannah tried to straighten her face, but that only made the urge to smile stronger. 'Okay, okay, I did meet someone this week, but –'

'I knew it!' Sandra declared clapping her hands together. 'Go on, who is he?'

'He's nobody, just someone I met in the park walking his dogs.'

'He's a dog lover? Must be alright. All men who like dogs are good-uns.'

Hannah wasn't totally sure she agreed with that logic, but didn't challenge.

'What's his name?' Sandra asked.

'Steve.'

'What does he do?'

'He's a plumber, and also runs a dog training class two nights a week. I went along to it yesterday, and he asked me out for a drink afterwards.'

Sandra's eyes were giddy with excitement. '*And?*'

'And nothing. We had a drink. It was nice, but then I started feeling guilty about John.'

'Guilty about what?'

'I don't know… betraying his memory?'

'It's been a year, Hannah. He wouldn't have expected you to remain celibate for the rest of your life. You can bet if the situation was reversed he'd be back on the horse by now.'

The smile disappeared from Hannah's face, hurt by the

suggestion. 'What's that supposed to mean?'

Sandra's face reddened as she realised she'd spoken out of turn. 'I'm sorry, I didn't mean any offence, but you know he was always quite flirtatious with people. All I meant was I could imagine he wouldn't have been short of offers, as I'm sure you're not.' She sipped her drink to compose herself. 'So when are you seeing this Steve again?'

Hannah shrugged. 'I don't know. I tore off so quickly that I didn't get the chance to arrange anything.'

Sandra sucked her cocktail through the straw. 'I'm glad you called actually. That strange girl was sniffing around your old house again today. You remember the one I told you about?'

'Did you speak to her? Who is she?'

'Sorry, she didn't knock on my door this time, and then I had to go out. You still don't know what she's after?'

Hannah had no idea, though her gut told her it had to have something to do with the mess surrounding John and Patrick.

'My John was a good man, wasn't he?' Hannah asked, frowning.

Sandra considered the question. 'I always thought so. He was always happy to chat, always smiling whenever I saw him. Why do you ask?'

'Just some stories I've heard flying about recently, suggesting he wasn't quite the man I knew.'

Sandra reached out and squeezed her hand. 'Are you sure you're alright? You don't seem… you just don't seem your usual self. I know things have been tough, but you shouldn't punish yourself for what happened. John *was* a good man. Don't let anyone else tarnish your memories of him. You were married to him, and probably knew him better than anyone.'

Hannah's phone rang; DI Chandler calling.

'Hi Jeanette, thanks for calling me back.'

'No worries. I assume it's regarding our last conversation. Seamus Fahey is back in prison, and if you're willing to –'

'Yes,' Hannah blurted, cutting Chandler off. 'I'll meet him.'

'You will?'

Hannah had never heard Chandler lost for words. Despite her previous reservations about being anywhere near the man who had assaulted her, and killed John, there was part of her who just wanted to look into his eyes and find out for certain that the police had arrested the right man.

'Um, how quickly can you get up to Manchester?' Chandler said, flustered.

'I'm in the city right now. How quickly can you get me in to see him?'

'Let me pull some strings and I'll call you right back. Thank you for doing this, I know it can't be easy.'

Hannah hung up the call and looked anxiously at Sandra. 'I'm going to need a proper drink before I go.'

THIRTY-SIX

Hannah had never been inside HMP Manchester, but had driven past it plenty of times. She'd never imagined she would ever have cause to pull up at the gate and present her identification to the guard.

He looked at the photo card licence, back at her and then back at the card, before returning it to her. 'Visiting time is finished.'

'I'm supposed to be meeting someone here. Detective Inspector Jeanette Chandler? She said she'd meet me in the car park.'

The guard returned to the small hut and spoke with his colleague, before returning. 'Okay, go through the gate and follow the signs to the staff car park. Your DI Chandler is waiting there for you.'

Hannah thanked him, trying to ignore the growing sense of unease and tightening of her shoulders. The staff car park was at the rear of the prison, and as she pulled into a vacant space, she saw Chandler standing near the staff entrance to the building smoking with another of the prison guards. Wearing her usual biker leather jacket, Chandler didn't look all that much different to how Hannah remembered her. Barely five feet high with a rotund waist

Chandler squashed the cigarette under foot as Hannah approached waving her hand in front of her face to clear the air of smoke. 'Good to see you, kid,' she said, with a strained smile. 'Hannah, this is Tom, and he's going to escort us through to a secure location where Fahey will be brought to. Now, you'll need to leave your bag and coat in the guard's office, and Tom will need to pat you down and pass a metal detector wand over your person. It's nothing personal, but they need to make sure you're not smuggling any weapons or contraband in. Okay?'

Hannah could barely hear the words, the blood pumping through her ears drowning out everything else.

'It could be worse,' Chandler added, cocking her head. 'If you were a prisoner you'd be strip searched and Tom here has very cold hands. Believe me!'

Hannah wasn't sure what she was supposed to take from that statement, so remained tight-lipped, following the two of them into the building, relieved it was a fraction warmer than the car park. Handing over her coat and handbag, she raised her arms and allowed the wand to be passed over her back, chest, bottom and legs.

'Can you give us a minute, Tom?' Chandler asked when he was finished.

He nodded and left the room, closing the door behind him and waiting patiently outside the glass door with his back to them.

'You don't have to go through with this, kid,' Chandler said, staring hard at her. 'I pulled a load of strings to get us in here tonight, but don't let that keep you here if you've had a change of heart. I wouldn't blame you, and won't be offended.'

'I'm fine,' Hannah replied, unable to keep her voice from cracking under the strain of emotion.

'You may be many things, our kid, but fine isn't one of them. You look as pale as a ghost and twice as thin. In fact, seeing you before me right now is giving me major flashbacks to the first night we met in your neighbour's kitchen. Tell me to but out and mind my own business, but you don't look fine.'

Hannah finally met her gaze, unable to keep her eyes from welling. 'It's just… I never ever pictured myself coming face-to-face with him. You know? The pictures of him that I saw in the papers haunt my dreams, but in them he is just a two-dimensional monster who I keep locked away. Seeing him in person… it just makes him more real. After today I'll know how tall he is, whether he talks with a raspy voice or sounds educated. I'll know how he walks and how dark or pale his skin tone is. All of that absolutely terrifies me. I know if I don't go through with this – if I don't confront him head on, and look into his eyes – I'll never be able to move on myself. When I was a child my mum always used to say the easiest way to defeat the monster I believed lived under the bed was to crawl down to his level. I spent a week sleeping under my bed, until I was able to accept that there wasn't any monster there, just dirt, fluff and spiders.'

Chandler looked ready to cry herself, but instead pulled Hannah into a warm embrace. 'Don't think this is some kind of chat-up line, but I think you just became my personal hero.'

Hannah pulled herself away. 'Does he know we're coming?'

Chandler nodded. 'He was told at the same time I called you. Bear in mind he'll have been planning this encounter in his head since the day he was arrested. He'll have thought about what he wants to say, what kind of reaction he's hoping for, and seeing your face may trigger all sorts of memories for him too. You just need to be ready for anything. Now, I'll be in the room with you, so if you suddenly feel uncomfortable and decide you want the meeting to end, all you have to do is give the word, and I'll pull it. He'll be escorted back to his cell and you'll never have to hear from him ever again.'

'I thought you said he just wanted to apologise; seek my

forgiveness.'

Chandler nodded reassuringly. 'That's why we've arranged this get-together. That's what he's told us, but I just want you to be prepared in case it doesn't quite go to plan.' She sighed loudly. 'Being in somewhere like this... it changes a person. For some it is a wake-up call, a realisation that their behaviour needs to change. For others, it steers them further down the slippery slope to hardened criminal life. Fahey hasn't been outside unaccompanied for the best part of a year. He'll have had to grow accustomed to a life behind bars, living in the pockets of other – and far worse – men. I've been in this game for too long not to expect the unexpected.' Chandler paused. 'I still don't like the colour of your cheeks, kid. It isn't too late to cancel. I'd rather we bin it off than you undergo any further trauma.'

'No, it's okay,' she said with a deep breath. '*I'm* okay. I want to do this. I'm ready.'

Chandler took one further hard look at her, before tapping on the door, and allowing Tom to open it. He led the way along a narrow and dimly lit passage, until they reached the first of five barred gates. Each one was opened with an individual key from the set on the ring attached to Tom's belt. Each time the gate slammed shut and was locked, Hannah jumped, even though she knew it was coming.

They finally arrived at a large metal door, with a small hatch at eye-level. Tom lowered the grate, looked through, before sliding another key into it, and pulling it open.

'There are cameras in all four corners of the room,' he said, pointing at each. 'They are there purely so we can monitor behaviour inside the room. They don't have audio ability, but recordings will be kept on record until the standard retention period expires. If we see any behaviour that contravenes normal conversation, myself or one of my colleagues will enter from this door or the one across the room and the meeting will be terminated. Is that clear?'

'As clear as the outline of the penis in your trousers,' Chandler replied with a wink.

Hannah simply nodded.

A large sheet of hardened glass bisected the room, with two chairs positioned centrally on this side, and a vacant chair on the other. A similar metal door was visible in the wall on the other side of the glass.

Chandler waited for Tom to close and bolt the door, before moving forward and sitting in the closest chair. Hannah slowly sank into the chair to Chandler's right, her entire body tingling with nervous energy. The sound of keys in the lock of the other door echoed off the walls, and then the door opened.

THIRTY-SEVEN

It was difficult to see Fahey at first, the overweight guard dressed in navy trousers and woollen jumper filling the entire doorway. The breath caught in Hannah's throat as the guard stepped aside, and the barely visible prisoner shuffled in behind him, the bracelets around his tiny wrists looking like they might slip off at any moment.

The monster who haunted her nightmares was based on the few images she'd seen of him in the newspapers at the time of the trial; dressed in his military fatigues, very much a soldier gone rogue. That was how the press had described him. The man before her now bore little resemblance to what she had expected.

Grey straggly hair hung down past his ears and shoulders, covering his eyes and nose. His lips were dry and cracked, and his chin covered in white fuzz. The stone-coloured tracksuit bottoms and sweater swamped his tiny shoulders and waist, and looked like they were the only thing keeping him upright.

As the prison officer removed the handcuffs, Fahey actually looked like he might collapse under the weight of expectation. The officer held out a wrist, which Fahey leaned on unsteadily as he allowed himself to be escorted to the seat before the glass. Once the guard was satisfied that Fahey wouldn't keel over, he left the room, locking the door behind him.

Hannah still hadn't taken a breath since he'd arrived in

the room, and it was only because her vision was beginning to blur that she remembered to inhale again. Glancing over Chandler's shoulder, the door on their side of the partition was only a couple of metres away, and she had to fight every instinct in her body not to rush to it and start hammering for escape.

'You alright?' Chandler whispered, noticing Hannah's gaze still on the door.

Hannah forced her head to nod, as she couldn't get the lie out of her throat.

Chandler turned her attention back to the shadow of a man on the other side of the glass. 'Morning, Seamus,' she practically shouted, causing him to shudder and raise his head a fraction.

Hannah allowed her eyes to take in his full appearance. His cheeks were almost as grey as the mop of hair on his head; the skin beneath his chin, which hung from his collar bone like a chamois leather, was an unpleasant mixture of purple, brown and yellow tones, in a sickening line where the noose had left its stain. His appearance didn't fit with the maximum security protocols that were the bricks and mortar of the place. Fahey would struggle to escape an unlocked room, let alone scale a three metre wall.

'How was last night?' Chandler bellowed towards the glass.

Fahey shrugged, at least it looked like a shrug, though it was difficult to tell beneath the baggy clothes.

'No more attempts to bump yourself off, I hope?' Chandler certainly had a way with words. Never one to pull any punches, it didn't look like her bedside manner would be making an appearance today.

Fahey didn't answer, but his face shifted slightly, like he'd suddenly realised Chandler wasn't alone on the other side of the glass.

In the newspaper, Hannah could remember he had dark

brown eyes, though it was impossible to tell through his thick fringe. His gaze was burning into her, and she took another glance at the door.

Chandler cleared her throat, keeping her eyes on Fahey's reaction. 'Do you know who this woman is?'

His voice when he spoke was gruff and quiet. 'Should I?'

Hannah turned back at the sound, her body tingling with fear as some distant memory sparked a little.

Chandler snorted. 'Well, given the number of times you've written to her in the past year, I'm surprised you don't know what she looks like.'

His posture shifted, straightening his back and shoulders as if someone had just told him to stand to attention.

Hannah's heart pounded in her chest, but she dared not speak.

The skin on Fahey's hands was blistered and cracked, as he raised them to brush the hair out of his eyes. The fingertips stained yellow from nicotine and tar, and the nails chewed to the quick. He opened his mouth to speak, before thinking better of it. As he looked away for the briefest of moments, Hannah saw the overhead light reflect off the shine in his eyes.

'I… I've imagined this moment for so long,' he finally whispered, the strain on his voice a combination of years of smoking and the bruising to his neck. 'I…'

Hannah's eyes hadn't left his face, studying every contour, looking for anything that would shine a light on the black hole in her memory. When he'd spoken, something had fired, but it had only been a glimpse and now it was gone. Her breaths were strained and only coming in short bursts. She had to concentrate. She wasn't going to cry, and she didn't want him to see her fear, but if it meant she could get it over with sooner then so be it.

Fahey suddenly leaned forward, resting his hands on his

knees, and Hannah instinctively recoiled as if he might somehow be able to reach through the glass and try to throttle her again.

'I… I am so sorry,' he said, as a tear rolled down the dry skin and blotted. 'I know how hard this must be for you. To know that I could have… that I caused you so much pain, I – I am just so sorry.'

His cheeks were now damp through, offering a touch of colour against the pallid grey surrounding them.

'The woman next to me is Hannah Davenport,' Chandler continued. 'She is the woman whose house you invaded last October, the woman whose husband you brutally stabbed with a kitchen knife.'

Fahey was blinking rapidly as more tears escaped, and as Hannah watched, willing herself to hate everything about this monster, she found herself filled with nothing but pity. If Chandler was right, he would never step outside the red brick walls; would never watch the sun rising or setting, and would be forced to spend his remaining days relieving the horrific events of that night. If ever there was an advert for a fallen hero, this was it.

As she continued to watch him now freely sobbing, using the backs of his dry hands to wipe his eyes and nose, she couldn't see the one thing she'd come for: recognition, either on her part or his. Could he really have been so drunk and stoned that he couldn't remember her face either?

'I know… I don't… deserve your forgiveness,' he stuttered between sobs. 'I want you to know… how sorry I am. For everything.' He lurched forwards, dropping to his knees. 'I beg you… I beg your forgiveness.'

Chandler put a protective arm across Hannah. 'Back on your feet now, Seamus. Don't make me call the guard in and cut short this meeting.'

He finally stopped staring at Hannah, and nodded at Chandler, reaching for the chair and hauling himself back onto it, wiping his face with the sleeve of the stone-coloured jumper.

'That's better,' Chandler confirmed as he composed himself. 'Now, is there anything you would like to say to the inmate, Hannah?'

Hannah's head snapped round in shock. She hadn't anticipated needing to speak, and her mind was blank as she searched for any kind of response. 'Um, I don't know,' was the best she could offer.

Chandler leaned closer, her voice barely more than a whisper so Fahey wouldn't hear. 'There's something else I should have told you before we came in here. Seamus isn't long for this life. They ran tests on him a couple of months ago when he started pissing blood. Reckon the cancer started in his lungs and is spreading like maggots on a corpse.'

Hannah couldn't stop herself looking over at him. The skin hanging from his bones like the clothes from his body, and why he'd been so desperate to meet was to clear his conscience before meeting his maker. Was it wrong that he was acting so selfishly? If anything it only made her pity him more.

'Does he know?' Hannah whispered back.

Chandler nodded. 'It would be impossible to miss the signs even if the doctors hadn't told him. It's only going to get more painful, another reason why he attempted what he did last week.' She paused, summoning the courage to ask the next question. 'I know it's asking a lot, but do you think there's any way… any way you could tell him you forgive him? You don't have to mean it, just say the words. I'm sorry, I know I'm asking you to do the last thing anyone could expect.'

'He took *everything* from me.'

'I know, kid, and I think karma is delivering you the justice you deserve. You don't have to do it if you don't feel up to it, but I think it would do the world of good.'

Chandler straightened, the brief interlude over. 'Now, Seamus, I think you owe this lady a real apology. So take a deep breath, and utter those three little words.'

Fahey nodded, closing his eyes and taking several deep breaths, before fixing Hannah with a sincere look. 'I am sorry for everything I did to you and your husband. I have no excuse for my actions or behaviour. I'm not an evil person. If it wasn't for the police finding my DNA at your house, I would have said I couldn't have done the things they accused me of. I can only assume that with my mind and body in a bad state, I lost control or something.'

A flash of memory from her childhood; her mother leading her onto a hospital ward, holding her hand, and then seeing her grandfather asleep in the bed. She hadn't realised then, but it was the last time she would ever see him. She'd tried to shake his arm to wake him, but he had remained at peace, while her mother had quietly wept.

Hannah closed her eyes, picturing John's smiling face. 'I… forgive you.' The words tasted bitter as she uttered them, but when she opened her eyes, for the briefest of moments, Fahey looked as at peace as her grandfather had.

THIRTY-EIGHT

Watching the prison guard lead Fahey out of the big secured door, Hannah finally allowed herself to focus on steadying her breathing.

'How are you bearing up, kid?' Chandler asked, her attention now fully back on Hannah.

'I'll be okay in a minute.'

'I take my hat off to you. I don't know how you managed to stay so calm.'

'I was hardly calm,' Hannah replied, feeling the sweat gluing the shirt to her lower back.

'You were serenity personified. If it were me coming face-to-face with the man who did… what he did to you, I would have been banging at the glass trying to find a way through to get revenge. That moment when he dropped to his knees, I was preparing myself to restrain you, but you remained resolutely still. Them Shaolin monks have got nothing on you.'

Hannah smiled weakly, feeling the pins and needles evaporating from her hands and fingers. 'I'm just glad it's done. Do you think… what I mean is, do you think it helped? Do you think he'll be okay now?'

Chandler stood and moved across to the door, giving it a good bang with her clenched fist. 'I wouldn't let any of that worry you. Listen, he's in the best place; metaphorically and physically speaking.'

Hannah joined her at the door while they waited for Tom

to unlock it and allow them out. 'What do you mean?'

Chandler smiled. 'In here, he's entitled to medical treatment that probably would have been beyond him out on the streets. He has regular check-ups with a team of oncology specialists, and although he is too far gone for treatment, when it worsens, they'll be able to give him palliative care. Whether or not he tries to end things again before that is anyone's guess, but if you ask me, when he left it looked like a huge weight had been lifted from his shoulders. Did you notice? He walked out far easier than he came in. You did that, and you should be very proud of this last act of kindness. It's more than he deserved for what he did, and I am in genuine admiration of you. Believe me, there's not many I give two stuffs about in this world, but you're one of them, lady.'

The sound of the bolt turning was followed by Tom's cheery face at the door. 'All done?'

'Yes thanks,' Chandler said, leading the way back to the first locked gate. 'What time you knocking off here tonight, Tom?'

'I'm on all night,' he replied glumly.

'That's a shame, because I feel like getting twatted.' She turned to Hannah. 'I guess it's just you and me then, kid. I'm buying you the largest gin and tonic you can imagine, and I'm not taking no for an answer.'

Hannah smiled again, more resolutely this time. A drink was exactly what she needed.

'And then the driver said, "No, it's just the way I tell the time".' Chandler erupted into laughter, slamming the table with her hand as she did, causing the two glasses to wobble.

Hannah strained a smile, not finding Chandler's brand of humour as funny as the detective clearly did.

Chandler wiped her eyes, as she continued to chuckle. 'Shall we have another?'

Hannah checked the time on her watch. It was nearly six, and she didn't want to be late getting to Wendy's for dinner. The stress of the day had taken its toll and she was looking forward to climbing beneath the hotel's duvet cover and putting it all behind her.

'I'd better not, I'm driving,' Hannah cautioned. 'Don't let me stop you. In fact, I should buy you a drink as it's my turn.'

Chandler held up a finger of warning. 'Your money is no good here. After what you did today, I won't allow you to spend a penny. Besides, you could always leave your car where it is and get a taxi home. Or better still, I could call the station and have us personally escorted home.'

Hannah was pretty sure Chandler wasn't the sort to take advantage of her role, but chose not to challenge the statement.

'You look pensive,' Chandler said, fixing her with a studious stare. 'Are you still thinking about Fahey?'

Hannah's cheeks flushed. 'Is it that obvious?'

'I told you: don't worry about him anymore. He can't hurt you where he is, and health-wise he's in the best hands.'

Hannah bit her lip. 'It's not so much that, more something he said.'

Chandler frowned. 'Go on.'

Hannah took a deep breath. 'He said: but for the police finding his DNA at my house, he wouldn't have thought himself capable of what he did.'

'And?'

'I don't know, it just stuck with me.'

'I think we're all capable of doing more than we can imagine if we find ourselves in the wrong situation. Did I ever tell you why I decided to become a police officer?'

Hannah finished her drink and shook her head.

'When I was nineteen and at college, my best friend was raped on her way home from the university bar. I'd known her since we were seven, and we'd seen each other virtually every day since. I wasn't with her that night as I was working at a pub away from the campus. When I got back to our digs, she told me what had happened and she told me who'd done it as well. I told her we had to report it to the police, and she reluctantly agreed. These two female officers turned up at the house, took her statement, and then escorted her to the hospital where she was examined. She told the police what she'd told me, and I remember spending the night in her room, because she was so terrified he'd come back to get her again. The next morning I went to lectures, but she stayed home. I told her I'd buy us some grub and be back at lunchtime.

'I knew something was wrong the moment I walked in through the front door. I could hear bath water sloshing, and as I raced up the stairs I could see the water overflowing, and that's where I found her. Face as white as a sheet, the water around her as red as the blood that had spilled from her veins. I called an ambulance, but she was long gone, and there was nothing I could do for her. She didn't leave a note.

'I missed the next week of lectures, and I was shocked when I returned. There he was – Ryan Gerrard – walking about freely. The police had questioned him about the assault, but because he had a mate providing him with an alibi for the night, and because he'd used a condom, it came down to her word against his. With her dead, there wasn't any interest from the CPS in taking the case to court. So, because of what he'd done, I lost my best friend, and there was nothing the police could do.'

Hannah reached out and squeezed her hand. 'My God, that's horrible. I'm so sorry.'

Chandler pulled her hand away, staring off into the

distance. 'I was livid. *So* angry. I wanted to kill him. As far as I was concerned, *he* was the one who had dragged the razor blade against her veins. I went after him. I remember this feeling of pure hate coursing through my body. I remember selecting the knife from the kitchen drawer, and hiding it up my sleeve, and I remember stalking from bar to bar until I found the one he was in, laughing and joking with his mates. I remember waiting. I ordered drink after drink, waiting until I could get him alone. Then when they left, I followed them away from the bar. They left him at the top of this dark pathway that led down to the street he lived on and that's when I raced across the road after him, kicking his legs from beneath him. He was pretty pissed and flopped to the floor. We were all alone, and I could feel the knife's blade pressed against my wrist, and it would have been so easy to pull it out of my sleeve and do him in there and then. Nobody would have seen, and I doubt many would have cared. I couldn't go through with it though. I tried picturing my friend's pained anguish and willed myself to end his life, but I didn't. I didn't bottle it. I could have killed him in that moment. I kept thinking of how I would spend the rest of my life seeing his terrified face in my dreams, and that I'd cross a line I could never return from.

'I left him in that alleyway, stinking of piss, and went home. The next day I applied to join the police force. I knew that killing Ryan wasn't the legacy my friend would want me to leave behind. She'd want me to go after the other men who thought they could get away with it, and bring them to justice. Thirty years later, here I am.'

Hannah asked the question burning inside of her. 'Apart from the DNA evidence, was there anything else that convinced you Fahey was guilty?'

'His prints were on the knife, his bloody footprint was on the carpet, and John's blood was on his coat when he was arrested less than a mile from your house. I've known people convicted on far less evidence.'

'Were there any other suspects considered during the investigation?'

Chandler eyes her suspiciously. 'Like who?'

Hannah thought back to the photographs Patrick had described. 'I don't know, like business acquaintances?'

Chandler scoffed. 'Your husband ran an IT company, not exactly a business synonymous with villainy.'

'Was Fahey the only suspect, or did you investigate anyone else?'

Chandler wasn't laughing anymore. 'What's all this about? You heard Fahey confess less than an hour ago.'

Hannah screwed up her face, before relaying what Patrick had told her about the thugs who had turned up, the contract and demands for money. For now she left out the part about the threat to Wendy and the children.

Chandler's nose wrinkled. 'So you think John – who nobody had a bad word to say against – was mixed up with local villains who then came and offed him?'

It sounded so silly when phrased in that way. 'Apart from Fahey's DNA, was there any other DNA found at the scene?'

'None that wasn't expected. Listen, in my experience, serious villains don't break into houses and butcher their victims with a kitchen knife. They hit them when they're away from home, and would just as likely use a gun as a knife. Think about it: if your brother-in-law is right and John had got himself mixed up with some shady characters, why would they kill him? If they invested their money in the company, with him gone, so is access to their money.'

'I suppose you're probably right.'

Chandler slurped the remains of the G&T from her glass. 'If your brother-in-law is getting troubled by some local heavies, I can put you in touch with a colleague of mine who works those sorts of cases. She's not as charming as I am, but she knows her stuff.'

Hannah checked her watch again. 'Thanks, I'll think about it. Listen, I need to make a move. Do you want me to buy you another drink before I go?'

Chandler checked her watch. 'No, I should probably head home too. Getting wasted isn't as much fun on your own. Could you give me a lift home on your way?'

Hannah nodded and reached for her coat.

THIRTY-NINE

Time enough to quickly shower and change, and race across to Wendy's. Pulling into a space in the busy Travelodge car park, there was nothing Hannah wanted more than to crash out in bed. It would be so easy to message Wendy and tell her she was just too tired, order room service and relax, and if it wasn't for Barney that's what she would have done. He'd been left with the houseful of strangers for long enough, and she needed a cuddle from him.

The woman behind the counter was preoccupied with a foreign-sounding couple, and didn't even look up as Hannah passed by, through the lobby door and into the ground floor corridor. Her room was at the end of the narrow passage, nearest the fire escape. In total there must have been twenty rooms, ten each side, and at least another forty on the floors overhead. Reaching into her handbag, she fished out the plastic key card, and slotted it into the mechanism above the door handle. It clicked and the LED inside the lock glowed green as she pulled the key card out. Pushing the door handle open, she froze as her eyes fell on the figure dressed head-to-toe in black, standing at the foot of the bed.

It was like she'd been transported back twelve months to their old home. Panic gripped her, and as her eyes widened, she desperately wanted to scream, but was incapable of making any noise. The intruder rushed forwards and placed a gloved hand over the lower half of her face, pulling her into the room, pressing a gloved finger to his lips hidden beneath the balaclava. She could only see his eyes, but with the only light coming from the corridor behind her, it was difficult to identify the colour.

She remained perfectly still, fearing what he might do. Keeping the finger to his lips, he yanked the handbag from her arm. She wanted to resist, but it was like her spirit had left her body and was hovering somewhere overhead watching the scene unfold.

The punch to her gut winded her, and she doubled over, crumpling to the floor. With that he was gone, out of the door, leaving her in a mess, as her body finally thawed and a single tear dripped to the carpet.

Perched on the end of the bed, Hannah held the hot mug of tea close to her face, savouring its warmth, as one of the uniformed officers examined the open window. It was her fault. That's not quite how they'd put it, but had she not left the window open, the intruder never would have got in.

'It's not the first crime like this we've seen in recent months,' the female officer standing close to the bed said. 'They prey on unsuspecting holidaymakers, wait until they leave, and then use bolt cutters to snap the safety cord that keeps the window from opening wider. You weren't to know. These hotel chains really should warn ground floor guests not to leave their windows open when they go out.'

Hannah didn't remember opening the window, and would have argued that it had already been open when she'd checked-in, but there seemed little point in arguing. The contents of her rucksack were scattered over the bed and floor. She'd wanted to tidy up, but had waited in case the police wanted to photograph the room or dust for prints, not that either had been offered.

'Most of the time these perps are looking for things they can sell quickly to buy drugs or booze. You were just in the wrong place at the wrong time. He probably thought it was easier to exit through the main body of the hotel than back through the window.'

'No obvious sign of prints,' her colleague said, approaching them. 'You said he was wearing gloves?'

'Yes,' Hannah nodded. 'Black leather gloves I think.'

The male officer nodded glumly. 'I'm afraid there's little else we can do for you than provide you with a reference number so you can contact your insurance company. You'll probably find your home insurance policy will cover it, but it's best to check. Now, apart from your handbag, is anything else missing?'

'My mobile phone was in my handbag, as well as my purse and cards, and a bit of makeup. It doesn't look like he's taken anything else. Thankfully I still had hold of my car keys.'

A sudden commotion in the corridor was followed by DI Chandler's flustered face appearing at the door. 'Now then, now then, what's going on here?'

The two uniformed officers didn't look surprised to see her, both acknowledging her arrival.

'The thief came in through the window, stole a mobile phone and the contents of this lady's handbag,' the female officer said, standing.

'Are you two done here?' Chandler asked, her gaze never leaving Hannah.

'Yes, ma'am,' the female officer replied.

'Good. Go and find the manager and see what kind of CCTV this dump has.'

They didn't argue, quickly leaving the room and disappearing into the brightly lit corridor, as Chandler joined Hannah on the bed.

'It just isn't your day, is it, kid?' she offered

empathetically.

'They didn't need to call you. I'm okay, just a little shaken.'

'I feel bad for not coming back here with you now.'

'It isn't your fault. You weren't to know he'd be here waiting.' Hannah paused, her mind slow to process the potential significance of the attack. 'You don't think… Given everything I told you about my brother-in-law and those thugs, you don't think this could have anything to do with that?'

Chandler weighed up the odds. 'Based on how you described the three heavies, I wouldn't have thought they would have come here to steal your purse. No logic to that in my head. For starters, how would they know who you are, that you were staying here?'

It was a fair point, but it felt too much of a coincidence that she'd been burgled in a hotel on the same day Patrick had told her about John's troubles.

'More than likely kids,' Chandler concluded. 'After anything electronic they can sell on to fund drugs or booze. You should still contact your bank, and get your cards cancelled just in case.'

'But what if the person who came here tonight was the same one who attacked me and killed John?'

Chandler smiled warmly, but there was pity in her eyes. 'Because I arrested and locked up the man responsible for that. Listen, kid, I know you've been under a tremendous amount of stress, but you're making crazy leaps and bounds here. I understand why you'd want to see a connection, but real life doesn't work like that. Not every loose end gets tied up with a pretty bow on the top. I'm sorry.'

Hannah nodded her understanding, but couldn't help feeling ashamed that she hadn't been more assertive when she'd entered the room. Over the last year she'd spent countless hours training her mind to react differently to confrontation. She'd told herself that had she been better prepared for what happened last year, she could have protected herself better, and maybe the outcome would have been altered. Yet her first chance to put that approach into practice had failed spectacularly. The masked man could have done whatever he'd wanted and she had to think herself lucky that she'd escaped with just the sucker punch.

'I don't think you should stay here tonight,' Chandler continued. 'Is there anyone else can put you up? Family? Friends?'

Sandra would be happy to offer her a bed for the night, but Hannah didn't want to be anywhere near her old house, which only left Wendy.

'My sister-in-law's house isn't far.'

'Good. We'll give you a lift, and I'll have a word with the manager and see about getting you a refund for tonight.'

'No. It's okay. Thank you, but I feel fine to drive. My sister-in-law has enough on her plate without me arriving in a police car adding to her worries. Honestly, I'm fine to drive myself, but I appreciate the offer.'

The car journey to Wendy's was slower than Hannah had anticipated, and as she pulled up ten minutes after seven, she hoped Wendy would forgive her for not messaging to say she would be late. Her only reason for returning to the hotel room had been to shower and change, and she hadn't managed either.

With her new phone now gone, she reached into the glove box and pulled out the Nokia. She couldn't remember how much credit the phone had left, but it wouldn't be too hard to top it up. Hopefully Wendy wouldn't mind her using the landline to contact her bank and put a stop to the cards, and to get fresh ones sent to the loft.

She stopped as her paranoia kicked into gear again. Surely whoever had been in her hotel room hadn't been after the Nokia? It had no valuable information on it; just that telephone number. What possible reason would someone have for wanting to steal it from her? The only person she'd mentioned the Nokia to was Patrick, and she'd already agreed to take it to him tomorrow, so he wouldn't have broken into her room to take it. Besides, although she'd told him which hotel she was in, there was no way he could have guessed which room she was in.

'You're just being paranoid,' she told her reflection in the rear-view mirror. Chandler was right: it was just a punk kid trying to fund a habit. With that thought in mind she hurried to the door, and knocked.

'Auntie Hannah,' Ben and James yelled, as the door opened and she saw their beaming faces.

'Hello, boys,' she said, quickly squeezing the phone into the pocket of her jeans, as they both wrapped their arms around her and squeezed. 'I hope you've been looking after Barney for me.

'He's brilliant,' said James.

'You're so lucky to have a dog. Mum says we can't have one,' Ben echoed.

'Well, when you're older and own your own houses, you'll be able to have as many dogs as you like,' she said, nodding towards Wendy who was holding two steaming plates in the kitchen.

'I want to buy a dog like Barney,' James said.

'Well I'm going to have two dogs,' his older brother boasted.

Hannah closed the door behind her and allowed the boys to each take a hand and drag her through to the front room. The pen and Daisy were now gone, presumably tucked up in bed. There was no sign of Barney, but with Wendy cooking, there was no doubt he was keeping her company in the kitchen waiting to mop up any scraps that might fall to the floor.

'I scored a hat trick today,' Ben declared proudly.

'Well done you!' Hannah beamed, already relaxing in their buoyant company. 'I wish I'd been there to see it.'

'Are you moving back for good?' Ben continued, his younger brother now lost to the television.

'No, I'm just back for a couple of days,' Hannah said, 'but you'll have to come and visit me in Southampton soon. Both of you, I mean. I have a spare room where you could sleep, and I'm sure you'd love the area. There's loads to do, and there are beaches a short drive away.'

'Oh, yeah, that would be ace,' he said, his eyes brightening.

'We might have to wait until next year though,' Hannah warned, remembering she'd have to check whether Wendy would be happy with them visiting. 'Too cold for the beach at this time of the year.'

'Come on, boys. Time for bed,' Wendy called, Barney trotting obediently behind her as she joined them. 'Dinner's on the stove and should be ready by the time I'm done with these two,' she said to Hannah.

'Great. Do you need me to do anything?'

'No, just relax.'

'Is it alright if I use the phone. Just need to call my bank.'

'Feel free. I'll only be a couple of minutes getting these two into bed. I said they could stay up to see you, but now they need to get to sleep.'

The two boys gave Hannah a big hug, and headed out of the room with their mother. Barney hurried over excitedly when he realised Hannah was there, and pushed his head between her knees so she could rub her ears. Burying her face in the fur on his head, she kissed him, so grateful to have him by her side again.

FORTY

Hannah pushed the plate away, wiping her mouth on the cloth napkin. 'That was delicious.'

Wendy collected both plates and carried them over to the sink. 'Just some chicken, rice and double cream. I think I'll have to delay my application for *Masterchef*. You're lucky I'd miscalculated how many fish fingers Ben and James would devour between them. Gannets sometimes those two.'

'You're far more adventurous in the kitchen than I am. These days, my choice of dining is based on whatever is on offer at the local supermarket.' She reached for the glass of wine, and took a long drink. 'John always used to love coming to yours for dinner.'

'We loved it when the two of you came over. You may not be a maestro in the kitchen, but your choice in wine is second-to-none. This one tonight is one you bought for us.'

There was a clatter as Wendy dropped the plates into the sink. Hannah turned at the sudden noise, and saw Wendy with her head bowed, and her hand over her eyes.

Moving across, Hannah gently rubbed her hand in a circle over Wendy's back. 'I'm sorry, I didn't think to ask how you're coping with everything you've got going on.'

Wendy straightened, lowered her hand and took a deep breath to compose herself. She wasn't one who enjoyed outward shows of emotion, and although her mask had briefly slipped, it was now firmly back in place.

'Is there a towel for me to dry up?' Hannah asked.

'We air dry in this house. More hygienic that way. Please sit down. You're my guest, and scrubbing the plates will only take me a minute or so.'

'Are you sure? I feel like I'm taking advantage in forcing myself on you without notice.'

Wendy smiled at her. 'Nonsense! You're my guest, and I will be offended if you don't embrace my hospitality. If you really want to do something, you can top up my glass with some more wine. The bottle's in the fridge.'

Hannah pulled open the fridge door, unsurprised by how well-organised the contents were: yoghurts, cheeses, and butter on one shelf; ham, chicken, and salami grouped together on the top shelf; and a drawer crammed with vegetables at the bottom. The half-empty bottle in the door wasn't the only one. Carrying it back to the table, Hannah shared the remains between the two glasses, and retook her seat, Wendy joining her a moment later.

'I've put some clean sheets on the bed in James's room. Hopefully it won't be too uncomfortable for you. Ben and James were giddy when I told them they would be in the same room tonight.'

'I appreciate you letting me stay over.'

'Don't mention it. After what you said happened at the hotel, nobody can blame you for not wanting to stay there. What did the bank say?'

'They've cancelled my cards, and will send new ones out tomorrow. Reckoned I should receive them by the end of the week. They ran through recent transactions, and it doesn't look like the thief tried to use them.'

Wendy took a long drink of her wine. 'Was Patrick okay when you saw him?'

Hannah relayed what Patrick had told her about John's apparent involvement in criminal activity. Wendy listened without interrupting, but the blood had drained from her face by the time Hannah told her about the bruising to Patrick's face.

'He's sleeping at the office?'

Hannah nodded. 'From the looks of it. I said I'd go back in the morning and show him this.' She lifted the Nokia phone, which had been sitting on the edge of the table.

Wendy's face crinkled in confusion. 'A phone?'

'I found it amongst John's things. I managed to switch it on but couldn't see anything that might explain what he was up to.'

Wendy reached for the phone, turning it over in her hands. 'I remember having one like this, must be… at least a decade ago, if not longer. And it was just in with his belongings?'

'That was the weird thing. I probably wouldn't have thought twice about it had it not been hidden inside a stuffed toy in with his work items.'

Wendy handed it back, but as Hannah went to grasp it, the device slipped and fell to the tiled floor, the battery unclipping on impact and scattering across the room.

'Oh sorry,' Wendy said quickly, moving to collect the battery, as Hannah reached for the main body of the device.

'It was my fault,' Hannah said, accepting the battery from Wendy and putting the phone back together. 'Doesn't appear to be broken.'

'What's that?' Wendy asked, stooping and collecting something small from where the phone had landed. She held it in her palm for Hannah to see. 'Looks like some kind of memory card.' She took the phone from Hannah, scrutinising the sides. 'Doesn't look like it came from any kind of slot in the phone, so it must have fallen out when the battery fell out. Weird.'

Passing the Nokia and memory card to Hannah, Wendy stood and left the room, returning a moment later, carrying a laptop with her. 'This has slots for reading memory cards,' she said, putting the laptop in front of Hannah, and pulling her chair over.

Hannah handed her the card, and watched as Wendy inserted it in the memory slot. A folder opened on the laptop's screen a moment later, containing just a single Microsoft Word file. The file listed John as the owner, and more alarming was the confirmation that the file was last modified the day he died.

Wendy slid the laptop closer to Hannah, angling it away from herself. 'Maybe you should be the one to open the file. I'll give you some privacy.'

Hannah's eyes hadn't left the screen. His full name written, including both his middle names, the same way it had been in their wedding register. The date that was permanently etched to her memory. The blood in her veins so icy, slowly working down her entire body, until she suddenly shuddered with the cold.

She grabbed Wendy's hand, and pulled her closer. 'Please don't go.'

Wendy nodded, and double-clicked on the file. It opened with an embedded video on the first page. Both gasped when they saw John's face frozen on the screen.

FORTY-ONE

Hannah ran her fingers the length of the screen, almost able to feel the sting of his stubble as she had so many times when she'd held his face. Gripping the mouse, her hand trembling, she started the video, John's face suddenly expanding to fill the screen.

'If you're watching this, then it probably means that I'm no longer around.'

The lump in Hannah's throat was cutting off her airway, making it almost impossible to breathe. Not that she cared, when she could hear his sweet voice once again.

The face on the screen looked away from the camera for the briefest of moments and the light flooding in through the window beside him reflected off the shine in his eyes. Then he was staring back into the lens.

'The first thing you should know is how sorry I am that I can't tell you any of this in person. All things being equal I will tell you when we're next together, but I'm making this video in case I don't get that chance. I am so sorry... for everything.'

Hannah felt the familiar splash on her own cheeks, making no effort to wipe the tears away.

'I wish I could tell you how all of this started, but I don't know. All I can tell you is what I found, and what I'm planning to do. If you ever get to watch this video, then it means I failed.'

Wendy paused the recording. 'Are you sure you

wouldn't prefer to watch this alone? It seems a bit personal, and I don't want to intrude.'

Hannah fixed her with a teary stare. 'I can't do this on my own. Please?'

Wendy nodded, but quickly moved to the fridge, pulling out the second bottle and topping up both their glasses. 'If we're going to do this, then I need a stiff drink. It's like… it's like seeing a ghost.'

Hannah didn't want more wine; she didn't want anything that might taint the memory of him talking to her. She couldn't disagree that it was like being messaged from beyond the grave, and although she'd wished for this moment for so long, it wasn't like she'd expected. She tentatively recommenced the video.

'In June, I stumbled across an anomaly in the company's records. Someone – and I'm pretty sure I know who – has been pouring surplus cash into our accounts. From what I've managed to pull together, the monies have been drip-fed into the accounts to hide their source, and I have my suspicions about what the money represents, and if I'm right then… I don't even want to consider the consequences for the company and me as one of its directors.

'I'm recording this video in my office at work, but only because I know I'm alone and nobody knows what I've found. In the file below this recording you will find the evidence that supports my suspicions. I don't want to believe any of it's true, but no matter which angle I look at it from, I can't see any other outcome. I believe Patrick is laundering money through our company accounts.'

Wendy paused the video. 'Hold on, hold on, now he's accusing Patrick? He's clearly made this recording to cover his own back, and shift the blame onto my husband.'

'I think we need to watch the rest; hear what he has to say, before passing judgement,' Hannah said breathlessly. 'I know how you feel: when Patrick told me earlier about what he suspected John had been doing, I didn't want to believe it – I still don't – but I think we should hear both arguments before we determine which brother is telling the truth. Don't you?'

Wendy didn't answer, reaching for her wine, her demeanour noticeably frostier.

Hannah restarted the video.

'In total I have discovered funds in excess of a quarter of a million pounds hidden in the accounts. If this is what I suspect, then it may already be too late for any of us. I've wanted to confront Patrick about it so many times, but whenever I try to book time with him to discuss the accounts, he avoids me, and tells me not to worry. "That's what the accountants are for," he says, but I suspect that he knows I've found something alarming, and he's trying to figure out a way to cover his actions. A couple of months ago, we took the team out for food and drink to celebrate our end of tax year results. Patrick received a phone call, and disappeared for ages. I eventually went looking for him and saw him in a heated discussion with three men I can only describe as looking like extras from some kind of gangster movie. Unsavoury doesn't do them justice. When I asked him who they were, he said they'd stopped him for directions, and acted blasé about it.'

John blinked away his tears. 'I've thought about phoning the police so many times, but he's my brother, and I don't want to drop him in it. I need to get to the bottom of what he's been doing, for whom and why. In the meantime, I have been subtly cleaning our accounts of that money, hiding it away in a shell company, until I can figure a way out of this mess. If the worst has happened, and I'm no longer around, I want you to take this video and my notes in the file to the police. They should be able to unpick what I have done, and find the money in the account details I have left.'

He looked away again, before grabbing the side of

whatever device he had recorded the video on. 'There's something else you should...' He paused and looked off-screen, and then the screen went black.

'Wait, what happened?' Hannah asked, checking to see whether the laptop's battery had died.

Wendy fiddled with the mouse. 'That's where the video ends. He must have been interrupted.'

Hannah pushed herself away from the table, eager to stretch her legs, but not wanting to be too far from the clip of John. 'Play it again. From the start. There has to be more. What else was he trying to say? His last words to me can't be that. He'd want to tell me how much he loved me, and how he was sorry for not confiding any of this in me sooner.'

Wendy wasn't listening, instead, she'd now minimised the video window, and was reading the notes in the rest of the document. 'This is it,' she declared, pointing excitedly. 'This is the missing money. We need to give these account details to Patrick. This will get him out of the trouble John left him in.'

Hannah stopped pacing. '*John left him in?* Didn't you hear what he just said? It was Patrick who was laundering money, *not* the other way around.'

'We only have John's word for that. Patrick said it was John who was at fault – and I'm sorry – but I'm inclined to believe my husband over yours.'

Hannah now wished she hadn't insisted on Wendy staying to watch the clip, but wasn't her reaction natural: to trust the man she loved over all others?

'I think the best thing to do is take this to the police. DI Chandler gave me the name of someone who –'

'Whoa, whoa, whoa,' Wendy said, standing. 'Hang on a minute. Don't do anything hasty. Regardless of whichever of them was responsible for the mess the company is in, this money, *that* account will get those heavies off Patrick's back, and then we can work out a plan to go forward. Why involve the police?'

Hannah couldn't believe what she was hearing. 'Because it was probably this mess that got John killed. The police need to know that. It's possible that Seamus Fahey wasn't responsible for what happened.'

Wendy raised both hands in a passive gesture. 'Tonight has been a shock for the both of us. 'I think the best thing we should do is sleep on it, and make a decision in the morning when we've had some rest and our heads are clearer. It's already quite late, and I'm not sure it's a good idea either of us making plans when we've been drinking.'

Hannah's instinct told her to call Chandler regardless, but she needed to give her subconscious a chance to process this new information. 'Okay, we'll discuss it further in the morning, though if I still feel it's right to phone the police, you won't be able to convince me otherwise.'

Hannah stretched out her hand, so there was no doubt who would be keeping custody of the memory card while they were both in bed. As much as she loved her sister-in-law, something told her not to put too much faith in trusting Wendy.

FORTY-TWO

The room was so dark, almost impossible to see anything. The carpet beneath her felt rough against her body, as she forced herself to crawl forwards, knowing that she couldn't remain where she was. The one thought that kept pushing to the front of her mind: you must get out, you must get out.

Progress was slow. Her muscles ached and her body felt like it was on fire, as if the carpet was made from hot coals. Her head throbbed, and the copper-like taste in her mouth reminded her of the beating she'd taken. Punched, kicked and throttled, her entire body stung.

You must get out.

Up ahead the darkness began to dissipate. Suddenly she could see the pattern of the carpet, though much darker than she remembered it. The tiny bursts of green and blue, like pictorial fireworks blazed on the material closest to her eyes. She threw her arms forward, using them to drag herself onwards: the carpet's frayed cords ripping at her flesh, further increasing the stabbing pain deep in her abdomen.

You must get out.

Her hand touched something sticky and cold, and as she drew her fingers nearer to her face, she wasn't surprised to see the crimson colour of blood on her fingertips. Turning to look behind her sent a sharp jolt through her neck and down through her shoulders, but she had to see; she had to know. The thick trail stretched beyond her feet, like something a giant snail would leave, only so much darker; so much redder; so much bloodier. Her blood.

You must get out.

She wanted to scream, to tell the world how angry she was at what had happened to her, but her mouth refused to obey, leaving her screaming internally, but silently.

You must get out.

She could now see that the light on the carpet was coming through the pane of frosted glass in the front door. It was night outside, but the street lights were casting an orange glow through the glass and onto the carpet. The door had to be at least three metres away. If she could only stand, force herself to her feet, she would close the distance in no time, but her legs couldn't take the weight; too badly bent out of shape.

You must get out.

She couldn't recall the beating or the minutes that had led to it, but she could remember the pain, and the sheer terror that death was close at hand. That terror hadn't left, and only the thought of making it to the front door, and out into the forgiving shower of rain was what drove her to continue moving.

You must get out.

She heard the certain thud, thud, thud of heavy footsteps moving about somewhere in the distance? Upstairs? She couldn't be sure, but definitely close by. Filling her lungs, she urged herself forwards, no longer caring how much noise she made as she groaned and roared, digging her nails into the carpet for extra grip.

You must get out.

The heavy footsteps sounded so close now. If he caught up with her he was sure to finish the job. She just needed to make it to the door. Through that door was redemption and freedom. Remaining inside meant pain and death.

You must get out.

She felt the stare upon her, burning through the skin in her forehead. Craning her neck as far as the pain would allow her – almost passing out with the exertion – she strained to see the eyes of the figure behind the window in the lounge, off to her right. Tall and dark, his shadow loomed beyond the glass, which was cloaked in condensation. His grey hair covering the top half of his face, she instantly recognised Seamus Fahey's whiskered chin, as he continued to watch.

You must get out.

Suddenly she felt hands reaching for her legs and body, dragging her back the way she'd come; through the trail of warm, sticky blood; away from the light and freedom of the front door; back into the shadows.

Hannah woke screaming, sitting bolt upright in bed, uncertain where she was, or who it was trying to grapple with her.

'Let me go, leave me alone,' she yelled, batting away the grasping fingers, the only light coming from the open doorway of the unfamiliar room.

'Hannah, Hannah,' Wendy was shouting. 'You're okay. It was just a dream.'

Hannah continued to bat at the hands, until she allowed her eyes to focus on the terrified face of her sister-in-law, dressed in a nightgown. Without a word, she pulled Wendy into an embrace, relieved, as her mind began to process the reality of the situation.

She was safe. She was at Wendy's. She was no longer back in *that* house.

'You were screaming,' Wendy explained. 'You woke us all up.'

Hannah dared to look towards the open door, the landing

light switched on and two sets of worried young eyes staring in from behind the safety of the doorframe.

'Were you having a nightmare? Can you remember what it was about?' Wendy pushed gently.

Even as she said the words, the memory of the dream was already disappearing into nothing like sand in an hourglass.

Hannah shook her head. 'I just remember feeling so scared.'

Wendy turned and looked at her children's faces. 'It's okay, boys. Your Auntie Hannah is better now. Just a bad dream, like you sometimes have. Go and get yourselves into bed, and I'll come and tuck you in, in a minute.'

Hannah mouthed the word 'Sorry,' in their direction, but wasn't sure either had seen it.

Wendy turned back to her, a hand on each shoulder, and staring into her eyes. 'Are you sure you're okay? Do you want me to sit up with you for a bit? Wait until you drop off again?'

Hannah resisted the sting in her eyes threatening to break free. 'I'll be fine. I'm so sorry I woke you up. It seemed so real again, and... I'm sorry.'

'I have some pills the doctor gave me to help with my insomnia. I'm sure it wouldn't hurt if you took one. Might help settle your nerves.'

'Thanks, but I don't think that's such a great idea. I'll be okay.'

Wendy continued to watch her for a moment, before relenting with a sigh, and standing. 'Okay, well if you change your mind the pills are on the top shelf in the bathroom cupboard. The label says to take two, but I find one usually does the trick. If you need anything else, you know where I am.'

As soon as the door was closed, the room plunged back into darkness. Hannah heard the rattle of Barney's collar, and a moment later he was at the side of the bed, his big, wet nose, pressing against her hand, checking she was okay.

'Do you want to come up and keep me company?' she whispered.

Barney hopped up onto the duvet and settled in next to her. Usually she would search for something to distract her from the flashes of nightmare, but with no television in the room, she was left to dwell on the remaining fragments, unable to forget the image of Fahey outside the window looking in.

FORTY-THREE

Wendy and the children were already up and eating breakfast in the kitchen as Hannah entered, feeling every hour that she'd remained awake until the first signs of dawn had crept beneath the curtains.

James bounded over and threw his arms around her legs and bottom. 'Auntie Hannah, you're still here.'

Fighting back the pain and confusion of the nightmare, she put on her most effervescent smile and stooped down for a proper hug. 'Yes, I'm still here. I couldn't go without saying goodbye to my favourite nephews and niece.'

Daisy squealed something unintelligible from her high chair, a bowl of porridge on the tray in front of her, and a porridge-covered spoon precariously hanging from her fingers. It seemed half her breakfast was on her cheeks rather than swallowed.

Wendy was over by the counter, moving backwards and forwards, grabbing a knife from the cutlery drawer, then a plate from the cupboard on the other side of the room, then back to the fridge for cheese, and back across to the bread bin. She had yet to acknowledge Hannah's arrival in the kitchen, but looked too flustered to interrupt as she prepared the boys' lunches.

'How is Ben this morning?' Hannah asked the eldest of the children, who was scowling sullenly at the cereal box in his hand, while he held a spoon in the other.

'Don't feel well,' he said, without looking up.

In fairness he did look peaky.

'Oh dear,' Hannah said, straightening and moving across to him. 'What's the matter?'

'Feel sick, but Mum says I have to go to school anyway.'

Hannah dared to look over to Wendy who was now still and staring up at the ceiling, counting silently to alleviate her stress.

'Well, I'm sure your mum knows best,' Hannah said, not daring to interfere.

There was no sign of a tea pot on the table, or any unused cups, so Hannah moved across to the kettle and filled it from the tap.

'Do you want a cuppa?' she asked, leaning closer to Wendy.

'Please,' Wendy said, not looking up, once again focused on making the sandwiches.

'Will you be here when we get back from school?' James asked.

Hannah had no idea what the day would bring, or whether her chosen course of action would warrant her a welcome back to the house that evening. 'We'll have to see,' she said. 'I do need to get back to my home before people start worrying about me.'

She was conscious that she hadn't spoken to Bea since the car journey yesterday afternoon, but without her mobile she didn't know what Bea's telephone number was.

'Would you mind if I borrowed your laptop again?' Hannah said to Wendy. 'I just want to message my neighbour on Facebook. Let her know I'm safe.'

'Sure, it's over there,' Wendy said, nodding to the countertop behind her.

Hannah picked up the device and carried it over to the table, lifting the lid and switching it on.

'You have to stay,' James said, as Barney trotted in, keen to investigate what breakfast scraps might come his way.

'We love having Barney here, you can't take him away so soon.'

There it was: the real reason James wanted her to stay, and probably the same reason Ben was hoping to stay home sick.

'Right kids,' Wendy said, turning, and clapping her hands together. 'Shoes on and teeth cleaned please. We're leaving for school in five minutes.'

Ben's chair scraped back, and James gave Barney a loving cuddle, before both boys trudged off, their footsteps hurrying up the stairs to the bathroom.

'What about your tea?' Hannah asked, as Wendy wrapped the sandwiches.

'Don't worry about it. I'll have it when I get back.'

Hannah watched as Wendy effortlessly wiped Daisy mouth, before lifting her out and strapping her into the pushchair waiting in the hallway. The laptop finished loading as the front door closed, leaving Hannah and Barney alone in the kitchen. Opening an internet page, Hannah logged into Facebook, and searched for the message portal Bea had shown her the other day.

A message window immediately popped up.

> ***From: Lucy_Davison***
> *Hi Hannah, I understand why you might be ignoring me, and I don't blame you for what happened. I really do think it would be good if we spoke in person. You deserve to know the real reason that we drifted apart. I'm home all day. Please get in touch.*
> *Lucy xxx*

Hannah frowned at the message. What did she mean by *the real reason that we drifted apart*?

It certainly hadn't been an intentional separation as far as Hannah was concerned. Their priorities had changed and their paths had taken them in different directions. It happened all the time.

I don't blame you for what happened.

What did that mean? Why did Lucy think Hannah was to blame for their drifting apart?

The window minimised as a box appeared in the bottom corner of the screen, advising that Bea was calling. Accepting the call, the laptop's screen suddenly filled with Bea's face, the reading glasses precariously perched on her neighbour's nose.

'Oh thank God!' Bea declared. 'You're alive.'

Hannah wasn't surprised by Bea's overly-dramatic statement. 'Hi Bea, yes, I'm alive. How are you?'

'Relieved to speak to you. I tried phoning your mobile but it says the line's been disconnected. I was fearing the worst.'

'It was stolen,' Hannah explained, 'so the mobile company has cancelled the number and is sending me a replacement. I was going to ask if you'd look out for it for me, as they said it should arrive today or tomorrow.'

Bea smiled. 'Happy to. Thank God I created that Facebook profile for you, or I'd still be thinking Nigel had done you in too.'

'We don't know for certain that he had anything to do with Melanie's disappearance. Did you manage to find out any more about that ex-boyfriend of hers?'

'I spoke to Chris, but he doesn't remember anyone called Billy at school being close to Melanie, so he must have been someone she met later. I could try asking that detective again, but I doubt he'd tell me Billy's surname.'

'How is Chris? Did he mention our run-in from Sunday night?'

'I asked him about it, but he said it hadn't bothered him.

He still fancies you, and I got the impression he was going to ask you out again.' Bea paused. 'I know you said the age gap worried you, but I don't think you should let it. There's no harm in going out for a bite to eat and giving him a chance to show you what he's really like. I'm not saying you have to start dating him, but just give him a chance.'

Hannah could feel her cheeks reddening, and hoped it wouldn't be noticeable to Bea on the video. 'I'll think about it.'

'He's sent you a friend request on Facebook. Have you accepted it yet?'

Hannah could see the red indicator over the friend icon, and clicked it, seeing a link to Chris's profile, and confirmed the request. 'Done'

'He will be pleased. Have you befriended the dog tutor yet?'

'I'm not sure how, or whether he'd be on here, or whether he's even speaking to me since I dashed out on him on Sunday night. Probably thinks I'm a nutcase.'

'Don't be daft. Anyone who's anyone has Facebook, especially if he owns his own business. Just type his name in the search box and when you find the image that looks like him, click on it.'

Hannah did as instructed, and more than a dozen Steve Williams appeared on the screen, but she recognised the chin dimple sixth on the list. The cursor hovered over the 'Add friend' button. 'Maybe I should message him first and just explain why I ran off.'

'Just add him, and worry about the rest later. What are you so afraid of?'

Hannah clicked the button, nervous energy filling her gut. 'There, done. I hope you're happy now.'

'Ecstatic. I've made it my mission to get you back out and socialising, and then when you've met someone you like, he can introduce me to his even more handsome friends, and we'll both be sorted.'

Hannah caught a glimpse of herself smiling on the screen, and instantly wiped it away. 'Have you noticed anyone strange going up to my apartment or acting suspiciously while I've been away?'

Bea thought for a moment. 'No, and I believe Nigel might be away too, that's why I was panicking that he might have taken *you*. His car's not been back in his usual space, and I'm sure I didn't hear anyone come into the block after me last night. Do you know when you're coming back yet?'

'I'm not sure. Got some family stuff to sort out up here first. Maybe tomorrow, maybe Thursday.'

'Will you do me a favour then? Send me a message through Facebook tonight, just so I know that you're safe. I'll reply so you know I'm okay too.'

'Agreed,' Hannah nodded, and ended the call, closing the lid of the laptop and tilting her head towards Barney. 'I suppose I should get dressed and take you for a walk, shouldn't I?'

Barney chased his tail in agreement.

The pavement was covered in moist, brown leaves, fallen from nearby trees. Autumn was definitely here, though the temperature felt mild and pleasant this morning. The ground under foot was wet from the heavy rain overnight, but the sky was reasonably clear.

Barney made a beeline for every tree, bush and lamppost, sniffing and cocking his leg whenever time allowed. She was glad she'd brought him with her on the trip. Especially after last night's traumatic dream. He hadn't minded her clinging to him for warmth and comfort, though she was certain she would live to regret allowing him to spend the rest of the night on the bed with her. The last thing she wanted was to encourage bad habits.

Thirty minutes after leaving the house, she found herself back at the front door, and it was only now that she even thought about how she would go about getting back in. She hadn't asked Wendy for a spare key, and there was no telling when she would return from school, but the sound of her voice on the phone growing louder, indicated she was returning too.

A moment later, Daisy's pram appeared on the driveway, with Wendy behind it. She quickly ended her call, and threw her keys in Hannah's direction. 'Sorry,' she said, 'I totally forgot to give you a spare key.'

'Not your fault,' Hannah replied, opening the door for them all.

Wendy pushed the pram in, extracting Daisy and placing her in the pen in the lounge, before joining Hannah in the kitchen. 'Before we discuss what we found on the memory stick, can you tell me the truth? How many of those nightmares have you been having?'

Heat rose to Hannah's cheeks again. 'What do you mean?'

Wendy sighed, her full attention on Hannah now. 'I didn't want to say anything when you turned up yesterday, but you looked tired, even more so now. I never asked how you're coping with the anniversary looming tomorrow. It can't be easy.'

'I'm fine,' Hannah said, but even she wasn't convinced by the lie.

'Hannah, I don't want to be rude, but I'd say you're not coping well at all, certainly if last night was anything to go by. You were shouting and screaming when I came in. Loud enough to wake the boys, and our James is usually a heavy sleeper. Are you going to tell me what the nightmare was about?'

Hannah didn't want to admit that she hadn't been

coping, but she'd been lying to herself for too long. Leaning into the counter for support, she let out a pained sigh. 'It's not the first nightmare I've had in the last few weeks. In fact, they're a daily occurrence at the moment.'

'Is it always the same dream?'

Hannah shook her head. 'No, but variations on a theme. I'm in all of them, and most seem to start or end in our old house on that night. I don't know whether some of it is flashes of the memories I can't access or stuff my imagination has created to fill in the blanks. I'm usually helpless to prevent whatever is happening, and I nearly always wake screaming.'

Wendy's pale face suggested she hadn't expected that answer. 'I'm so sorry, that sounds horrific. Are you still seeing that psychiatrist? What was her name again…?'

'Dr Yenny. No, I've spoken to her a couple of times since I bought the loft, but only because she was checking up on me and encouraging me to make an appointment with a more local counsellor in Southampton. I went to an on-call GP on Sunday, but he couldn't give me anything and until the new GP receives my medical notes, I'm a bit stuck.'

'Is there anything else troubling you, or just the nightmares?'

Hannah shook her head again. 'You're going to think I'm cracking up, but a few times now I've thought I've seen John when I'm out and about. I see him as clear as I can see you now. At the market, at work; I'm sure it's just my mind playing tricks on me, but for those tiny moments it's like what happened last year wasn't real, and that he's still alive out there somewhere. Stupid, right?'

Wendy moved across and placed a supportive arm around Hannah's shoulders. 'Not at all. You're a woman still grieving for the man she loved. There's nothing stupid about that. I saw your reaction when his face appeared on the laptop last night. It's okay to admit you need help.'

'About that…' Hannah began, nervous to broach the subject. 'I spent a long time thinking about it last night, and… I still think the best thing to do is speak to the police.'

Wendy's eyes widened, and she opened her mouth to speak, but Hannah cut her off.

'I didn't mention it last night, because Patrick asked me not to, but the men who are threatening him had a picture of you and the children. They've made it clear that they will come after all of you if they don't get their money.'

'All the more reason to give the memory stick to Patrick, so he can pay them off.'

'No, Wendy! If John was right then it was Patrick who put the company and your lives at risk; I don't trust him to put it right.'

'It's John's word against Patrick's though. What if you're wrong about John? Have you considered that? What if John was the one responsible and then hid the money but made the video to frame Patrick? You give that confession to the police and they'll have Patrick bound and in cuffs before the sun sets tonight. You'd be sending an innocent man to prison when all he wants to do is protect his family. Protect *us*.'

Hannah knew it wouldn't be easy to convince Wendy, but her mind was already made up. 'For all we know, these men have already acted. We don't know that they aren't the reason John died that night.'

Wendy forehead crumpled into a frown. 'What?'

'Think about it. John made that clip only hours before we were attacked and he was killed. Coincidence?'

'What about the guy they charged? His DNA was all over your house.'

'I'm not certain he's guilty.' Hannah pulled a face, disgusted with herself for even considering it. 'I thought he was because of what the police told me last year, but now…

I saw him yesterday, and he isn't the monster I expected to see. He has no memory of being at the house, and what if someone framed him to take the blame?'

Wendy was cringing. 'Hannah, you're under a huge amount of stress; you've admitted that this morning. How can you be sure you're thinking straight now? I understand why you want to believe John was innocent in all of this, but just consider for a moment that he might not be. Please, let's invite Patrick over here and talk about what we found. If we sense he's not telling the truth then I'll phone the police myself.'

Hannah shook her head, as a thought she'd been trying to ignore popped to the front of her mind: what if it was Patrick who had killed John?

She shook her head to clear the thought from her mind. He couldn't have; he wouldn't. Yet, what if he'd realised John had moved the money, or he'd overheard John making the video? Maybe he'd come round to have it out with John and things had turned nasty.

'No,' Hannah said, for her sake, as much as Wendy's. 'My mind is made up. I will speak to DI Chandler and explain the situation. She's a straight arrow and won't take liberties. We can trust her.'

Wendy's eyes were watering, but she remained composed. 'So be it, but for your own sake I think you should make an appointment with that counsellor today. It isn't healthy to be having all these nightmares. Hold off calling the police until you've spoken to her or another counsellor. Please? Once you've spoken to your Dr Yenny, I'll go with you to the police station and we can tell them everything. Okay?'

Wendy handed Hannah the landline, and she reluctantly dialled Dr Yenny's number from memory.

FORTY-FOUR

Dr Yenny smiled pleasantly as Hannah entered the small office. 'You're lucky I was only planning to complete paperwork this morning, so I could squeeze you in. How have you been?'

Hannah made her way to the straight-backed chair and perched, but before she could get the words out, she felt the tears pooling in her eyes. 'Not good.'

Dr Yenny handed her a box of tissues, while simultaneously picking up her notepad and recorder. 'Are you happy for me to record the session? It helps with tidying up my notes afterwards. I know I ask every time, but legally I'm required to do so.'

Hannah dabbed her eyes with one of the tissues. 'It's fine.'

Dr Yenny frowned empathetically. 'I have to admit, I wasn't that surprised to receive your call this morning. After our video call last week, I sensed things weren't quite as rosy as you were making out. Sorry, you have to get up pretty early to pull the wool over my eyes.'

'I thought I was doing okay,' Hannah said, trying to choke down the sobs. 'I love my new home, and I secured new employment, and even made some new friends… but now I think I was just trying to mask what was really going on.'

Dr Yenny crossed her legs, leaning back in her chair. 'What's really going on?'

Hannah wasn't even sure where to begin, but started with the events leading up to the apparitions of John, before relaying the nightmares she'd been experiencing. Dr Yenny listened intently, only interrupting to clarify what had been said, and frantically scribbling the answers in her notebook.

'I was determined to battle through, and avoid going down the medication route, but I think it's all getting to be too much. To make matters worse, there's now an issue with my brother-in-law and financial difficulties in his company. Oh and one of my neighbours might be a crazy psychopathic killer. I really don't know where to turn.'

Dr Yenny's eyes widened, causing Hannah to laugh through the tears.

'He isn't really a psychopath,' Hannah clarified, 'at least I don't think he is, but one of my neighbours is convinced he had something to do with the disappearance of someone that used to live in my apartment.'

'It certainly sounds like you have a lot on your plate, and we may not have time to cover everything, but I would like to dig a little further into these visions of John's face you mentioned. Was it just the three occasions?'

Hannah nodded. 'He's appeared a couple of times in the nightmares too, but I put that down to my grief.'

Dr Yenny nodded. 'Yes, it probably is a symptom of your grief, but I wonder if it goes deeper than that. In the months when you were seeing me after what happened to John that night, we never really discussed your life prior to what happened. I don't want to wash over that clearly traumatic experience, but I wonder whether these apparitions – or whatever you want to call them – are the result of something more deep-rooted.'

Hannah blew her nose, disposing of the tissue in the waste paper bin beside her chair, and reaching for another. 'I'm not sure what you're asking.'

'Would you mind telling me a bit more about John?

What were his likes and dislikes? What first attracted you to him? Was he a considerate lover? Did you argue much?'

The flurry of questions made Hannah's head spin. 'I don't see what that has to do with –'

'Humour me. How did the two of you meet?'

'It was just after I'd graduated. We both wound up at the same party, playing truth or dare. His mate knew he fancied me and dared me to kiss him. I did, and then he spent three weeks begging me to go on a date with him. I thought he was cute, but wasn't looking to settle down with anyone. I eventually relented, and said yes just to stop him asking.' Hannah smiled at the memory. 'I'd thought he would take me for the standard first date – dinner or cinema – but instead he took me to a cookery class at a local college. He told me he wanted to learn to cook what I liked, so he could cook for me every night. It was such a cheesy line, but we ended up having fun. I would never have believed cookery could be so competitive, but he bet me that the teacher would prefer his version of the honey chicken over mine. I wasn't much of a cook back then, but the recipe was quite straight forward. Even so, John managed to mess it up but I could see he was trying so hard…' Her words trailed off as she focused on the memory.

'Who won?'

'Oh, I did, of course. His meal wasn't even edible.'

'You agreed to go out with him again?'

'Not at first. He asked once more, and when I said I was happy being single for a bit, he stopped messaging me. Then about six months later he turned up at my house, his hands full with two bags of shopping. He said he'd been to every weekly cookery class since, and now had twenty-odd recipes he could make, and had bought everything he needed to make any of them. I don't know why I invited him in, but there was this eagerness to impress that I lapped up. He recited a list of the recipes, and I challenged him to make three of them at the same time, just because I thought it would be a hoot to watch. He managed all three and I was surprised at how well he did. I figured after that much effort I should give him a chance.'

'So you enjoyed being pursued?'

Hannah frowned at the question. 'I wouldn't say that. I liked that he managed to surprise me on both occasions.'

'How long were you married?'

'It would have been our tenth wedding anniversary this year.'

'Did he continue to surprise you after you were married?'

'Occasionally, but I think we became accustomed to each other. I loved him very much.'

'I don't doubt that. Did you argue much?'

Hannah didn't like the directness of the question. 'No more than any other couple. Do you argue much with your wife?' Hannah instantly regretted the blunt come-back.

Dr Yenny wasn't the least bit offended. 'All the time! She drives me nuts sometimes, but I know she loves me.'

'I know that John loved me.'

'Good. That's important.'

'So why ask that question? What does arguing have to do with me seeing his face when he's not there?'

Dr Yenny uncrossed her legs and re-crossed them the opposite way around. 'Often, seeing a deceased partner's face in unfamiliar surroundings can be a sign of unresolved trauma. In your case there's reason to assume it's as a result of the way John died, but it's also possible that your unresolved trauma could be related to your relationship prior to that night. You mentioned meeting new friends earlier. Are any of those friends someone you might be attracted to?'

Hannah pictured Steve and Chris, and the feelings of guilt when she'd thought about betraying John's memory.

'There is a guy who… he's just a friend, if that.'

'I bet when you made your wedding vows, you meant them for life though, didn't you? Maybe the fact that you're trying to mentally adjust to the prospect of essentially breaking those vows is what is causing you to see visions from the past. You're still grieving and beating yourself up for allowing that prospect to enter your thoughts. It's perfectly natural, and something that many widows and widowers experience.'

'And the nightmares?'

'Exist because you still don't have closure for *that* night. If you knew exactly what had happened, *how* John was killed, then you'd probably find the dreams stop.'

'How do I get that closure? I've tried meditating, I've tried hypnosis, medication, and none of it has worked.'

Dr Yenny checked her watch. 'I'm so sorry, but I do have a referral call to make in a few minutes. Are you sticking around in Manchester for a few days? I'd really like to follow-up with you on this. I think we've made a bit of progress, and I'd prefer to do it myself. If not, then can we arrange a regular time to meet via video call?'

Hannah said she would call later when she knew what her plans were. Heading down the stairs to the ground floor, she froze when she spotted Patrick outside, leaning against the bonnet of her car.

FORTY-FIVE

Pushing open the large glass door of the building, the sudden bitter wind caught Hannah off-guard, and in that moment's hesitation, she realised Patrick wasn't alone. The lead strained as Barney spotted his owner, and he pulled to get closer. Patrick wrapped the end of the lead tightly around his hand, but remained leaning against the bonnet.

'You know why I'm here,' he called out across the car park, apparently unconcerned about anyone that might overhear. 'Wendy called and told me about the memory card.'

So Wendy definitely had gone behind her back and consorted with her husband, what else had she worked with him on? Had her lack of awareness about the re-mortgage been just another lie? Had they been playing her from the start? Hannah hoped not, because if they had then Wendy was a better liar than Hannah had ever given her credit for.

'I just want the money,' Patrick called out again, yanking Barney closer to him. 'There's no reason this needs to end badly for anyone.'

The threat was against Barney, even if he didn't actually say the words. The poor creature, looked tense as he continued to be restrained. Maybe he could sense her anxiety, and was reflecting it in those sad, brown eyes.

Hannah continued across the car park, but left a five metre distance between them. She didn't want to believe that Patrick was the man who killed John and left her bruised and bloody, but his actions now weren't providing any reassurance. Why would he have brought Barney with him if not to threaten her?

'It was you, wasn't it?' Hannah shouted, louder than was necessary in the hope that Dr Yenny's receptionist or some stranger nearby would hear and realise she was in trouble. 'You were the one who laundered that money through the company. It wasn't John.'

Patrick considered the statement, before a sick grimace broke out across his swollen face. 'You're right, of course. I wasn't sure I'd convinced you yesterday, and then when Wendy told me what the two of you had discussed, I figured I should just come clean with you. All the rest was true though. They did threaten Wendy and the kids, and they will kill me if I don't return their money. That's why you need to help me.'

'They're criminals, Patrick! How could you get yourself wrapped up in something so... so reckless?'

He lowered his voice, but it was still loud enough to carry across the gap between them. 'What can I say? The bank was dragging its heels on approving our loan to buy the second office building. John said it was fate's way of telling us to hold back, or consider renting instead. He didn't have the same level of ambition or foresight as me. I knew – and I still maintain – that had we gone ahead and set up the second premises, the two of us would be bankrolling close to half a million each this year, post-tax. So I looked to find the money by other means. I was doing what I thought was right for the company, and for us. That money was supposed to be used to branch out, but I couldn't drop it straight into our accounts as I knew John would question where it had come from, so I was slowly depositing a bit here, and a bit there, until I could convince him we didn't need the bank's loan.'

Hannah pushed the hair from her face, as the cold wind

blew it loose of the pony tail. 'He did find it though. I watched his video message, and he said he didn't trust you, and I can understand why. Did you really think you'd get away with it?'

'I would have done, had he not interfered. I had no idea he'd even found the money until I spoke with the accountant this year. John never spoke to me about the money or his suspicions, and allowed me to blindly forge forwards, knowing something like this could happen.'

Hannah casually glanced around the near-vacant car park. Nobody else had arrived for an appointment, nor exited the building. She was on her own, and wishing more than ever that she'd just phoned DI Chandler last night when she'd first seen the video. It had been Wendy who had convinced her otherwise, and all along had been hatching this plan to set Patrick on to her.

'I know this must have come as a shock to you,' Patrick continued, 'and believe me when I say I never wanted to involve you, but it was John's actions that dragged you into it. There's no reason for anyone else to get hurt.' He paused and rubbed at his bruised and grazed cheek. 'I've learned my lesson, and I just want to reset the balance by returning what's owed to them. The business can survive – *will* survive – I just need to get these thugs off my back. I need your help, Hannah. We're family after all.'

Hannah choked down the urge to vomit at the word *family*. 'You don't know the meaning of the word,' she spat. 'Family means putting your loved ones first, not going after the quick money. It's about loving and supporting one another. I lost my family the night John died –'

Patrick's bitter laughter cut her off mid-sentence. 'Such a hero, our John, wasn't he? Such a kind and loving man; butter wouldn't melt, and all that. You have *no idea* what he was really like! I've allowed you to mourn him this last year for your own sake, but if you knew the truth, you wouldn't want anything to do with him.'

The tears stung her eyes as the wind continued to blow. 'Don't you speak that way about John! He was ten times the man you are!'

'Oh yeah? Then how do you explain Katrina?'

The picture of John in their room with the woman in a crimson dress filled her mind. 'Who?'

Patrick was grinning maniacally now, almost laughing at her. 'If John was such a fucking hero, how come he was banging another woman – younger than you – in the six months before he died?'

She felt winded by the sucker-punch. 'You're lying,' she shouted, but didn't believe herself.

The grin remained on Patrick's face. 'You really don't know, do you? I was convinced you'd find out. Maybe discover a receipt for a hotel in one of his pockets, or question the number of *business trips* he took last year. I was even convinced that he might have told you, and you being the wet blanket you are, decided to give him another chance. That would be so typical of the two of you. He fucks up, and you simply turn the other cheek, like Mr and Mrs Proper.'

Now the thought of the arguments they'd had about the number of business trips he was taking filled her mind. At one point they'd been almost weekly, and only ever away for one night, two at most. He'd said it was because they were trying to expand the business into Europe, and she'd believed him every time. Had there been other signs in those last six months?

'I don't believe you,' she proudly declared. 'John loved me.'

'Ha! He was planning on separating from you. He'd even discussed divorce proceedings with our solicitors. Phone them if you don't believe me. His dying was the best thing that could have happened to you, because if he hadn't the two of you would now be divorced, and you wouldn't be living off his life insurance money.'

She tore forwards, no longer caring about her own safety, and wanting to lash out at him. Her sudden surge caught him off balance, and as she began to slap and punch at his arms, it took him a moment to regain his composure, and put up hands and arms to protect himself. He dropped the lead, and Barney raced away, stopping after a few metres and turning to see whether he could help his owner, but she was already short of breath, and rapidly retreating.

'You killed him,' she yelled, breathlessly.

'What? No. I couldn't.'

'You found out he'd taken the money, and then you went after him, and when he wouldn't give it back, you stabbed him.'

Patrick took two large strides forwards. 'You've got it wrong. He was my brother, there's no way I could... do something like that.'

Chandler's words suddenly echoed through her mind: *we're all capable of doing more than we can imagine if we find ourselves in the wrong situation.*

'I don't believe you, and I'm going to tell the police as much. You came to the house wanting to have it out with him, but didn't expect to find me there? Then the two of you went upstairs so you could argue out of sight, but something went wrong, you overreacted and John ended up stabbed. You wanted to cover your tracks, so you pushed me down the stairs.'

The grin was gone, wiped clean by the look of disgust clawing at his features. 'No! Absolutely not! I wasn't anywhere near your house that night. The police checked my alibi. I was with a client on the other side of town.'

'Convenient! The moment your brother was murdered, and you were across the city. It couldn't possibly have been you, but that doesn't mean you didn't pay someone to do it, or maybe sent your thuggish new friends to do it. Is that what happened? They came demanding their money back, and you sent them after the man who'd hidden it from you? That still makes you just as guilty in my book.'

'You're out of your fucking mind! Listen to me carefully, because this is the first and last time I'm going to say this: I had *nothing* to do with John's murder. I loved my brother, and wouldn't be able to live with myself if I'd done something like that. I'm sorry he's dead, and even more so as I wouldn't be in this fucking mess if he was still around.'

He suddenly took two more strides forwards. 'Now give me that SD card and then you never have to see me again.'

Hannah didn't think twice, turning and racing towards the large glass door of Dr Yenny's building, calling Barney to her side. By the time Patrick reacted, it was too late, and she was behind the door, and moving over to the safety of the reception desk and the woman behind it.

Patrick looked on, glaring at them through the window, until he saw the receptionist raise the telephone to her ear, and at that point he moved away, but something told Hannah that wouldn't be the last time he came after her.

FORTY-SIX

Staring down at the memory card in the palm of her hand, Hannah couldn't believe how something so small could be so damaging. Hand it to Patrick and she'd be supporting his illegal activities. Hand it to the police, and she would not only be condemning him to potential prosecution, but would also be signing death warrants for Wendy and the children.

How had life become so complicated in such a short space of time?

She'd always been a firm believer that everything happened for a reason, though she'd been unable to justify such an optimistic outlook since John's death. She'd never been able to make sense of why they'd been attacked that night, as it served no greater purpose. To learn that it may all have been driven by John's discovery, as detailed within the memory card, didn't bring any additional comfort, even if it did explain why he'd died.

Hannah had been sitting in the waiting room for fifteen minutes, and she'd seen no sign of Patrick returning. The receptionist had been sending furtive glances every couple of minutes, but had yet to pluck up the courage to question what Hannah was waiting for, or why she now had a dog with her. Poor Barney was lying on the carpet tiles, head resting on his paws, waiting patiently for her to forge a plan of action.

What would John do? The fact that he'd taken the money out of the company and hidden it from Patrick suggested he wouldn't be in favour of her handing the memory card and advantage back to Patrick. But then neither had he consulted the police. Doing nothing wasn't an option either as Wendy and the children's lives were at stake.

She shuddered as Patrick's voice filled her mind: *how come he was banging another woman?*

Was it really possible that John had been having an affair in the six months prior to his death? She'd had her doubts about their marriage before, though no more than any other wife terrified that something would burst the idyllic bubble of life. That didn't mean he was capable of the deceit and planning to keep it from her.

She didn't know anybody called Katrina, so who was she, and how did Patrick know about her? The thought of John lusting after someone else made her want to retch. That he hadn't only been attracted to another woman, but had also acted upon those feelings, was heart-breaking. The man who she'd held on a pedestal for the last 12 months was suddenly rapidly falling.

What if Patrick was right? What if involving the police resulted in something happening to Wendy or the kids? As much as she felt betrayed by Wendy's actions this morning, Hannah couldn't bear the thought of anything harming Ben, James or Daisy. It wasn't their fault that life had become so complicated.

Hannah stood, picking up Barney's lead and began to pace just inside the large glass doors. Call the police, or call Patrick. It was as simple as that. If she gave Chandler the memory card and told her of the threat to Wendy and the children, couldn't the police put them in some kind of protective custody? Wasn't that the best option?

Switching on the Nokia without breaking stride, she tried Chandler's number. When it went to answerphone, she left a brief message asking Chandler to call her back urgently.

With the receptionist still firing furtive glances her way,

Hannah pushed open the large glass door, Barney trotting obediently beside her. There was no sign of Patrick's car in the car park, nor could she see him lurking behind any nearby buildings. Reaching her car, she opened the driver's door and helped Barney into the passenger seat, securing his harness to the seatbelt, closing and locking the door behind her.

She remained still, scanning the horizon for any sign of Patrick's car, but it didn't reappear. Maybe he'd got the message. Burying her face in her hands she took several deep breaths to compose herself. The stench of Patrick's aftershave on her hands transported her back to the hotel room last night. The man who'd been waiting in her room and had stolen her bag and tablet had been wearing the same cologne.

Her heart skipped a beat as the thought developed. He'd known about the Nokia phone, and she'd been naïve enough to tell him where she was staying. Had he been that desperate that he'd gone there and broken in?

She felt like such a fool. Of course it had been him. Had the Nokia not been safely stashed in the glove box she might never have seen John's video. She felt sick to the stomach, yet his words still continued to reverberate around her head: *how come he was banging another woman?*

Without a beat, another voice clamoured to be heard: *you deserve to know the real reason that we drifted apart.*

Had Lucy Davison known about John's affair? Was that the reason she'd reached out after his death?

There was only one way to find out. Starting the engine, Hannah headed for Lucy's house.

FORTY-SEVEN

Staring at the large oak door, Hannah closed her eyes and steadied her breathing. It wasn't too late to turn around and sneak away without Lucy being aware that Hannah had even stopped by. Opening her eyes again, she jabbed the doorbell; she'd buried her head in the sand for too long. If she was ever going to find the closure that Dr Yenny championed, Hannah would have to face her demons head on.

Lucy looked exactly how Hannah remembered her: hair held up by two chopsticks, a face clean of makeup – Lucy had always had such perfect skin – and the sleeveless vest hanging from her shoulder.

'Hannah? Oh my God, I can't believe you're here,' Lucy exclaimed, pulling Hannah closer and then into a tight squeeze. 'You look so well.'

Hannah broke free of the embrace, and offered what she thought was a grateful nod, but concern instantly tautened Lucy's cheeks.

'Gosh, Hannah, what's wrong?'

Hannah nodded towards Barney, patiently sitting by her feet. 'Should we go somewhere to chat? I don't want to leave him in the car.'

Lucy looked down at Barney and her concern was instantly replaced by joy. Placing both hands either side of Barney's face, Lucy made a fuss of him. 'Don't be silly, he's more than welcome to come in. I think the cats are out, so he should be safe. This is a pet friendly home. Come in, come in.'

It had been two or three years since Hannah had last stepped over this threshold, and it felt strangely odd to be doing so now. She was certain the hallway was a different colour to what she remembered, but the interior was bright and breezy, opening into a large lounge, beyond it, doorways to a kitchen, dining room and conservatory at the side of the property, into which Lucy beckoned her.

'You'll have to forgive the state of the place,' Lucy cooed, collecting a cushion from the floor and throwing it onto one of two wicker settees. 'If I'd realised you were coming over I'd have tidied up.'

Despite the comment, the house looked immaculate, the sort of place that would feature in a glossy haberdashery magazine.

'Before I sit, would you like something to drink? I've got fresh lemonade, or I can make you a tea or coffee?'

'Lemonade would be lovely, thank you,' Hannah said, perching on the wicker settee nearest her.

Lucy returned a moment later carrying a tray with two tall glasses and a jug. Resting the tray on a large trunk in the corner of the room, she filled both glasses, and handed one to Hannah.

'I still can't believe you're here,' Lucy said. 'It feels like a dream.'

Hannah sipped the lemonade, enjoying the sharp sweetness as she swallowed. 'You said in your message that there was something you wanted to talk to me about.'

Lucy's demeanour changed as she recalled the flurry of Facebook messages, and she joined Hannah on the settee. 'It's hard to know where to begin. How have things been since… since John passed?'

Blinking tears away, Hannah focused on her breathing. 'Hardest year of my life.'

Lucy nodded empathetically. 'When I read about it in the newspaper, I desperately wanted to reach out to you and offer my support, but I didn't think you'd welcome it after... so when I saw your name appear in a list of people I may know on Facebook, I figured fate had intervened and given me a second chance to make things right between us.'

Hannah was conscious of time, knowing Patrick was still out there looking for the memory card, and that there was a potential threat to Wendy and the children. 'I don't have a lot of time, Lucy. Can you tell me what it is you want?'

Lucy's shoulders tensed. 'I assume John told you about our confrontation?'

Hannah stared blankly back at her. 'What confrontation?'

Lucy gave her a sceptical look. 'He didn't tell you the reason he banned me from your house?'

'What? He didn't ban you from our house.'

Lucy's hand shot up to her mouth. 'Oh my God, you really don't know.'

'Know what, Lucy?'

'What do you think happened between you and me? Why did we go from being great friends to strangers?'

Hannah shrugged, not able to recall a specific reason. 'Our lives spurred off in different directions. I wanted to focus on building a home for John and I, and you wanted to go back to university to complete a Masters. We just drifted apart. It happens.'

Lucy was shaking her head in disbelief. 'That's not what happened. Yes, I became a mature student, but that had nothing to do with us losing contact.' She shuffled forward and took Hannah's free hand in her own. 'Do you remember the night you hosted a barbeque for John's thirtieth? There must have been at least a dozen people in the back garden, John's brother was in charge of cooking the meat, and you'd made that boozy fruit punch?'

Hannah allowed herself a brief smile at the memory of the night. 'What about it?'

Do you remember John having a go at you about not buying enough ice? It was a really warm night, and he'd filled a large container of ice with cans of lager, but then moaned because there wasn't any ice left for people's drinks.'

'I remember not buying enough ice, but I don't recall John having a go at me.'

'I was coming out of the toilet and the two of you were in the kitchen, and he was yelling at you, calling you all sorts of names, saying you weren't good enough and you'd embarrassed him. You really don't remember?

Hannah shook her head. 'Are you sure it was me and John you overheard?'

Lucy pulled a face. 'I know it was the two of you because I heard your voices through the door. He told you to get out of his sight, and as I pushed the door open I saw you hurrying into the garden to check whether anyone wanted a fresh drink. He glared at me like something he'd trodden in. I told him he was out of order, that nobody gave a shit about the lack of ice, and that he had no right to speak to you in that way. He told me it was none of my business and he'd speak to *his woman* – that was how he described you – however he liked. I couldn't believe his audacity. I told him you were my friend and deserved more respect, and do you know what he did? He made a pass at me. Pressed me up against the kitchen wall, telling me I looked so hot when I was angry and how we should sneak off as a birthday treat. I pushed him away and told him what a dick he was, and how I would tell you just as much.

'He threatened me, saying he had you under his spell, and how nothing I could say or do would change that. He said if I mentioned it, he would simply say I had made a pass at him, and then you'd turn your back on me as well.

'I remember trying to get you alone for the rest of the night, but every time I tried he would come over and tell you he needed something, and like always, you'd jump to it.'

Hannah had been biting her tongue, but Lucy had no right to be dishonouring John's memory like this. 'Why are you making up these stories? I remember that barbeque, and I remember everyone having a good night. It was my fault there wasn't enough ice, but I learned from it.'

Lucy ground her teeth. 'Can you hear yourself? I can't believe you're still defending him, even when he's gone.'

'He was my husband and I loved him, of course I'll defend him against such wicked allegations.'

'He treated you like a doormat, Hannah. How many times would he intimidate and threaten you? Every time we met up he would criticise and undermine you, telling you what you could and couldn't do. He was a bully and he was psychologically abusing you. I would have thought in this last year you would have realised how much of your life he controlled.'

'Stop it, stop it, stop it!' Hannah screamed, covering her ears with her hands. 'Why are you being so mean? Tomorrow is the anniversary of his death and you are attacking him.'

Lucy reached out and gently pulled the hands from Hannah's ears. 'No, sweetie, I'm not attacking him, I'm just telling you what I witnessed. I came round to your house the day after the barbecue, determined to tell you how badly he'd been treating you, but when I got there you weren't home. He invited me in, but I didn't trust him, so I said I'd wait in my car on the driveway. He phoned the police and told them I'd been stalking him and was refusing to leave the property. He wanted charges filing against me. I was escorted away before you got home, and when I tried to phone you at home, he blocked my number.'

Hannah stood, wanting to leave. Coming here had been a mistake; it was no wonder they'd drifted apart. 'You were always so jealous of what John and I had, weren't you?'

'What? No!'

'Yes you were. You'd always been more popular than me in school, and you hated the fact that I'd met a decent man and married before you. You always thought you were better than me. I remember John saying as much once. He couldn't understand why I tolerated your attention-seeking.'

Lucy's eyes watered. 'About a month after the barbeque I saw the two of you at the Trafford Centre, and I decided just to confront him there and then. I approached, but he saw me coming and made a beeline for me, asking how my degree course was going and stating how he was good friends with the dean of the faculty.'

Hannah recalled the awkward meeting while out shopping, how Lucy had been evasive and hadn't wanted to hang around and chat. As far as Hannah could remember that was the last time the two of them had spoken.

'What about it?' Hannah asked. 'John was only taking an interest in your life, and you hurried away. Quite rude as I remember it.'

'Don't you see? His comment about his friend was a threat that if I tried to get between the two of you he would make life difficult for me at university. Surely, you must see what he was like?'

'He loved me, Lucy. That's what I remember. He was my rock, and I've been a mess without him.'

'You weren't a mess before you met him, Hannah. That's what he did to you. He even made you give up on your passion. For as long as I'd known you, you'd loved everything about photography, and I was so proud when you set up your own business so you could indulge that passion. But after marrying John, you suddenly gave it all up.'

'I didn't have a choice. The business was failing; I couldn't afford to keep it going.'

'It wasn't like you needed to make money from the business though. John's company was doing well enough that you could become a housewife, so why couldn't it afford you the chance to fulfil your dream? You must see how he manipulated and isolated you?'

Hannah had heard enough. Grabbing Barney's lead, she marched to the front door, Lucy calling after her.

'Hannah don't rush off, I can prove to you what he was like if you'll just stay and listen.'

Spinning around, Hannah glared at her former friend. 'Never contact me again. You've revealed your true colours.'

Slamming the front door behind her, Hannah took deep gulps of fresh air, racing to the car and securing Barney inside, willing the tears not to break free.

She had to be certain. She had to know whether John was capable of lying to her face for so many years. Starting the engine, she put the car into gear and drove to the one place she hoped might shed some light: home.

FORTY-EIGHT

The butterflies in her gut were fluttering wildly as Hannah passed the old red post box, and slowed, flicking down the indicator as she had done so many times before. The fish and chip shop on the corner had its shutters down, and she could remember how excited John had been when their offer on the house had been accepted.

'We'll have fish and chips every night,' he'd said the day contracts were exchanged, and for the first three nights he'd stayed true to his word, but it hadn't been long before the novelty had worn off.

The once shiny metal shutters were now caked in multi-coloured tags. The shop itself had changed ownership three times in the years they'd lived on the street, and none of the owners had ever managed to stop the graffiti. It was part of the youth scene in the area.

Pulling into the road, her fingers were throbbing with pins and needles. The last time she'd been here she'd vowed never to return, and now she was about to dig up the past she'd strived for so long to bury.

Her t-shirt and jeans were stuck firm to her clammy skin. Switching on the air conditioning, she cranked it to the max and adjusted the blowers so they were aimed at her face, but it did little to cool or ease the ache burning behind her eyes.

Then she saw it. On the edge of the horizon, the large green hedges at the front of the property, which had once shielded them from intrusive eyes, now looked overgrown and in dire need of trimming. The couple who had bought the property from her had had plans to rent the place out, but it didn't look like they'd put any work into it.

Driving past the property, she parked up further down the road. Sandra answered the door on the second knock, a bathing robe around her shoulders and her long blonde hair tied up in a towel on her head.

'Hello, hun,' she said, leaning in and kissing both of Hannah's cheeks. 'Can't keep you away from me.' Her playful nature reverted to a look of concern as she saw Hannah's tear-filled eyes. 'Whatever is the matter? Come in, come in.'

Hannah dared herself to have one final look back at the old place, before following Sandra through to the kitchen at the front of the semi, and promptly dropped into one of the chairs around the small square table in the corner.

Barney's lead fell from her hands, and he made a beeline for the chocolate Labrador watching warily from its basket on the kitchen floor.

'Do you think John could have been having an affair?' Hannah hadn't meant to be so direct with the question, but there was no point in beating around the bush.

'No, don't be silly,' Sandra replied, turning away and filling the kettle.

It was the answer Hannah had been longing to hear, but she knew Sandra was lying. 'I want you to be honest with me,' Hannah continued, her voice cracking under the strain, and her eyes filling.

Sandra lowered the kettle to its stand, but remained with her back to Hannah. 'All you need to remember is how much John loved you.'

'Don't lie to me!' Hannah squealed, surprised by the aggression in her tone.

Sandra faced her, face sombre. 'Why are you asking this? Why now?'

'John's brother told me John was having an affair in the months before he died, and was planning to divorce me. I need to know whether you ever saw John with another woman, or ever suspected he was up to no good.'

'How could I? I barely knew him. He'd already left for work most mornings before I woke, and wouldn't get home until after me. The only time I ever really saw him was when the two of you were together, or when he was putting the bin bags out.'

Hannah watched her former neighbour squirm, unable to hide the lie despite her best efforts. 'What aren't you telling me? Please, Sandra, it's important.'

Taking a deep breath, Sandra dropped into the chair across from Hannah. 'Okay, okay, but I don't want to upset you. What I'm about to tell you is only because you're demanding to know. Okay?'

Hannah nodded, one of her tears splashing onto the table's dusty surface.

'It was probably three months before that night… I think you were out somewhere, at the cinema or something. You'd told me you were going to some premiere in the city because a friend of yours had been part of the production crew and had invited you along.'

Hannah remembered the night well. Lucy had invited her. The movie was independently produced, and she had enjoyed dressing glamorously and pretending to be a celebrity on the red carpet for a night. She'd drunk too much Prosecco and the hangover that followed had wiped her out for most of the next day.

'I left work early that day because I had a raging cold and felt awful,' Sandra continued. 'I was surprised to see John's car in the driveway, but didn't think any more of it until I was stood at that window,' she nodded her head to the front window, 'and saw him emerge from the house with a slim woman. I couldn't see her face, but I was pretty sure it wasn't you. Even more so when I saw how furtive he was acting. Our eyes met at one point, and his cheeks immediately flushed with guilt. He hurried away, but alarm bells were ringing in my head.'

'Why didn't you tell me any of this?'

'I didn't feel it was my place. Besides, he called round later that evening and explained that the woman had been a client who'd been caught short, and as they'd been passing, he'd pulled in and allowed her to use your toilet. He asked me not to say anything to you, because you became easily jealous of other women and would jump to all the wrong conclusions.'

'You believed him?'

Sandra shook her head. 'I can spot when a man is lying. The first sign is his lips moving.' She offered a sympathetic smile. 'I know I should have told you, but it was difficult. I didn't know how you would react, or whether you'd think I was just trying to stir trouble. I couldn't find the words. I'm sorry.'

Hannah felt like the rug had just been pulled from her feet. How many of her other friends had suspected John of being up to no good and had kept it from her? Didn't she deserve more respect?

Sandra moved a box of tissues from the window ledge to the table, as she stood to make the tea.

Hannah pulled out a tissue, and dabbed her eyes. 'Who was this woman? Describe her to me?'

'I didn't get a good look to be honest. She was shorter than you, and very slim – stick-like, you know – the sort of waist you see in those glossy magazines that only a tiny percentage of women will ever achieve. I mean, you're way slimmer than I am, but she was even thinner than you. The sort that needs a good meal inside her.'

'You didn't catch a name? Patrick said the woman was called Katrina.'

Sandra shook her head. 'Sorry, I didn't hear her speak. He shuffled her into the car so quickly, constantly checking to see if anyone had seen. I really didn't get a good look. What does it matter anyway? He was your husband, and you shouldn't let some rumour about infidelity spoil your memory of him.'

Hannah had heard enough. Not for the first time she couldn't help feeling that returning to Manchester had been a huge mistake. Pulling out the Nokia she checked to see whether Chandler had returned her call yet, but the display was blank. With the memory card burning a hole in her pocket, she stood suddenly, keen to put as much distance between herself and the house next door. Without a word, she peeled out of the kitchen and headed towards the front door, but stopped in her tracks as she saw the pair of eyes staring back at her through the letterbox.

FORTY-NINE

Pulling the door open, Hannah gasped as she saw the full face of the young woman crouched on the door mat. As slim as Sandra had described, straightened, caramel-coloured hair hung just below the woman's shoulders. She couldn't have been much older than twenty at most, and as she straightened, revealing the designer t-shirt beneath her faded denim jacket, Hannah suddenly became aware of the sound of a baby snuffling. The young woman twisted and tended to the infant in the pram behind her, before turning back to face Hannah.

'You're a difficult woman to track down,' she said matter-of-factly.

Sandra now appeared at the doorway to see where Hannah had gone, and gasped. 'You?' Pulling on Hannah's arm, Sandra added, 'This is the woman I was telling you about; the one who was asking about you; pretending to be your friend, and who said she was from a debt-collection agency.'

The young woman nodded coquettishly. 'I'm sorry for the deceit, but I had to get hold of you somehow.'

Hannah's mind was racing. 'Who are you? What do you want?'

The woman frowned. 'I'm Katrina Wainwright, do you remember me? We met a long time ago.'

There was certainly something familiar about the face, but Hannah couldn't place where she'd seen it before.

'What do you want?'

Katrina reached into the pram and pulled out the snuffling infant, hugging her close. 'I want you to meet John's daughter.'

Sandra had reluctantly agreed to take Barney for a walk to allow the two women some space to talk without interruption. Having fed the baby with a bottle of milk, the infant was now sleeping soundly in the pram as Katrina gently rocked it.

'I'm sorry to just turn up unannounced like this,' Katrina said quietly. 'I didn't know how else to get you alone long enough to explain. The last thing I want to do is upset you, but you need to be aware of a few facts. For starters, yes this is John's baby and I will agree to any kind of DNA test you want performed to prove the fact. I've only ever slept with one man in my short life.'

Hannah swallowed down the urge to retch. It felt like she was dreaming, only pinching the skin of her hands was doing nothing to wake her.

'I know you'll find this hard to believe,' Katrina continued, showing no shame, 'but I really loved John, and I think in his own way he loved me too.'

Each statement was like a knife being plunged into Hannah's heart. 'How old are you?'

'Nineteen. I first met John a month before I turned eighteen. He came to my college to fix some IT issue, and I was instantly attracted to him. I don't expect you to believe me, but I'm telling the truth. I was a good student, predicted to achieve high grades in my AS Levels, and not the sort to throw myself at any boy. John was different though. I knew he was much older than me, but he was sweet, and so helpful when I told him I was having difficulties with my laptop.

He said he'd take a look at it, and found this malicious virus I'd accidentally downloaded. He fixed the computer and I was so grateful. He drove me home one day after college, and I told him I fancied him. He told me he was flattered, but happily married. The rejection hurt, but that only made me want him more.

'I looked him up on Facebook, and added him as a friend. I was surprised when he accepted, and then we started corresponding through the Messenger app. I knew he was interested, but didn't want to do the wrong thing. He wanted to honour his marriage vows, and I didn't want to come between the two of you. I'm not that sort of person, despite what you might now think. I didn't mean to fall in love with him, but sometimes fate moves the pieces around the board without consulting us first.'

Hannah wanted to storm out, return to Southampton and never look back. How many months had she wasted mourning a man capable of lying to her face for so long? She didn't move, however, knowing she needed to hear what else Katrina had to say.

'The way I figure it,' Katrina continued, fixing Hannah with a stern stare, 'my daughter is entitled to half of John's estate.'

So that was what this was all about: money.

'How dare you!' Hannah exclaimed. 'To come here and claim that this child is my late husband's in order to extort money out of me. Have you no shame?'

Katrina's jaw tightened as she ground her teeth. 'It hasn't been easy for me either, you know. It's alright for you. You get to play the grieving widow while all around stoop to offer sympathy. Nobody's offering any support to me. I was five months pregnant when John died, and I've had to cope with giving birth and providing for her single-handed. While you've been able to move away and start a new life, I've been trapped here with nobody to give me and my daughter the helping hand we deserve. That's why I had to track you down. I don't blame you for leaving, but you need to know that my daughter is legally entitled to the money you're living off, and if you're not prepared to reach a settlement with me, I'll have no choice but to take you to court.'

'Don't threaten me.'

'It isn't a threat. I've been to Citizens Advice and I understand my rights. When the DNA test proves beyond doubt that she's John's you won't have a leg to stand on.' Katrina paused, taking several breaths to compose herself. 'I didn't come here to argue with you. I know this isn't ideal, and I also bet you'd rather John's name not be dragged through the mud if this does go to court. I'm not unreasonable, and I'm willing to discuss options with you. I just want what's right for my daughter.'

The blood boiling in her veins throbbed in Hannah's ears.

'I know it's a lot to take in,' Katrina continued, checking on the baby, 'and I don't expect you to reach a decision today.' She bent low and removed a padded envelope from netting beneath the pram. 'I've put a sample of my daughter's hair in the first test tube. All you need to do is put something of John's in the other, and post it. They'll send us both a copy of the results, and then we can talk again once you've seen the truth. My mobile number is on the page inside as well, so we can keep in touch. There's no reason for any of this to be any more awkward than it already is. I just want what's best for my little girl.'

Katrina was so self-assured, and showed no sign that any of her story was bluff or bluster, though that didn't necessarily mean she was telling the truth. 'When I answered the door, you said we'd met before. Where?'

The first flicker of doubt appeared on Katrina's face, as she frowned. 'It was the night he died. Don't you remember? I was waiting in the car when he returned home to pack his bags. He sent me to the shops to give you guys some space, and when I returned the police were all over the street. I thought it had something to do with what his brother had been up to, and I went home, expecting him to phone me, but he never did. I saw on the news that he'd been murdered by some homeless guy. I came to the hospital to see you, but I chickened out of telling you who I was. I knew then I was on my own.'

Hannah remembered the only number she'd found in the Nokia's call history, and suddenly picked up the phone, reading it out. 'Is that your number?'

'It was. I lost that phone ages ago.'

'John phoned you an hour before he died. What did you talk about?'

Katrina looked away as the memory played out before her eyes. 'He told me he'd spoken to his solicitor and would start to complete the necessary paperwork for divorce in the coming weeks. I've replayed that conversation over and over in my mind so many times. I was so happy. We were finally going to be together properly, and although I knew the first few months would be difficult, I could only picture a happy future for us with our child.'

Hannah had heard enough, and couldn't bear to stay in the same room a moment longer. She needed air, and time to clear her head. She didn't like the thought of leaving a stranger in Sandra's house, but she had to get out. Rushing to the front door, she stumbled out onto the mat, her vision blurring as her eyes filled, and she crashed into Sandra and Barney.'

FIFTY

Burying his head between her legs, Barney nuzzled into Hannah's knees until she ran her fingers through his soft fur. An hour had passed since Katrina's bombshell, and she'd only agreed to leave when Hannah had said she'd phone her in the coming days.

Glancing down at the blank screen of the Nokia on the kitchen table, Hannah couldn't believe DI Chandler still hadn't returned her call.

Sandra wobbled from one foot to the other, keen to ask something, but holding back.

'What is it?' Hannah eventually asked, when she could no longer handle the suspense.

'That Katrina girl,' Sandra blurted. 'I didn't realise it until today, but she could very well be the woman I saw John smuggling out that time. You think she's legit?'

Hannah had been trying to push the memory of Katrina's revelations from her mind. 'I don't know what to think. She seemed so certain of her version of events that my gut tells me there is something to it, yet I'm sure she was holding something else back; I just can't work out what it was.'

'Are you going to have the DNA test done?'

Hannah looked at the padded envelope, still on the table where Katrina had left it. 'I don't know. I'm not sure where I'd find a sample of John's DNA. I don't think I kept any of his combs, but maybe I'll find a stray hair on one of his jumpers or something. I think I should probably speak to a solicitor before taking any action to be honest.'

'And if it turns out she was telling the truth…?'

Hannah allowed the question to pass without response. She didn't have an issue with sharing John's estate with his illegitimate daughter, but she sensed Katrina's motivation for reaching out now was less moral than she'd claimed.

Hannah grabbed her phone and tried phoning Chandler for the umpteenth time, surprised when the phone connected this time.

'Hey, kid,' Chandler said, exhaling. 'Everything okay with you?'

'Um, no, not exactly. I'm sorry to keep pestering you, but are you free to meet me? It's about what I told you last night; about the money and other suspects in John's murder.'

'No can do, kid. I'm tied up at the prison. Long-story-short, Fahey has demanded to see me, claiming he's now ready to share the truth of that night. You can understand why I need to be here. I can meet you later if that helps?' Another audible exhale; Chandler was outside smoking.

Hannah took a deep breath. 'I found a memory card containing a video message from John. His brother Patrick was the one laundering money through the company, and I'm sure it's tied to what happened to us that night. You mentioned a colleague who might be better placed to help, but the thing is a threat's been made against my sister-in-law and her children, and I'm worried that –'

'You're just making things worse?' Chandler concluded. 'Listen, I understand, and God knows you don't need the additional stress. I tell you what, as soon as I'm finished here, I'll come and get you and we can go to my colleague together. Sound okay? Listen, I need to run as the solicitor says he's ready. I'll call you back when I get a moment.'

'No, wait –' Hannah tried, but the line was already disconnected. Hitting redial, she was frustrated when the answerphone kicked in straight away.

She was about to try again, when the phone burst into life. She recognised Wendy's home number and answered it, expecting an apology from her sister-in-law. What she was not expecting was to hear Patrick's anguished voice.

'They've taken them.'

FIFTY-ONE

'What?' Hannah exclaimed. 'Who's taken who?'

'I just came home to see Wendy and Daisy, see what I could do to patch things up, and I found the front door open, and there's no sign of the two of them. I've phoned the school and the boys are there, but there's no sign of Wendy or Daisy.'

Hannah's pulse quickened. 'Have you tried her mobile?'

'Her phone and bag are here. She wouldn't have gone out without them, and she wouldn't have left the front door open. It looks like they smashed in the boarding over the window to get in.'

The thought of Darlene's overreaction to Hannah's own sudden disappearance rang in her mind. 'Don't panic. I'm sure there's a reasonable explanation –'

'No,' he interrupted, the anguish in his tone heightening. 'You don't understand. They phoned me this morning, saying I had until tonight to get them the money. That's why I ambushed you in the car park. I'm sorry, I wouldn't have come there if I wasn't desperate. They're going to kill my wife and daughter. Oh God! Please, Hannah you've got to help me. Bring me that card and I can end all of this. Please?'

Hannah's instinct told her to try Chandler again, but if she'd now gone into the prison, there was no chance she'd be reachable until much later. Where would she begin trying to explain what was happening to another officer? Would they even take it seriously in time?

'I'll come straight over,' Hannah said, a long-buried maternal instinct kicking in. 'Do you think you can get hold of the money in time?'

'I don't know. I hope so. I have to try.'

He hung up, leaving Hannah at the table, her muscles tightening as the adrenaline pulsed. Grabbing the phone and Barney's lead, she knew it was too late to choose between helping Patrick and waiting for Chandler.

Katrina's words fired at the back of her mind: *sometimes fate moves the pieces around the board without consulting us first.*

The front door was still open when Hannah screeched the brakes at the kerbside. Leaving Barney belted into the seat, she raced to the house, seeing the cracked window now broken through where the captors must have gained entry. Patrick was in the living room, pacing back and forth, a glass in his hand and an open bottle of scotch on the table, next to Wendy's handbag and phone.

'Oh thank God,' he said, seeing her enter, and rushing over to hug her. 'Thank you for coming. I realise this is all my fault, and you'll never know how sorry I am. Did you bring it?'

Hannah fished into the pocket of her jeans, and pulled out the memory card. 'Here it is. How are you going to get them the money? Did they leave you any other instructions?'

He didn't answer, slamming the glass onto the table and leaving the room, returning with Wendy's laptop a few moments later, plugging the card into the slot and booting up the computer. He opened the file, and suddenly John's nervous face filled the screen once again. He looked different this time; somehow the revelation of his deceit had coloured her view of him.

How many other lies had he told down the years that she had no idea about? Had he even meant for Hannah to find the file? As she listened to the message again, at no point did he mention her by name.

Patrick listened intently, avoiding Hannah's questioning gaze as John explained what he'd found and how he'd hidden the money. Patrick scrolled down, finding the account details recorded in the rest of the file, and scribbled them down on his hand with a pen.

'What will you do?' she asked, as he slammed the lid of the laptop.

'I'll go see if I can get the money and then I'll phone them about the exchange.' He leaned closer and put his hands on her shoulders, pulling her closer, and kissing her cheek. 'Thank you so much for this. You're a lifesaver. I promise we'll sit down and sort out all this shit when they're safe.' He turned to leave.

'Wait, is that it? You're not going to phone the police?'

He stopped still. 'No police. They said if they got the impression I wasn't flying straight they'd kill them and I'd never find the bodies. I have to do this on my own.'

It was that kind of gung-ho attitude that had resulted in John's death. 'You can't do this on your own. I'll phone DI Chandler; she'll know what to do.'

He glared at her, the blood draining from his face. 'No, please. Just trust me. I'll get them back, just let me do it my way, okay? Please, Hannah. Don't phone the police. I'll call you as soon as I've spoken to them. Please just wait here until you hear from me.'

Then he was gone, leaving the front door swinging, as he tore through it and out onto the street. She followed him to the porch and watched as he jumped into his Land Rover and accelerated away, the mobile to his ear.

Hannah stepped out and collected Barney from the car, leading him in through the front door, and managing to push it closed with her bottom. Barney padded through to the living room, jumping up onto the sofa, before curling into a ball. She joined him, allowing her fingers to play with his fur, trying to determine whether she'd done the right thing. Every bone in her body told her she should have insisted on phoning the police before handing Patrick the memory card, but maybe he was right. If the thugs had threatened to kill Wendy and Daisy if the police were involved then he had no choice but to obey.

The sound of keys in the door, followed by the shrill cry of a hungry toddler had Hannah staring at the living room door. It opened a moment later, and Wendy appeared, startled when she saw Hannah and Barney on the sofa.

'What are you doing here?' Wendy asked.

Hannah leapt up and hugged her close. 'I could ask you the same question. Did they let you go already?'

Wendy extracted herself, her face gripped with confusion. 'Did who let me go? What are you talking about?'

A feeling of dread began to wash over Hannah. 'Patrick phoned me and said you'd been abducted. He said if I didn't give him the memory card they'd kill you.'

Wendy's face reddened, but it wasn't clear if she was embarrassed for herself or Hannah. 'I've been at the toddler's gym with Daisy. We go there every Tuesday to play and sing.'

'You didn't take your handbag or phone.'

'I never do. There's nowhere to leave them securely at the gym, and I usually have Daisy's bag with nappies and changes of clothes; there just isn't room for a handbag too. Oh, Hannah, I don't know how to say this…'

The blood boiled beneath Hannah's skin and she desperately wanted to lash out. 'He lied to me. *Again!* I fell for it.' She raised a hand to her forehead, trying to calm herself down, and determined more than ever to phone the police and show them the video clip. Patrick had crossed the line too many times and the consequences of his actions were all on him. If they sent him down for life, it was the least he deserved.

FIFTY-TWO

Dropping the phone to the kitchen table, Hannah growled in frustration.

'Still no answer?' Wendy asked, pulling a sympathetic face, as she busied herself at the sink.

'Keeps going straight through to answerphone,' Hannah said in acknowledgement. She could remember how strict the rules had been with personal belongings in the prison – everything left at the guard's station by the entrance – and until Chandler emerged from her meeting with Fahey, she'd be unreachable.

Perhaps it was time to just phone the regular police and report what Patrick had done. Everything in John's message *suggested* Patrick had broken the law, but she didn't know where to begin trying to explain exactly what he'd done. She dreaded the thought of having to explain the last year to a stranger. At least Chandler knew the family and the backstory.

A thought fired in her mind.

'Can I borrow your laptop for a second?' Hannah asked.

'Sure,' Wendy said absently. 'I think it's in the living room.'

Hannah scraped the chair back, and hurried from the room, finding the laptop where Patrick had left it. The battery indicator in the bottom corner was flashing, and threatening to turn the device off.

'Where's the charger?' Hannah asked, carrying it back

into the kitchen.

Wendy dried the soap suds from her hands with a towel, and disappeared out of the kitchen and upstairs, returning a moment later, and handing the snake-like length of cable to Hannah.

If Hannah was to stop Patrick, she needed first to locate him. She didn't have a clue where to start looking, but she knew someone who would. Logging into Facebook, she located Chris's profile, found his number and dialled. It connected after two rings.

'Hello,' a tired-sounding Chris answered.

'You sound different on the phone,' Hannah said, standing and carrying the phone through to the living room, away from Wendy's prying ears. 'It's Hannah Davenport.'

'Hannah? Oh wow, it's great to hear from you. You changed your number already?'

'It's a long story,' she explained, too tired to fill him in on everything that had happened. 'The old one was stolen so this is my temporary number.'

'Oh I see. How are you?'

'I'm…' she wasn't sure how to answer. 'I need a favour.'

'What sort of favour?'

She hadn't spoken to him since he'd seen her with Steve at the pub on Sunday night, and would have understood his reticence to help her, and appreciated him not making things awkward.

'The other day you were able to run a telephone number and check who it was registered to. If I give you a different number, would you be able to tell me its current location?'

'Give me a second,' he said, returning a moment later. 'Right, I've got my computer open. Who are you trying to trace? Give me the number and I'll see what I can find.'

She relayed Patrick's number and made up a story about him cheating on his wife, and them trying to catch him.

'Signal is broadcasting in Manchester,' Chris replied. 'The app is just zooming in on the nearest cell towers to pinpoint probable location. I should warn you that this won't be a hundred per cent accurate. It's just a free site I've accessed from the internet, but it should give you a rough location.'

'Thank you,' she said, once again grateful for his support.

'It's an industrial estate,' Chris confirmed, reading out a postcode.

Hannah recognised it instantly. 'He's at the office,' she mouthed to Wendy. Of course that's where he'd retreat to when the pressure was on. 'Thanks, Chris. I owe you one.'

'Dinner then?'

Hannah closed her eyes, remembering what she'd promised Bea: *just give him a chance.*

'Yes,' she said. 'Dinner sounds good.'

'This weekend when you're back from Manchester?'

'Yeah…' her words trailed off in confusion. 'Wait, how do you know where I am?'

'Oh, sorry I was just looking at Facebook and it said that's where you were when you accepted my friend request. Sorry, I wasn't stalking you, it was just there. When you're back I can show you how to deactivate it if you want? Just need to adjust your settings.'

'Sure, okay, thanks again.' She disconnected the call, and looked at Wendy. 'I'm going to go and see Patrick, and try to make him see sense. He needs to admit what he's done, and if he won't see reason, then I will tell the police exactly where he is. He's lied to all of us, Wendy. You must see that now.'

Wendy didn't answer but the look of resignation in her eyes told Hannah she did.

The laptop beeped.

From: Chris_Ryland
Do you like spicy food? I know a great Mexican restaurant that's just opened in town. I'll make a reservation for Saturday at eight. That okay with you?

Hannah swivelled the laptop screen so Wendy wouldn't see the message, concerned her sister-in-law might judge.

From: Hannah_Davenport
Sounds great. I'll see you then.

Logging off, Hannah closed the lid of the laptop and pulled on her jacket. 'Will you watch Barney for me? I don't know how long I'll be, and it'll be easier if I don't have to worry about him.'

Wendy nodded, not really listening. 'Are you going to be okay?'

Hannah shrugged. 'For the first time in a long time I know what I need to do. Patrick needs to be stopped, and I'm not giving him any more of a head start.'

FIFTY-THREE

Traffic back to the industrial estate was thick with parents collecting children from school, and workers heading home early for the day. As was the way whenever Hannah was in a hurry to get somewhere, she seemed to get stopped at every traffic light and pedestrian crossing along the way.

Finally arriving at the office, she was surprised to see lights on inside the building. Had the lack of power been another lie of Patrick's? Nothing would surprise her anymore. Not wishing to alert him to her presence, she avoided the office's own car park, and parked alongside the neighbouring building instead. Killing the engine, she took a moment to compose herself.

What did she want to achieve from this confrontation? Patrick had the account details from the memory card, and no doubt would be busy trying to gain access. That wasn't what was bothering her at the moment. How far back did his lies go?

Gripping the Nokia, she tried Chandler's number again, but the answerphone cut in once more. 'Hi Jeanette, I've been trying to get hold of you all day, but I'm guessing you're still at the prison. Can you call me back as soon as possible? It's about my brother-in-law Patrick. Do you remember what I told you about him? Well it's *all* true. I've come to the company office to intercept him, but I could do with your help. He's the one who's been embezzling money with those local villains, and…' She took a deep breath to steady her nerves. 'I also think he's the person who killed John. I can't prove it, but I'm going to try and get him to admit it. Please hurry.'

Disconnecting the call, she couldn't ignore her shaking hands, and the terror pulsating through every cell in her body. Despite everything Lucy had told her, she wished John was with her right now.

Flicking through the Nokia's limited apps, she located what she'd been hoping for and switched on the voice recorder.

Holding the phone at arm's length she said, 'Testing, testing, one, two, three, four.'

Ending the recording she played it back, and heard her voice, much quieter, but loud enough. That meant she'd need to be standing close to Patrick when she challenged him. She just hoped she would be near enough.

Pocketing the phone, she opened her door quietly and slipped out. Then keeping her body pressed against the brickwork, she scurried along to the front door, relieved to find it unlocked.

The atrium's radio was playing music softly as she passed the reception desk, and headed for the stairs up to the top floor. Patrick was hunched over his desk, face buried in the screen as he busily typed. He physically jumped when Hannah cleared her throat to disguise her action of switching on the phone's voice recorder.

'Oh it's you,' he said, the smile spreading widely across his face. 'You almost gave me a heart attack.'

'I know you lied to me,' she said moving forward, and only stopping when she reached the edge of his desk. 'About Wendy being taken this morning.'

His eyes were temporarily pained, but he shook it away dismissively. 'In my defence, it wasn't a complete lie. They did phone me this morning and threaten her again, but I told them I would get them their money. Thanks to you that's now going to happen.'

'You lied to me,' she said again bitterly.

'You didn't leave me much choice, and neither did John. I did what I had to do to get things back on track. If he hadn't... well, we wouldn't be in this mess now. For what it's worth, I am sorry I lied to you. I always used to think of you as my sister, and not just my brother's wife.'

She snorted. 'Even when you broke into my hotel room and stole my bag?'

A flicker of shame in his eyes confirmed her suspicion. 'I didn't mean to frighten you. I didn't expect you to come back so quickly. I thought I had more time, and when you came through the door, I panicked.'

'What did you do with my bag?'

He splayed his fingers on the desk. 'I threw it in a dumpster. I figured the police would check all the local bins and recover it for you. Not my finest moment, but no lasting damage done. I'll buy you a new bag if needs be.'

His lack of remorse angered her. 'Is that it? Is that all you have to say for yourself?'

'What else do you want? An apology? Okay, I'm sorry for breaking into your hotel room. I needed to get my hands on these account details and I just knew deep down that John would have left them for someone to find. When Katrina said she'd had nothing from him, I knew he had to have left the details with you.'

Hearing her name again sent a shiver along Hannah's arms. 'You went to see Katrina?'

'Only to find out whether he'd given her the account details. It became pretty clear she had no idea what I was talking about, but she did make some claim about that brat of hers being John's. I told her to take it up with you.'

'You have no shame!'

Patrick slapped the desk hard, and pointed a finger of warning at her. 'If John hadn't started interfering in my business, none of this would have happened. If you want somebody to blame, you should look no further than him.'

A solitary tear rolled down her cheek. 'Is that why you killed him?'

Patrick's face contorted into confusion. 'I told you: *I* didn't kill John.'

'Don't lie to me, Patrick,' Hannah shouted. 'I know you were desperate to get the money back, and John knew you were onto him. I saw the fear in his eyes in that video the day he died. What happened? You came to the house looking for him, and a fight erupted?'

'No! Hannah, listen to me, you've got it wrong. I was nowhere near your house when John was killed.'

'You came to the door, you attacked me, and murdered John. Just admit what you did once and for all!'

Patrick slammed the lid of his laptop and stood, his finger still pointed at her face. 'I had nothing to do with any of that. I loved my brother, despite his flaws, and back then I didn't even know he'd taken the money. Do you really think I'm capable of something like that?'

'I don't know what you're capable of; not anymore. I never would have said you would get mixed up with criminals and risk the company you built together.'

'I did what I thought was best for the company, but that doesn't make me a murderer.'

'Why are you still lying? Come on, Patrick, it's only you and me here, why won't you just admit what you did? I will help you with lawyer fees, but please just finally admit the truth.'

His eyes fell on her hands, where she was struggling to hide the bulge of the Nokia in her pocket. Pushing her away from the desk, he stormed from the office, and was heading down the stairs, as she forced herself up from the floor. Checking the phone's display, she ended the recording, and was disappointed to see Chandler had still yet to call.

If Patrick left now, she'd have no way of keeping him in sight until Chandler was able to get to her. She hadn't managed to record his confession, but Chandler would crack him, of that she had no doubt.

Chasing after him, Patrick was already behind the wheel of the Land Rover, as Hannah tore out of the building. Racing to her own car, she jumped in, and started the engine. The Land Rover was already heading for the exit on the opposite side of the car park, meaning she didn't have time to block him in. Reversing, she shot out onto the main road, swinging around to a chorus of horns and swearing, and back around towards where the Land Rover was now passing through the exit. Flooring the accelerator, Hannah no longer cared what would happen to her, so long as she stopped Patrick escaping again.

The cars collided almost in slow motion, the seat belt restraining Hannah's shoulders; metal crunching and scraping against metal; the airbag deploying, cool like a large pillow against her cheeks. Then the darkness came.

FIFTY-FOUR

The gentle sound of music playing quietly somewhere nearby was the first thing she heard, as her eyes remained clamped firmly shut. Whether it was the shock of what had happened, or the sense that she had experienced something so similar a year ago, the disorientation was bringing with it waves of nausea.

Was she back in the house? Had it happened again? She couldn't hear the smoke alarm nor smell the pungent aroma of meat burning in the oven. Despite the overwhelming heat emanating from every muscle, a cool breeze was blowing nearby.

Her head was pressed against something hard, and as she tried to raise it, a hot, shooting pain coursed through her neck muscles. The side of her face, between her cheek and temple stung with fresh cuts, and something wet and sticky was clinging to her chin. Running her tongue around the inside of her mouth, she tasted the familiar copper tang of blood, and the slightest movement had her grimacing at the ache behind her eyes.

Trying to raise her hands to survey the damage to her head, she found her right arm restrained by a firm brace, which stretched across her tender ribs and down to her hip.

The music ended with an excited voice telling her to get down to her local dealership for an offer too good to resist. The radio? No, the car stereo system.

The car crash exploded in her memory. Shifting her body

weight, she managed to free her arms from the seat belt, grip the steering wheel and peel her face from it. The hot poker-like pain tore through her neck again as she straightened. It wasn't the smartest idea to move after such an impact, but she couldn't remain where she was; that much was clear.

Opening her eyes, she was surprised at how dark it was outside of the car. The hull of Patrick's Land Rover was all she could see from the windscreen. She had no idea how much time had passed since the accident, but it didn't appear that anybody had stopped to check on them. To her right, a string of passing headlights, and the hum of traffic moved by on the main road, oblivious to the carnage just inside the industrial estate entrance.

She strained to raise her head further, trying to look in through the windscreen of the Land Rover, but the glass was too fractured to make out anything inside. There was certainly no movement, which meant Patrick had either scarpered, or was in a worse condition than her. Stretching her hand up, she flipped on the car's interior light, and surveyed the damage. The driver's side window was also cracked, with a large chunk of glass missing; this was where the cool breeze was blowing in.

The remains of the air bag hung from the carcass of the steering wheel, specks of red on both. Pressing a trembling hand to her chin, she saw fresh blood on her fingers as she studied them. She needed to get free, report the accident and check on Patrick's welfare. Nothing else mattered.

Pressing her thumb against the seat belt release button, she pushed and exhaled in satisfaction as the catch released and the belt slowly retracted, releasing her chest. Then, reaching for the door handle, she pulled on it, but the door remained stuck in place. Tentatively leaning all her weight against the frame, she tried the handle again, but it remained firm.

'No,' she whimpered, feeling the fight draining from her

tired and broken body.

Staring through the gap in the broken window, she could see the Land Rover's large front wheel at an awkward angle, but pressed firmly against the door panel of her car. She was in no state to apply the necessary force to use the door to push the wheel out of the way, meaning she was trapped unless she could summon the courage to slide her aching body into the passenger seat and attempt to exit through the door there.

She could feel her eyes watering again, when a face suddenly appeared at the passenger side window.

Hannah had never seen such concentration in Jeanette Chandler's face. 'Try not to move. There's an ambulance on the way.'

Hannah allowed her eyes to close, finally a glimmer of light at the end of the tunnel.

The paramedics arrived within ten minutes, and having provisionally examined Hannah, had her lying flat on a stretcher in the back of the ambulance, an oxygen mask strapped to her face.

'We'll take you in for further examination,' the woman in the green uniform said, smiling sympathetically. 'We need to get your ribs examined, just to check you've not done any lasting damage. Overall though I'd say you're pretty lucky to be walking away from a crash like that.'

Hannah didn't feel lucky, but appreciated the paramedic's positivity.

Chandler appeared just outside the doors, but her usual bounce and personality were muted. 'Your brother-in-law wasn't in the Land Rover when I arrived,' she said solemnly.

Hannah lowered the face mask, despite the paramedic's

disapproving stare. 'He was the one behind all of this. He was laundering money through the company, John found out, and so Patrick killed him. I have a video message from John explaining everything.'

Chandler's expression remained stone-cold. 'We'll catch up with your brother-in-law.' Chandler hoisted herself into the ambulance as the paramedic left them alone. 'I'm sorry I wasn't there for you today, but I need you to come with me now.'

'Come where?' Hannah croaked.

'I'll explain when we get there. There's something you need to hear.'

FIFTY-FIVE

The high walls and cold face of HMP Manchester came into view as Chandler cut through the traffic, the flashing blue of the lights in the grill reflecting off the damp road.

Hannah had been unable to say much during the journey, battling every urge to shout out in pain at every turn. Her knuckles were white from gripping the arm rest in the door. Chandler had offered little by way of conversation either, probably too shocked by the lengths Hannah had gone to in order to stop Patrick.

Chandler held her identification out to the guard, who signalled for the barrier to be raised. Then following the road round to the staff car park and entrance again. The windscreen wipers' squeaking out a warning of what might transpire.

Prison guard Tom met them at the entrance, but the mood was more sombre than yesterday, replaced by a chilly professionalism to their exchange. Tom led them through to the office where he waved his metal detecting wand over them both, before signing their names into the visitor book. Then he led them along the maze of narrow corridors, until they reached the room with the large iron door.

Hannah couldn't ignore the look of shock that still gripped Chandler's features, and as the door's lock clunked with the turn of Tom's keys, fear and regret hovered near.

Inside the room, Fahey was already slouched at the table, his face swollen from tears, and a defeated look in his eyes.

The woman sitting on their side of the glass, wearing a bright green suit jacket and cream-coloured blouse, had to be a solicitor. She had that air of arrogance required for the role. Hannah and Chandler took their seats, and Hannah couldn't ignore the sense that something significant had unfolded in this room today. Even the solicitor looked drained.

'Perhaps it would be better if you were to leave,' Chandler said to the woman in green. It wasn't a question.

'Actually, Detective Inspector, I think –'

'Leave us!' Fahey grizzled, startling Hannah.

The solicitor glanced over to him, checking he was certain, before moving across to the door where Tom was still patiently waiting. Once she was through, he closed and locked the door, leaving the three of them alone in the room.

'What am I doing here?' Hannah whispered to Chandler when she could take the suspense no longer.

The detective didn't answer at first, as if the question was alien to her, or she couldn't quite find the words. She eventually adjusted her seat so she was facing Hannah.

'There's something you *need* to hear. Seamus and I have been talking all day, and now you need to hear what he has to say. I know this won't be easy, and I have no idea how you will react, but it's important you give him the space to speak.'

Dread crept ever closer.

'Well, Seamus,' Chandler continued, turning back to face him through the glass, 'it's over to you.'

Slumped in the chair, his stick-thin legs stretched out beneath the table, he looked like death was lurking near, and for the first time Hannah realised just how ill he looked. His hair was even more unkempt than when she'd first laid eyes on him, but the giant bags beneath his eyes made it look like he hadn't slept since they'd last spoken.

'Last night,' he began, his voice croaky, 'I remembered

everything. It was a dream, but it was like reliving every moment over again. Maybe seeing you yesterday, or hearing your voice triggered... I don't know. At first I thought it was my mind playing tricks on me, but those images... I can't stop seeing them.'

Hannah braced herself for his imminent confession. That had to be why Chandler had spent the day here, and why she'd insisted Hannah come so late at night. Why else would Fahey's solicitor been here?

'I was there,' he said after a breath. 'In the garden. That night. I saw what happened... and I know what I did. I think you saw me at the window at one point, but by then you were in such a bad state that I'm not sure it registered.'

Hannah dry swallowed, the walls of the room suddenly seeming to shrink closer. Her dream of Fahey at the window, had it been a fragment of memory, rather than an imagined moment triggered by their meeting?

'I don't know when I stumbled into the garden, but I remember seeing you busy inside, preparing food I think. I remember the aroma coming from the extractor fan. It smelled so good. I sat and I waited until you weren't in the room, and then I planned to break in.'

The knot in Hannah's stomach tightened. It had been six when she'd put the turkey in the oven. He'd been watching her and she'd had no idea.

'I saw you leave the room for a moment and head to the front door. A younger woman came in to the house. The two of you sat at the kitchen table, and I could see that she was upsetting you. I must have fallen asleep as the drugs took hold. Next, there was a man in the kitchen with you. His face was red; angry. The two of you were arguing, and I saw him slap you hard across the face. That angered me; it's not right for a man to ever strike a woman. I think I shouted something at the door, but my body wouldn't allow me to take a stand.'

The breath caught in Hannah's throat. Had Fahey witnessed what Patrick had done? Had Chandler even shown him a picture of Patrick to confirm his identity?

'My memory is… hazy,' he said, sitting up and clearing his throat. 'The two of you disappeared from the room, but as I entered through the door, I heard him upstairs shouting and laughing at your anguish. I wasn't sure if what I was seeing was real, or just some film. It was almost like I wasn't in my body, hovering above and watching but unable to stop what was happening.'

Chandler hadn't moved, transfixed by the narrative, her knuckles pale from how hard she was balling her fists.

'I heard you begging him to stop what he was doing, and then I heard you screaming, and this banging sound. I raced to the noise, and found you in a heap at the bottom of the stairs, your arm bleeding. You looked so peaceful that I thought he'd killed you. I wanted to confront him, and I must have gone upstairs, and that's where… that's where I found him.'

A flash of Hannah's own memory fired to the front of her mind: crawling up the stairs and finding John on the bed, the knife in the pool of blood on the mattress.

'I saw the blood,' Fahey continued. 'Even though there was so much of it, I think I must have thought there was a chance to save him, which is why I pulled the knife out of his abdomen, but it soon became clear I was too late. I panicked and hurried down the stairs. I don't even remember seeing you again, or how I got out. My head was spinning – so much blood – and I must have taken another pill. The next memory is of the police cuffing me.'

Hannah blinked several times. Was he claiming John was already dead on the bed? Did that prove that Patrick had been the one to kill him then? That had to be why Chandler had wanted her to hear Fahey's explanation.

Hannah doubted a dream would be enough evidence to

overturn Fahey's conviction, but if he could identify Patrick as the attacker, then maybe it would be enough for Chandler to reopen the investigation. Maybe that was why she looked so pale.

Chandler suddenly turned to face Hannah again. 'We spoke to a woman by the name of Katrina Wainwright this afternoon. Do you know who she is?'

Hannah nodded. 'What about her?'

'Were you aware that she claims to have been having an affair with John when he died?'

Hannah swallowed hard. 'I didn't until earlier today. She's not shown me any evidence to back up her claim.'

'Well, according to the statement she's now made, she knocked at your door around six on the night in question. Says she'd had an argument with John on the phone and had called round to come clean with you. Do you remember that?'

An image of Katrina standing at the door, dressed in that maroon mini dress and petite leather jacket fired in Hannah's mind, but she shook her head. 'I remember a knock at the door, but it's all blank after that.'

'Well she claims you invited her in, and she told you about the affair. Apparently you didn't want to believe her at first, but she was able to show you pictures and dates that corresponded with dates and times when John had claimed to be away on business. The two of you were still arguing when John returned home. He sent Katrina away so the two of you could talk. Do you remember what happened next?'

Hannah shook her head again, even as the flicker of John and Katrina together in the kitchen sparkled in her head.

FIFTY-SIX

'Tell me she's lying, John. Tell me this is all some elaborate prank.'

His eyes answered, even as his lips remained clamped shut.

She was shaking as she stood there in the kitchen, feeling as though her legs would cave at any moment. There they were: her sheltering behind his tall figure; him with flushed cheeks, all his lies unfolding before his eyes.

'How long has it...?' Hannah tried to ask, the words sticking in her throat.

Again, John and Katrina remained silent, exchanging shamed glances. He hadn't even apologised for the fact that his bit on the side had shown up and dropped such a bombshell. Was it worse that he'd kept it covered up so long, or that he hadn't even had the courage to come clean himself.

'I think you should go,' he said, turning to Katrina, and squeezing her hand.

It was like a knife had been thrust into Hannah's breaking heart all over again. So, that was that. It was over. He wasn't on his knees begging for forgiveness. If anything there was a hint of relief in his face. Relief that he would no longer need to keep his sordid affair a secret.

Katrina's watering eyes searched his for encouragement, and he nodded at her, a silent message of support exchanged. Katrina dared to look back at Hannah once more before heading to the front door and closing it behind her.

Hannah remained where she was, glaring at her husband, daring him to offer anything that could possibly explain how he could betray her in the cruellest way. 'How could you... after all we've been through...'

He moved across to the sink, staring out into the pitch black garden. 'You surely can't be surprised. I mean, look at how you've let yourself go.'

She smoothed the hair at the side of her face. 'But this is what you wanted. You made me into this.' Her heart fluttered, knowing she was treading dangerously. 'But I can change. Tell me what I need to change and I'll do it. You want me to look more like her? I'll dye my hair and grow it out. I'll go on a diet until I'm super thin again. Is that what you want?'

'It's too late for all that.'

The breath caught in her throat. 'No, it isn't too late. I can change, John, and be better, just the way you like. Just tell me what I need to do.'

He turned, staring at her, not with love, but pity and shame. 'Why would I want you when I can have her? You're no good to anyone anymore.'

'Do you love her?' The words tasted so bitter in her mouth, and she didn't want to hear his answer.

'I didn't know what real love was until I met Katrina. What you and I had, this, it wasn't love.'

She reached for his arm. 'Yes it was, John. I love you, and deep down I know you still love me too. We can put all of this behind us and things can go back to how they were.'

He yanked his arm away. 'Why would I want things to go back to how they were? You mean nothing to me.'

'She's barely of legal age, for goodness sake!'

'She's eighteen.'

Hannah scoffed. 'Is this some sort of midlife crisis? Is

that what this is? Your body clock is telling you you're nearing the grave, and you wanted some proof that you're not past it?'

He spun round quickly, shock swiftly turning to anger. *'That's not what this is about. I love her.'*

'You love her? You're old enough to be her father!'

The slap to her cheek happened so quickly that it didn't register at first. Her hand shot up to her face as the sting took hold.

'I'm sorry, John, I didn't mean to make you angry. Come on, let's go upstairs and I'll show you how much I love you. You'll see that what we have is worth saving. Please don't leave me.'

Shaking his head dismissively, he left the room, Hannah scurrying after him.

'I'm leaving you,' he declared, picking up a stack of CDs from the shelf in the lounge.

She was losing him, and had to find a way to keep him here. 'You want out of this marriage? Fine, but I'm keeping the house and I want my fair share of the business.'

She'd only said it to try and hurt him; to make him see sense. Divorce would be financially-crippling for him, and she'd have the court on her side. He was the one who had strayed.

'Screw that, and screw you!' he fired back.

'What did you think would happen? That I'd sign everything over and you could move your floozy in here in my place?'

He swallowed the space between them in three strides, forcing her to take several nervous steps backwards. 'Don't you refer to her like that! None of this is her fault. It just happened.'

'Oh, it just happened?' she roared back, the blood in her own veins reaching boiling point. 'Like dropping a pint of milk, or maybe slipping over on some ice? It just happened.'

She laughed bitterly in his face. 'What was it like? You just woke up one morning and realised your dick was inside her?'

She saw his hand fly up again, but she wasn't quick enough to duck out of the way.

'It's not like you gave me much encouragement not to look elsewhere.'

'So it's my fault? I thought we were happy!'

'Then you're more naïve than I ever gave you credit for!'

'We'll see how naïve I am when my solicitor strips you of all your assets, and you and that child are struggling to put a roof over your heads.'

She'd pushed too far. She knew that the moment he slapped her again, only this time he followed it up with a blow to her stomach. Doubling-over, she dropped to her knees, as he began to ascend the stairs. Her world was crumbling before her eyes and she had to do something to show him how much she needed him.

Pulling the carving knife out of the block in the kitchen, she crept up the stairs and into the bedroom. His back was to her as he scooped suits out of the wardrobe.

'If you go, I'll kill myself,' she declared.

The announcement forced him to turn and look at her as she pressed the cool blade against her arm and broke the skin.

He watched her, unflinching, making no effort to take the knife from her.

'Aren't you going to stop me? Do you really want my death on your conscience?'

He folded his arms. 'Go ahead, save me the effort of doing it.'

She didn't want to live. A world without John wasn't living anyway. Striding towards him, she held out the knife. 'Do it! I'd rather you kill me than leave.'

He batted her arm away and turned back to the

wardrobe. 'Don't be ridiculous.'

The fight left Hannah's body, and her shoulders slumped. It had been her one roll of the dice, but the house had won. Fresh inspiration struck. He'd said he didn't want to kill her, which had to mean that he still had feelings for her. Stepping forward, she opened her arms to embrace him, but she didn't see him turning back with a fresh handful of clothes, and suddenly the blade met resistance, and John yelped.

It was like a dream. Blinking several times she tried to wake herself as John stumbled back against the open cupboard door and then falling forwards onto the bed, the knife plunging deeper into his abdomen.

'What did you do?' he wheezed.

It was an accident, she wanted to yell. It was as much his fault for stepping into the blade as it was hers for holding it.

'I'll call for an ambulance,' she whispered, rolling him onto his back, and attempting to pull out the knife.

'No, leave it where it is,' he grimaced. 'You stupid bitch!'

'I'm so sorry,' she whispered, stumbling backwards out of the room, not wanting to take her eyes off him. What had she done? He would never forgive her now.

Her foot went from under her as it slipped from the top step of the staircase, and as she fell backwards through the air, the last thought in her mind was, how had things ended like this?

FIFTY-SEVEN

Chandler must have noticed the blood drain from Hannah's face as the memories played out before her eyes, like an old black and white movie late at night. 'It's okay, kid, I'm here for you.'

Hannah couldn't bring herself to make eye contact with her. 'I want to get out of here. Now.'

Chandler suddenly stood and moved across to the door, banging her palm against it. 'Tom? You can have Mr Fahey returned to his cell now, thank you. I'll let you know when we're done in here.'

Hannah kept her head bowed, but strained her eyes to watch as a prison guard entered the room on the other side of the glass, cuffed Fahey's hands behind his back and escorted him from the room, closing and locking the door behind him.

'You don't really believe any of that story, do you?' Hannah said aggressively, hoping Chandler didn't pick up on the doubt in her voice.

Chandler remained by the door. 'Why would I? A convicted murderer claims to be having an epiphany after a dream that nobody can prove or disprove he had. Suddenly the previous cloud of amnesia has shifted from his mind and he sees it all in picture-perfect clarity. Sounds like someone desperate to upset the apple cart.' She paused. 'Yet your reaction to the story, and that niggling voice in the back of my head, lead me to believe that there's certainly some truth in what he said.' Another pause, and an awkward shuffle. 'I never told you that something didn't quite sit right with me in this case. I had to ignore my gut instinct back then, because all the evidence pointed towards Fahey. He wasn't disputing the evidence, other than saying he couldn't remember doing anything wrong. Until today I've managed to keep that niggling voice quiet, but right now it's shouting at me through a megaphone.'

Hannah's head snapped up. 'You think I killed John, don't you? I couldn't. I loved him.'

Chandler returned to her chair, her voice calm and empathetic. 'I don't doubt that you did love him, petal. That will probably never go either. I've told you before we're all capable of doing more than we can imagine if we find ourselves in the wrong situation. I've seen good people do the most horrendous things when pushed to it. Nobody is saying you meant to kill him, but even you must see how things could have played out that night?'

Hannah was doing everything she could to shut out the thoughts that continued to fizz and flicker in her mind's eye.

'Here's what I think happened,' Chandler said, her voice still calm. 'You're at home, cooking dinner and waiting to break the news of your pregnancy. Katrina rocks up and brings your world crashing down, and when John – the man you loved – returns and fails to back you, an argument erupts between you. You both say hurtful things to one another and one of you lashes out. The other responds in kind, but things get out of hand. The wounds inflicted screamed a crime of passion, but as I said the evidence led us elsewhere.'

'You can't prove any of that's true.'

Chandler let out a heavy sigh. 'You're probably right. Too much water under the bridge now anyway.'

Hannah's brow furrowed. 'So what are you saying? Do you think I killed my husband?'

Chandler fixed her with a hard stare. 'I think you were attacked and may have done what was necessary to defend yourself. Tell me something, prior to that night, had John ever been violent towards you?'

Hannah screwed her eyes shut to hold back the tears. 'He didn't mean to... he could get stressed, and sometimes... he always apologised, and it only happened when I pushed him. I knew he loved me... at least I thought he did.'

'If I had a pound for every time I heard victims say their partner didn't mean it... well, I'd have a bigger pension to look forward to.'

Hannah kept her eyes closed, fearing the answer to her next question, but unable to stop herself asking it anyway. 'What happens next? Am I under arrest?'

Chandler patted her knee. 'Not at the moment, no. Officially the investigation into John's death was closed some time ago. My instinct is telling me not to go digging up the past.'

Hannah's eyes snapped open, as she searched Chandler's face for whether she was telling the truth. 'What about Fahey?'

'If he chooses, he can petition to appeal against his conviction, and there's a chance he could earn his day back in court, but I don't think he's likely to do that. In here he has a warm roof over his head, three square meals a day, a television in his room, and access to medical treatment he couldn't afford on the outside. Believe it or not, before I brought you in here tonight, he asked me not to take further action. He knows now he didn't kill John, and I think he is at peace with his future. He probably has a year to go at best, and he's far more comfortable where he is.'

'What about you? Don't you have a duty to report what he said? What about justice?'

Chandler laughed. 'Do you remember what I told you about why I joined the police? The story about my friend being assaulted and the perpetrator getting away with it?'

Hannah nodded, remembering the admission at the wine bar last night.

Chandler fixed her with a sincere stare. 'The question I have to ask myself is who will be best served if I start trying to prove what really happened that night. I don't think you're a killer; just someone forced to act in defence of her life. You lost everything dear to you that night, and for me that's probably punishment enough. John's death was tragic, but the world may be that bit safer with him not in it. I think there's probably a lesson for us all to learn somewhere in here, but I'm too old and busy to unpick what it might be.'

Chandler stood and moved back to the large door. 'I'll need you to come down to the station and make a statement about your brother-in-law and the car accident, but as far as I'm concerned, you've heard what you needed for the closure you deserve.'

FIFTY-EIGHT

Stepping out into the cold night air, Hannah didn't even notice the drizzle at first. Chandler had insisted on personally taking the statement about Patrick's activities, and had promised to follow-up on it directly. Apparently, an All Ports Bulletin had been lodged, meaning if Patrick tried to escape the country, he'd be swiftly apprehended. Not that Chandler felt it would come to that.

'I'll circulate his picture to our uniformed patrols, and I'm sure he'll turn up sooner or later,' Chandler had said.

They'd sat and watched the video on the memory card together, though Hannah had struggled to look at John's face and not re-picture the confrontation in the living room. She had to keep believing that Fahey's version of events and her own splintered mind weren't an accurate snapshot of what had happened. Chandler had made it clear she wouldn't be searching for more.

'Best just to put it all behind you and move on,' Chandler had said, but the look she'd given had been less-assured, as if her view of Hannah had now changed; Hannah was no longer quite the same innocent victim she'd once been.

'I'll do my best to keep your family's name out of the papers,' Chandler had promised. 'The last thing you all need is more headlines.'

Hannah had thanked her, somehow knowing it would probably be the last time the two of them spoke.

'Do you want me to arrange a lift back to your sister-in-law's house?' Chandler had offered when they had finished.

The fact that Wendy had delivered Barney to the station along with the bag of clothes Hannah had left at the house told her she wouldn't be welcome back there anytime soon.

'I'll be fine,' Hannah had said, hoping to catch a passing taxi to take her to the train station.

The truth was she desperately wanted to be as far from Manchester and her past life as swiftly as possible. It had been a mistake to come back and allow history to attack her future. Sorting out Katrina's paternity challenge, and the written-off car could wait until she'd had a decent night's sleep back in her own bed where she felt secure.

She'd missed half a dozen calls from Bea, and putting the phone to her ear, she listened to the three voice messages Bea had left. Calling her friend back, the relief in Bea's voice was palpable.

'Where've you been? I've been trying to get hold of you for hours. You never sent me a message on Facebook and I panicked. In the end, Chris told me the two of you had spoken and gave me this number. Are you okay?'

Hannah's ribs still ached from the accident. 'It's been a long day. I just want to come home.'

'Ah well, I have a surprise for you,' Bea giggled mischievously. 'Message me your postcode and your surprise will be there soon.'

Hannah narrowed her eyes. 'Why? What have you done?'

Bea giggled again. 'You'll just have to wait and see. I'll speak to you in the morning. Have a good night.'

The call ended, and Hannah couldn't help but suspect that Bea was trying to play matchmaker again. Finding a booth in a nearby café, Hannah texted Bea the address and waited with Barney.

When a van pulled up outside the café twenty minutes later, Hannah was amazed to see Steve exit it and approach the café. He waved when their eyes made contact and he collected Hannah's bag and offered her an arm as he escorted her back to the van.

'What are you doing here?' she asked.

'Your friend Bea messaged me and said you needed some help. She said you'd been expecting me?'

So that's what the giggling had been about. She would have to have words with Bea in the morning, but it felt good to have someone looking out for her again.

'You look in pain,' Steve commented once she was in the passenger seat. 'Is there anything I can do to make you more comfortable?'

It had been a long time since a man had looked at her the way he was right now. 'I know it's a lot to ask, but can you drive me back to Southampton? I just want to go home'

He nodded, starting the engine, before turning to face her. 'I don't want to overstep my mark, but the thing is… oh, what the hell, I'm just going to say it. I like you, Hannah. I mean, I *really* like you. I know we hardly know each other, but fate or something seems to have pushed us together, and I really hope you feel it too.'

Hannah wasn't sure she could ever really trust her own feelings again, but she couldn't deny that his handsome face and genuine warmth towards her made her feel more secure than she had in a long time. Leaning across she rested a hand on his hot cheek, and pulled him inwards, kissing his lips.

'Let's just take it one day at a time,' she said.

'I know it may be old-fashioned, and I'm not going to apologise for being set in my ways, but I want you to be treated how you deserve. I don't care if it takes a lifetime, but I will spend the rest of my days proving to you how worthy I am of your affection.'

She kissed him again, and then fastened her seatbelt. He took the cue, and pulled back onto the main road.

Hannah stirred some hours later, the bright lights of the motorway now gone, and the headlights barely lighting the narrow strip of road they were on.

'I'm sorry, I must have dozed off,' she said, stifling a yawn.

'That's okay,' he said, glancing over and smiling. 'You probably needed the rest after all you've been through.'

That was an understatement, and Hannah was so relieved that the rest had passed without any kind of visions or nightmare. As she stretched her shoulders, it felt like a huge weight had been lifted.

'Where are we now?' she asked casually, wiping condensation from the window with her hand.

'Traffic on the motorway was a nightmare,' he said. 'An accident of some kind. I hope you don't mind… it's late and I think we could both do with some shut eye. I have a friend who has a cottage up this way and I asked if we could crash for the night. She said she'd make up a bed for you, and I'm happy to kip on the sofa. Is that okay with you?'

The clock on the dashboard said it was nearly half past one, and she couldn't blame him for wanting to sleep.

'Are you sure she doesn't mind?' Hannah asked. 'I don't mind paying for a hotel if that's easier?'

'She's expecting us now, and we're not far from the cottage.

Barney pressed his head through the gap in the seats, and nuzzled her hand until she played with the fur on his head.

'Is she okay about Barney staying over?'

Steve turned and smiled reassuringly. 'Oh yeah, she loves dogs, and she's used to spending time with my two. I promise you, it's all fine. I think the two of you are going to get on like a house on fire.'

Hannah was too tired to argue, and a moment later the outline of a cottage appeared on the horizon, framed by the light of the full moon overhead. A thin trail of smoke rose from the brick chimney pot. The building was surrounded by fields as far as the eye could see, presumably farmland, and Hannah couldn't imagine ever wanting to live somewhere so secluded.

'She's probably already in bed,' Steve said, as he opened Hannah's door and offered a hand to help her out of the cabin. 'She said there's a key safe by the front door and we should let ourselves in.'

Hannah yawned as she reached for Barney's lead and allowed Steve to carry her bag around to the side of the building, where a single light illuminated the key safe screwed to the wall. Steve typed in a code she didn't catch, and unfastened the door with the key. The door was thick and heavy and it took him a while to push it fully open, but he stepped aside and allowed her to enter first.

Hannah heard the Nokia ringing in her pocket, and withdrew it to see Bea's name in the window.

'Give me a second,' she said apologetically to Steve. 'It's my neighbour, Bea.'

'No worries,' he replied, closing the heavy door. The cottage felt warm, and the narrow corridor led to a further door ten feet away.

'Hi Bea,' she said into the phone. 'Everything okay?'

'Chris went to the address you sent me but he says you're not there. Where are you?'

'Wait, why is Chris at the café?'

'Because I told him you needed help, and he offered to come and get you. That was the surprise I'd arranged.'

A sudden shiver ran the length of her spine. 'Chris was the surprise?'

'Yes, of course. Oh, and you will never believe it, we managed to track down Melanie's ex-boyfriend, Billy. Only, his name isn't Billy, that's just a nickname. Chris and I were going through Melanie's list of friends on Facebook when we stumbled across him.'

Hannah already knew what was about to be said, but she couldn't speak as the breath stuck in her throat.

'Chris recognised his face from school. This guy called Steve Williams was Melanie's boyfriend at school, and he still lives locally from what Chris was able to find out. He was going to tell you all about it when he got there. Where are you, anyway?'

Hannah wanted to answer, but Steve extracted the Nokia from her hand, and switched it off, removing the battery as he did.

'It – it was you...' Hannah stammered. 'You killed Melanie Fowler.'

In the lowlight it was difficult to see his expression, but she did see him shake his head. 'We'd better go in,' he said calmly, before unlocking the inner door, and opening it wide. 'Oh good, you're still up,' he said into the darkness. 'That's good. I brought someone to see you.' He turned and beckoned Hannah and Barney into the room. There was no light inside, but Hannah could just about make out a pair of slippers across the room. Steve closed the door, before fiddling with something on the wall, and suddenly the room erupted with bright light, and Hannah came face-to-face with the ghoulish figure in the slippers.

The woman's brittle hair hung down to her knees, and her gaunt cheeks and stick-thin frame looked light it might collapse with the slightest gust. The woman was alive, but barely.

'See, Melanie,' Steve said proudly, 'I told you I'd bring company.'

Hannah's pulse quickened.

The zombie-like woman bowed in his direction and shuffled towards Hannah, who recoiled in disgust.

Steve pushed Hannah further into the room, dropping her holdall on the small square table pressed against the boarded-up window.

Hannah's heart felt ready to burst through her chest, her gaze falling on the deep-set scratches in the door Steve had just bolted.

'Now we can be a proper family,' Steve said, plonking himself into the only chair at the table. 'Might have to make some adjustments though. For starters we'll need an extra chair. I'm sure after a while you'll come to realise just how lucky it was we found each other when we did.'

It had to be a nightmare. It *had* to be.

Rushing to the door, she pulled hard on the handle but it was stuck firm. 'Let me out of here, Steve. This isn't funny.'

He remained where he was, smiling in her direction. 'You need to calm down. There's no reason to be scared. I'm not a violent man. Just ask Melanie.' He looked at Melanie. 'Tell her. In the years you've lived here, have I ever raised my hand to you?'

The look of terror in the gaunt face spoke volumes, but she quickly shook her head submissively.

'See!' he continued. 'Now if we're all going to get along there are a few ground rules we need to set out.'

Hannah didn't hear the rest of what he had to say, as she threw her hands against the door and tried to make as much noise as she could muster. In her rage she thought about all the ways in which she'd failed to see through Steve's charm and good looks, as she had John's.

Then she thought about how nobody knew where she was. As far as Bea was concerned, she was somewhere in Manchester, and had simply disappeared as Melanie had. To have escaped one monster, she now found herself trapped with another, although this time the chances of escape were nil.

Dropping to her knees, she buried her face in Barney's fur and prayed to be woken from the nightmare. But nobody answered, and as Steve approached, lifting her into the air as if she was as light as a feather, she desperately clung to

the last ounce of strength in her bones.
　　This wouldn't be her end.
　　She would find a way to escape again.
　　All she needed was time.

THE END

AUTHOR MESSAGE

Thank you for taking the time to read **SNAPSHOT**. If you enjoyed it, please post a review on Amazon or Goodreads and share the story with your friends. If a book is written to entertain, then the reader is the target audience, and I feel honoured that you chose one of my books to read.

Please don't be afraid to contact me via Facebook or Twitter to let me know what you thought of the story. There's nothing more joyful for an author than hearing from a reader who loved one of their books (believe me!). I really do respond to *every* message.

Thank you again for reading my book. I hope to hear from you soon.

Stephen Edger

www.stephenedger.com
/AuthorStephenEdger
@StephenEdger

ACKNOWLEDGEMENTS

I'd like to say special thanks to the following people, without whom **SNAPSHOT** wouldn't be in existence today:

Parashar Ramanuj, my best friend for more than twenty years and my first port of call whenever I have strange questions about medical procedures and body parts. His knowledge of psychological illness was essential for this story, and any errors are my misinterpretation of what he explained.

Joanne Taylor who has been reading and providing feedback on my novels since the beginning

I'd also like to thank my incredibly supportive family, in particular my wife Hannah, who puts up with my mind wandering mid-conversation as a new plot twist strikes.

Final thanks must go to every reader of my books for encouraging me not to give up and to follow my dream.

Printed in Great Britain
by Amazon